1 Hate Surprises

Cassandra Roland

This is a work of fiction.
Names, characters, organizations, places, events, and incidents are either products of the author's imagination or are used fictitiously. Otherwise, any resemblance to actual persons, living or dead, is purely coincidental.

I Hate Surprises is intended for adult readers and contains mature content.
Read at your own discretion.

Copyright Registration Number: TXu 2-462-062
Effective Date of Registration: December 04, 2024

Paperback ISBN: 979-8-9923385-0-8
Hardcover ISBN: 979-8-9923385-1-5

For all of the flowers, growing in sidewalk cracks.
Not watered or nurtured, but thriving nonetheless.
And for all of the people they represent.

I Hate Surprises Playlist

Prologue: Don't Stop Belivin' - Journey
Chapter 5: Stargazing- Myles Smith
Chapter 11: Sober - Evanescence
Chapter 30: If You Love Her- Forest Black
Chapter 31: Beautiful Things- Benson Boone
Chapter 34: Therapy- Isabel LaRosa
Chapter 36: Head Above Water- Avril Lavigne

PROLOGUE:

Samantha

Ross's fingers are intertwined with mine as we walk down the sidewalk. We are in Orlando, where we've just spent the evening at a ball game. I live in a smaller up-and-coming town not far from here, called Glenbrook. I don't mind coming into the city for a fun night out, I couldn't live here though. It's too busy for me to be comfortable with it every day. I'm not sure how many dates we have even been on at this point, but most of them have been in the city. We have seen each other a few times a week for the last month or so.

Ross is wearing a basketball jersey with the number 5, underneath a player's name I can't even begin to pronounce. His light brown hair is swooshed back and faded on the sides. I think he runs his hands through his hair more than any guy I've ever met. On our first few dates, I assumed it was just nerves, figuring it would happen less the more time we spent together... but it hasn't. Ross is a lawyer at his family's big firm here in the city. He wears a lot of slacks and button-ups. He is not usually in a suit still, this jeans and jersey look is the most casual thing I have seen him wear.

"I can't believe our boys lost tonight," Ross says, going on about the basketball game while we walk back to the car.

"OUR boys?" I tease. "I warned you. I know nothing about this sport. I take zero responsibility for the butt-kicking those guys took tonight."

"Ah, lucky you have a boyfriend with such vast knowledge of basketball, isn't it?" he says giving me a flirtatious half-smile, right as we reach my car.

My eyebrows immediately shoot up.

"Boyfriend?!" I say a little louder than I mean to, shocked by his declaration.

I may not know how many dates it has been, but I would have known if we were an official couple. We definitely have not had this conversation. Is this his way of asking me to be his girlfriend? What do I say? Shouldn't I be doing backflips? Instead, I feel like a deer stuck in the headlights.

Ignoring the few other sports fans making their way down the sidewalk, Ross turns me to face him and says, "If you'll have me, that is?"

Yup. Definitely what I thought he was asking.

I should say something but I don't know what to say. I don't know what I want. I don't think Ross senses my hesitation though because he looks from my eyes to my mouth and back again slowly closing the gap between us. Just a blink before our lips meet my phone starts to blare the lyrics to "Baby Got Back." With a sigh, he takes a step back. I give him an apologetic smile, along with a sigh of my own. I hope it comes across as disappointment, like his. But truthfully I am grateful for the interruption, it gives me more time to process.

"Sorry," I fib.

"It's okay, you can get that." he shrugs, letting go of my hand.

I back away a little more before turning and pulling my phone out of my bag, I don't need to look at the phone to know who it is, it's Jess. He set that ringtone on my phone, goofing off a few months back. It's only assigned to his contact and I haven't bothered to change it.

"What's up, Jess?" I answer.

"You gonna be back home soon? We got a situation," Jess's rugged voice says.

"How serious is it?" I say loud enough to make sure Ross can hear me. Jess didn't sound worried, but maybe this will buy me some time.

"Chad needs us to go get him, he's piss drunk. Mel called and asked if we could get him home safe," He explains.

I'm not really sure why he needs me for this. They all knew about my date tonight. But I'm not ready to give Ross an answer to his relationship proposal right this second either, so I decide to overlook my friend's lack of forethought.

"On my way," I tell Jess, hanging up the phone.

Before I put my phone away I also notice a text from my roommate Leah, telling me she's borrowing one of my dresses. I don't bother responding to it though. She's gotten pretty comfortable about using my stuff lately and I don't really mind. I think it's her way of trying to bond since we've only lived together a little while.

I take a few tentative steps back towards Ross and start to explain. "I am so sorry about that, it's kind of an emergency. We can finish this tomorrow, right?"

Ross lets out another big sigh and forces a small smile and slight nod, giving me a short "Yeah, tomorrow," for an answer.

I'll take it.

I give him a quick peck on the cheek and turn quickly to get into my car. He was going to take an Uber home anyway since he doesn't live far from the stadium.

~

When I make it back to town I notice that Jess's truck is already parked out front of the apartment I share with Leah. I park my new Jeep next to his truck and lock it. The Jeep is a beautiful blue, the guy at the dealership said it was called "Chief Blue". I smile at the sticker on the back, that reads *"Tuna, no crust"* before I open the truck door to climb in. Jess is already backing out before I manage a greeting, or to even get my seat belt on.

"Nice dress," he says without looking away from the road.

"Oh, this?" I say pointing to myself. "Yeah. It's what someone typically wears when they're, ya know... on a DATE."

"Huh. Was that tonight?" Jess asks, feigning innocence.

Even in the dark of his truck cab, I can see the playfulness in his icy blue eyes. A stark contrast to his jet-black hair and the matching five o'clock shadow that I try not to appreciate as the streetlights we pass highlight his features.

"You knew it was." I roll my eyes, then start to kick off my shoes and pull my hair up into a messy bun on top of my head.

I don't need to worry about appearances with Jess. He and I have been friends since I was fifteen. Same with Chad actually, though Chad is slightly more Jess's best friend, and I suppose Mel is more mine. She and I have been glued together since 7th grade. We are making good on our promise of being BFFs since this year Mel and I both turn 24. Jess is 27 and Chad is 26.

We are all sort of a package deal most weekends. They all really banded together for me when my Dad died a few years ago. We just sort of fell into the comfort and routine of always being together after that.

"When Mel called asking us to come get Chad, I just

kinda assumed you let her know the date was already over and you'd sent pretty boy packing." Jess shrugs.

Pretty boy? Is he serious?

"And why exactly do you just assume that I would 'send him packing'?" I ask crossing my arms.

It took us no time to arrive and park outside of the sports bar just a few blocks away, waiting for Chad. *Again, he really didn't need me for this.*

"Just not the type of guy I thought you were into," Jess says staring out the window and lightly drumming his hands on the wheel.

Pfft. What does he know?

Before I can respond Mel appears at the passenger side window with Chad draped around her shoulder. I scoot over to make room for him because Jess's truck is an early 90's model single-cab he refuses to give up on. According to him, it is now considered a classic. Maybe we should have brought my Jeep, but I just got it and I really don't want Chad tossing his cookies in it.

"Thanks for coming to get him, Jess," Mel says across the cab. "Your date end early, Sammy?"

"Kind of. I heard there was an emergency." I say equal parts confused and annoyed that she didn't seem to be expecting me.

Did she not ask Jess to call me?

"Right... well I am gonna head back in with *my* date. Later guys." Mel says hooking her thumb over her shoulder towards the guy waiting for her.

"Why didn't Mel know I was coming?' I ask Jess, not bothering to greet Chad who was already leaning his head against the door.

"Beats me." Jess deflects, resting his arm over my left leg.

Another charming feature of his truck is that it is a manual, meaning with drunken Chad taking up so much space on the other side of me Jess has to shift the truck between my legs to drive it. I roll my eyes and turn on the radio because I know that prying never gets me anywhere with Jess.

It's quiet for the first few minutes of the drive to Chad's.

The radio changes to an old Journey song and Chad reaches across to turn it up and starts singing the words wrong... and off-key.

Jess nudges me shaking his head and laughing at our goof-ball friend. He starts to sing along, smiling at me until I respond with the next line. I cave and join the two men singing. That's all it takes for the three of us to put on an over-the-top performance of the rest of the song on the drive to Chad's. Unlike Chad, Jess knows every word, listening to classic rock and aimless driving has always been a core part of our friendship. I can't help but notice that I am having way more fun at this moment than I did the entire basketball game with Ross earlier, even if Jess was being weird before. When the song turns into a commercial break Jess reaches over and turns the volume back down.

"Good thing you remembered deodorant today." I tease him as he lays his arm back on my leg, his hand back on the shifter.

"Are you trying to tell me I smell good, Doll?" Jess grins at me, shifting in his seat. His leg is now pressed right against mine and I can't tell if he is actually trying to get closer, or if he just doesn't have enough legroom with me and Chad sandwiched into his truck.

Probably the latter.

"He thinks you smell good too." Chad lilts drunkenly, barely lifting his head from the window. I guess he just had enough energy left for the one song.

"Will you keep your yap shut?" Jess snaps "You're almost home."

"I'm just saying brother, you miss a hundred percent of the shots you don't take." Chad mumbles.

"*And* would you look at that? We are here. Goodnight, Chad." Jess says, pulling the truck to a stop.

"What is he talking about?" I ask Jess, not sure Chad is coherent enough to elaborate.

"Nothing." he shakes his head. "He's drunk."

"Just man up and tell her you got a big ol' crush on her dude." Chad slurs, slamming the door and then making his way inside.

He what?

I don't say anything and I forget to move back over now that Chad is out of the truck. I just kind of sit there, staring at Jess and waiting for him to say something, but he doesn't. He just puts his arm back across my leg and shifts the truck into reverse.

"Soooo…" I say, trying to break the tension we are obviously both feeling but I couldn't think of a single other thing to say. *Was he serious?* Does Jess like me as more than a friend? *Would it be so bad if he did?* It would explain his weird behavior when it comes to Ross.

"So?" he hardly glances at me.

"What was that about?"

My chest feels tight. Why am I so nervous?

Do I want Jess to like me? No, right? I'm supposed to be swooning over Ross right now, he's the one who just asked me to be his girlfriend.

"Nothing to worry your little pretty boy about," he says shortly.

"My what?' I ask.

"It's all good, you got a new boyfriend and apparently a newfound love for ball sports." he continues, obviously not knowing that I chickened out of the boyfriend conversation with Ross earlier this evening. "And besides, you know, sometimes I don't even think of you as a girl."

"Not a GIRL?!?" I snap.

"Yeah." he shrugs. "You know."

I most certainly do not know.

"I am not really close friends with most girls like I am with you. Plus there's the whole thing where you can wrench on cars and keep up with shit talk and basically you are closer to a brother to me than anything," he says.

"A brother?" I repeat, like a dumbfounded parrot.

"Yeah," he says, rubbing his hand behind his neck, clearly uncomfortable with this conversation.

"Right." I mean, what else am I supposed to say to that?

What kind of a thing to say is that? And why the heck do I feel disappointed? I wasn't even sure if I wanted what Chad was saying to be true. Now I am feeling rejected? Why? Ross doesn't see me that way, in fact, he looks at me like he can't get enough. I don't even know how to process the roller coaster of emotions I have been through this evening so I just stare out the window until Jess drops me off right back where he picked me up.

Maybe I'll send Ross a message and tell him yes. I mean, at least he can tell I am an actual female and not some spitting, grunting, crotch-scratching *bro* that Jess apparently sees when he looks at me. Not that I care.

Chapter 1

Samantha

13 Months Later

I am sitting in a booth at the small Jamaican restaurant in downtown Glenbrook, when the owner, Benjamin Randolph, sits across from me. Benny moved here from Jamaica when he was young, so his English is mostly good, if a little broken.

"You don't look so good today, Sam," Benny says, by way of a question.

Benny has known me my whole life. He was close friends with my father. He practically helped Dad raise me after my mom took off when I was little. She pops up every once in a while, like a cold sore. You don't really want her around, and it's never convenient, but she's in my DNA, so she inevitably comes around. Benny and Gramma are the only *real* family I have left. Gramma lives a few hours away though. I usually call her to check in more than I can make it over to visit. She's one of those cool grandparents who knows how to text, but thankfully no one has taught her how to use Facebook.

"I confronted Leah," I tell Benny, explaining my demeanor.

Benny already knows exactly what I am referring to. I vent to him sometimes, and other times he just hears me talking with friends while we are here and eavesdrops.

"Couldn't have gone well if you have Jerk chicken and still look upset." He says, waiting for me to continue the story.

He's not wrong. Benny's jerk chicken wins awards.

Leah and I have been roommates since I graduated college. We've grown close since living together, but I would still call her my roommate more than a best friend. Mel, my actual female best friend, didn't want a roommate. I thought it would be a good way to save a little during my first few years of teaching, having spent most of Dad's life insurance on school so I wouldn't have student loans. Leah's aunt, Maude, heard I was looking for a roommate when we were at the diner one day. One thing led to another and it seemed like the perfect fit, at first.

The issue is that after we moved in together Leah started to make subtle changes. It was small at first, so I didn't notice. Maybe I never would have noticed, if Jess and Mel hadn't pointed out when she cut her hair exactly like mine. Leah even had the ends of her brunette hair lightened to mimic how mine gets lighter from the sun over time. Other than that it was usually small things. Small enough that you'd feel stupid bringing it up. She would buy the same dress as me or change her profile picture to have a similar pose as mine. A few times she even seemed to get a bit jealous or possessive when I spent time with Mel or Ross. My friends notice the small things more than I do. They think Leah is creepy, which I chalked up to them being overprotective. I thought I could brush most of it off as a sign of flattery… until now.

"I don't know Benny." I sigh. "I have been trying to give her the benefit of the doubt, but it's too much."

"What'd she do this time, use your curling iron?" Benny

teases me. He tends to think my friends have been overreacting.

"She bought a Jeep. Same model as mine, in *Chief Blue*." I pause to wait for his reaction. I feel like an idiot for reading into this. I wait for Benny to laugh it off or tell me that I am overreacting, but he looks almost as stunned as I did when I saw Leah pull up in it.

"The same one?" Benny clarifies.

"Just missing the sticker," I tell him.

His head moves slowly up and down processing what I just told him.

"So what happened when you asked her about it?"

"She lost it," I tell him. "She started ranting about how selfish I was to not want her copying my every move. She said I had the perfect job, perfect boyfriend, friends, car, you name it. In a nutshell, she said we were in some sort of sick competition and she was tired of losing."

That was the final straw for me. I had noticed Leah flirting with Ross when he was around, but I thought it was harmless. I figured she just thought he was charming like everyone else does. I didn't think she was actually jealous of him being with me. I just figured she got jealous at times because the rest of us, aside from Ross, had been close for so long. I really thought with time she'd feel less on the outside. I am not sure if that's what this is all about, but nothing else makes sense.

"Wow," Benny says as I continue.

"Can you believe that? She thinks I have the 'perfect life', like we haven't told her about everything with Dad and Carol. How did I get roped into a competition that I didn't even know I was in?"

"She wasn't there Sam," Benny says. I almost think he's

defending her before he continues. "She didn't see how close you and your Dad were. She never watched you climb out from under a car with him covered in grease because his hands couldn't fit where yours could. She didn't watch the accident break you, or how hard you fought to put yourself back together."

"I know." I sigh, but Benny doesn't stop.

"I was here. Mel, Jess, and Chad were here and we know. We are all so proud of you Sam. You deserve to enjoy the good things when they come your way. Don't feel bad about your blessings because they make someone else jealous."

That's what my friends were, my blessings. Along with all the other things I have worked this hard towards. Benny is right.

"Thanks, Benny," I say, still feeling uneasy. "I just don't know what to do now. I have to live with this woman. It's not like I have anywhere else to go."

"Well, the apartment upstairs is still empty," Benny offers with a sigh. "Before, I said take time. But if you want out, it's yours."

It always makes me smile when he says "Take time". It's comforting, even if the rest of his offer is unexpected.

"That's going to *take time*," I say, mimicking his accent.

"Nonsense. The apartment is empty. It's yours. I will charge you less rent than you pay now, you can move in right away. No wait." He says fiddling with his keyring.

"Benny, you don't have to do that for me," I tell him, but it's no use.

"You are family, Sam. We take care of family, don't worry."

I know him well enough to know the matter is settled, he

won't take no for an answer. I am just grateful to not have to stay there tonight.

"Thanks, Benny for everything," I say hugging him.

"You know, your dad would be proud of you Sam, you're doing alright."

~

After Benny gave me the keys, I let myself into the apartment to look around. There is a door in the alley that leads to a landing upstairs, and then the door to the apartment which has its own lock. I don't have to go through the diner to get into the apartment, which is convenient. The power must be connected to the diner's bill because all the lights work. I make a mental note to check in with Benny about how to pay for the power tomorrow. There is already some furniture here, a sectional sofa, a coffee table, and some bar stools at the counter.

At least I won't have to argue with Leah about splitting up the furniture from our common areas. I just need to get my bedroom furniture, clothes, and other personal things. Then thanks to the even cheaper rent, which I am super grateful for, I should be able to start making the place my own. The living room window gives me a clear view of the business district on Main Street. It's mostly old buildings. Some are brick and some have fresh paint. The town council makes sure everyone keeps Downtown Glenbrook historic, but also holds high standards for keeping up with building maintenance. It's beautiful.

"Take time." I sigh to myself. Then I take out my phone to message my friends on our group chat. I don't want to bother

Ross about this, he is on an important work trip. We don't live together so it doesn't affect him anyway.

Samantha: SOS. I need trucks and muscles. Will pay in pizza and beer.

Mel: It's not Leah's body is it? I mean don't say so over text if it is. I just can't do felonies for pizza.

Samantha: No felonies, I promise.

Jess: When and where?

Chad: Trucks and muscles? What are you moving?

Samantha: Everything… from my bedroom at least.

Jess: Tonight? Where are you going to stay?

Samantha: Benny is going to rent me the apartment over the diner. I am here now. It's kinda cute.

Mel: Told you living alone was a better plan.

Samantha: There is a sofa I can sleep on tonight, I know it's last minute.

Jess: On my way.

Chad: Fine.. But it better be a big pizza.

Chad…and cold beer

Samantha: Thanks, guys.

While I wait, I think about why I don't have the strong urge to tell Ross about what happened. You're supposed to want to tell your boyfriend every little thing right? This isn't even little, moving is a *big* thing. I've always been a fan of rom-coms and romance novels, which all seem to agree that your boyfriend should be the first thing to pop into your head when something comes up. The only problem is, I think I am secretly a bit of a cynic. I have only had two men profess their love for me (Ross being the most recent of course) and my natural reaction both times was to say, "No, you don't." Of course, I did eventually say it back to Ross. I just think maybe love isn't this grand, earth-shattering force that consumes you. Perhaps that's just for the sake of selling books and in the real world love is just being lucky enough to feel safe.

I decide to call him in the morning and not worry about it anymore for now. I want to take a moment to soak in my surroundings now that this is going to be my new home. I imagine throw blankets and pillows on the couch and art on the wall. I've never had a place all to myself. I'm excited to decorate it how *I* want.

Jess is the first one here. His shop, *Adams Auto*, isn't far from here. Jess is the third generation of Adams men to run the family mechanic business. He took control of the shop when his dad decided to retire so his parents could travel. Being from Florida, they wanted to be the opposite of snowbirds. Naturally, he is wearing his usual Adams Auto t-shirt when I open to door to let him in.

"Hey, Doll." Jess drawls, he has called me that since the day we met. He says it's because of my petite size. He has one of those voices that just comforts you, or maybe it's just because I've had a rough day and I've known him so long.

"Thank you for coming," I say with a tinge of guilt.

He clearly worked all day, even though it was a Saturday. He's been working to make changes at the shop to bring it "into the present". When his Dad decided to retire and left him the shop it wasn't really set up to fix anything made in this century. According to Jess, that's bad for business, even though he and Chad both still drive old pickups. They both have other cars as well. I think Jess has three or four different vehicles varying in age and type because that's what car guys do.

"So.. Ross isn't helping you move?" Jess asks when I stand back to let him into my new front door.

"No, he is out of town." I shrug.

See? Boyfriends are supposed to be a part of life changes, my inner cynic mocks me.

Jess's *hmpf* certainly seems to agree, but he doesn't comment on it directly.

"Well, I don't want you sleeping on a couch that's been up here gathering dust. I already told Chad to meet us at Leah's, we'll get your bed and stuff over, and then tomorrow we can talk about having that couch cleaned before you sit on it."

"I wouldn't have minded," I tell him, but he just shakes his head.

"I would have. Let's go get your stuff." Jess says gesturing back to the door.

I wonder if Ross would have come to help me so quickly if he weren't out of town. I mean, it's not like he has a truck, but still. Would he have cared if I didn't have my own bed? I try to shake the thought out of my mind. I get in my Jeep to follow Jess to the apartment that I now officially no longer live in. The more vehicles, the more we can fit. Even if mine will only hold a few hampers or small things.

Luckily, Leah isn't home when we get there. She works at the market as a cashier. She must have a shift now because her smock isn't hanging where it normally is by the door. It's not long before Chad and Mel catch up. Mel takes over Jess's role of helping me gather things into whatever hampers, duffel bags, and boxes we have around. Jess and Chad make quick work of loading my bed into Chad's truck. Once the top of my dresser is clear they move it into the back of Jess's, without even emptying the contents. Then Jess loads the chair from the corner of the room carefully into his truck bed and covers it with a blanket for protection. I don't have to ask him to be careful, Jess knows how much it means to me. The chair belonged to my Dad, it was his favorite spot in our living room.

Once we finish loading up everything I care to take, I take my key off of my keychain and leave it on the kitchen counter. Then we head back to the apartment on top of Benny's diner. Everyone does basically the same jobs we did at Leah's, but in reverse, turning the empty apartment into my new home. It will take some time to get used to calling it that, but that's what it is now… I suppose.

Chapter 2

Samantha

"Don't forget, I am having Chad come over to fix that sink in the morning" I tell Ross as he heads into the bathroom to shower. We haven't officially moved in together. But it's Friday, night so I would usually spend the weekend with him at his place.

I have only been in my new apartment for a few weeks, which means I am still getting situated, so I convinced him to come here instead. I keep waiting for it to feel like home here, but it just hasn't clicked yet. I have mostly added a few cute things I have found from Amazon, yard sales, and thrift shops. I just haven't been able to make it feel right. I am hoping spending more time here with Ross and inviting my friends over more might help with that.

"Why don't you just call a plumber?" Ross asks, pulling his shirt up over his head.

"Because you can't pay a plumber in pizza and high fives," I tell him sitting cross legged on my bed. "Unless you wanna take a look at it?"

This is a variation of a lot of little talks we have that remind me of how differently Ross and I were raised. He's usually much quicker than I am to throw money at a problem. I try not to fault him for it. Honestly, I think that it's nice that he grew up with that stability. But I think there's always going to be that part of me that grew up having less. I'm used to doing things myself or leaning on your village to get by. That part of me will probably always try to save money every chance I could, even if I wasn't a new teacher on a starting salary.

"Oh no. I make the big bucks so I can pay someone to do that crap for me." Ross says shaking his head. "If I wanted to fish your hair out of the drain, I would've gone to some crappy trade school instead of law school."

He likes to pull that out of his sleeve as much as he can. It gets a little old. Humility isn't exactly his strongest personality trait. But no one is perfect, right? Besides the financial differences and the work hours of a lawyer, he's a pretty good boyfriend. He is around when I want him to be and isn't overbearing so he doesn't mind when I have a girl's night and eat a pint of ice cream with Mel whenever she has her latest breakup (which happens more than she'd care for me to admit). Plus he can be sweet when he wants to. Just not in a *roll-up-your-sleeves* kind of way.

"Yeah, yeah, listen," I say changing the topic. "Grades are due next week, so Mel is coming over to grade papers here tonight. That way hopefully, I will be completely done before we leave tomorrow.'

"Oh, yeah. Okay," Ross says.

"So I figured we could just have Benny send something up for us. You like the jerk chicken right?" The jerk chicken is my personal favorite. It always reminds me of backyard cookouts my dad would take me to with Benny's family.

"I do," Ross says not sounding too enthused. "But if you are just gonna be hanging out grading papers, I think I'll just go to Jason's for poker night."

Jason is one of his few friends outside of the city. He doesn't live terribly far, but still, poker nights are usually pretty open ended as far as when they end.

"Aw, are you sure?" I say, giving him fake puppy dog eyes.

Ross pulls me off the bed and wraps his arms around me.

"Yeah, but don't worry I am still whisking you away tomorrow for your surprise. Which means I will be back here tonight so we can get an early start." He says smiling, before leaning down to kiss me. Of course, I can't help but start smiling too.

Knock. Knock. Knock.

"Mel has terrible timing." Ross laughs, releasing me and heading into the bathroom to finally take his shower.

I am still smiling and giddy as I open the door for Mel and lead her into the living room to unload her workload for the evening. She and I both started teaching at the elementary school together last year. We take turns going to each other's places to hang out and grade papers usually once a week.

"Someone's in a good mood," Mel says noticing my smile isn't going away as I shuffle around some papers.

"I can't help it." I gush. "I told you Ross had a surprise for me right?"

"Did he get you a puppy?" Mel teases.

"No." I roll my eyes at her. "He said we are leaving first thing in the morning. He is whisking me away for the weekend. He won't even tell me where we are going!"

"No way!" Mel says "Wait, you don't think he's gonna propose do you?"

My eyes go wide and I look around making sure he didn't just hear her say that so loud. I still hear the shower though, so I think we are okay.

"Shhh," I tell her. "What if he hears you?"

"Maybe we should ditch the paper grading and go get manicures so your hands are photo ready!" Mel says, squeezing my arm.

"I can't. I have to get these grades done today. I don't know when we will get back." I explain.

"Fine, but we are celebrating," she says heading to the kitchen and pulling out two wine glasses. "And I insist on painting your nails when we finish."

"You always manage to find a reason to celebrate when we are grading papers." I tease, following her.

"This is true." My friend agrees popping the cork on a bottle of wine she pulled out of my fridge.

We are sitting at the counter waiting for Benny to send up our dinner orders, drinking our wine when Ross comes out of the hallway. He is freshly showered, not a hair out of place, as usual. Ignoring Mel, he sets his jacket down on the counter between us. Then he leans on it, cutting Mel off in the middle of her complaining that one of her students threw up on her shoes this morning.

"Excuse me, pretty boy, we are talking here," Mel says pushing Ross back away from the counter, so she can see me again. Jess's nickname for Ross didn't take long to spread.

"Yeah. Hi to you too, Mel." Ross rolls his eyes.

I don't think they really like each other. Of course, no one says that but there has always been a weird thing with my friends and Ross. They pretty much just deal with him politely for my sake, and vice versa. They'd probably never hang out with him if he wasn't my boyfriend. But Mel is always the supportive friend, so as long as I am happy she is the biggest hype girl.

"I'm outta here babe. Have fun grading." Ross says before heading out the door.

"You two could be a little nicer to each other, you know." I sigh at Mel once the door clicks shut.

"I know. I know," she responds holding her hands up guiltily. "I hereby promise to no longer call him 'pretty boy'."

"Thank you." I half smile at her.

"IF he proposes to you this weekend." she finishes.

I half laugh and half roll my eyes at the idea. Then something buzzes between us on the counter. Ross must've forgotten his phone in his jacket on the counter.

"Oooh! Maybe there's a clue for this weekend on this bad boy." Mel says, pulling the phone out of the jacket pocket before I can stop her.

"Oh shit."

"What?" I ask, looking over her shoulder.

And there it is. A notification from Leah on his phone reads, "Hurry up, or I'll start undressing without you."

What. The. HELL.

Ross comes back in the door, now remembering to grab his jacket and phone. Mel slips the phone back in the pocket quickly and hands him the jacket. Both of us act like teenagers who just got caught cheating on a test.

He smiles and says "Don't wait up, you'll need your energy tomorrow." before kissing me on the head and walking back out the door.

Either because I am in shock, *or because I am absolutely*

pathetic, I just freeze. I don't call him out, scream at him, or even whack him with the half-empty bottle of wine over the head like I want to.

I just freeze.

"So I guess there isn't really a guy's night?" Mel says slowly like she is trying not to spook me.

"I think I'm gonna be sick," I tell her.

"No honey, you just need more wine," she says putting one arm around me while topping off both our glasses.

I drink the whole glass in one breath, and Mel immediately refills it again.

"I don't think we are grading tonight," I say, still staring ahead in shock.

"No. Not tonight." she agrees.

~

1:37 AM

That's what time it was the last time I checked my phone. Mel left hours ago after I promised her I would be alright. I didn't want anyone else around when Ross got back. Mel, while being my biggest hype girl, is also a force to be reckoned with when she's mad. She offered about a thousand ways she could tear Ross a new one, and I knew she wanted to, but this is between Ross and me. If I unleash Mel on him I will never get out what I need to say.

I have spent the last few hours practicing in my mind a hundred different things to say to Ross when he comes back. *If* he comes back that is. I can't imagine the gumption you'd have to have to ditch your girlfriend to cheat with her ex-roommate and still come back to her apartment. My stomach sinks as I wonder if this wasn't the first time.

How many times has he cheated on me, right under my nose?

Was he sleeping with her before I moved out?

Maybe that would explain why Leah was so jealous.

I feel gross. I crawl into bed, now in my most comfortable sweatpants and oversized purple sweater. I flip through the TV for a few minutes but ultimately give up. I slink down into the comforter and lay on my side with my knees pulled to my chest.

I. Will. Not. Cry.

I haven't cried yet. I'll be damned if I let Ross strut back in here to find me crying over him.

I don't know what time it is when I hear Ross walk into my bedroom. I fell asleep at some point so I didn't hear him come inside. He leans over from behind me and gently kisses my head. Then I hear him putting his keys and phone on the nightstand. I don't move. I am still half asleep and have now forgotten all of my wine-fueled battle plans that I spent so much time on. Ross walks into the bathroom and the shower turns on... again.

Disgusting.

As soon as I know he is in the shower, I bolt out of bed and start rushing around the room, grabbing everything I see that belongs to Ross or reminds me of him. His jacket from the chair by the window, a stupid dolphin figurine he gave me for my birthday, and his shoes from the floor. I don't know why I didn't do this earlier.

It all has to go.

Arms full, I walk out to the kitchen to find an Amazon box by the garbage can. I stuff everything in my arms into the box and continue scouring my apartment for any other

Ross memorabilia. When I am satisfied I have gotten everything I take the box back to my room. I pick up his keys and phone, having decided the best place for these would be the bottom of the box so he has to dig for them. *Apparently, I am petty when scorned, who knew?*

Against my better judgment, I look at his lock screen and see another notification from Leah.

It says, "I can't wait for tomorrow." with a winking emoji.

TOMORROW?!?!!

I squeeze the phone in my hand, willing it to crumple like a soda can, but it doesn't. It stays the same, showing me the proof of the betrayal of my boyfriend and the girl who, until a few weeks ago, was one of my close friends. So close in fact that Leah used to always tell people we were more *like sisters than anything.* I don't have any sisters, but I am pretty sure that's not how you treat them.

All of the emotions are building into a rage that won't let my heart stop pounding. It's beating so loudly that it's all I can hear, so I didn't hear Ross turn off the shower and come up behind me.

"You didn't have to get up. I was just coming to bed." Ross says, coming out of the bathroom in sweatpants, and rubbing his hair with the towel.

I spin around with his phone still in my hand. "You missed a call," I tell him holding the phone out.

Right before he can get a grip on it, I let the phone drop to the floor. Unfortunately, it misses his foot.

"It was Leah," I say trying to keep my voice from shaking, as he bends over to pick the phone up. "She said you left our relationship in her bed."

He looks down at the cracked lock screen and then his eyes, wide, flash back up to mine. "Shit."

"Yeah…shit. We are done, Ross."

"Sam, I can explain…" He stutters.

"After a year? I would love to hear it. Please regale me with tales of how you tripped on your way to poker night and accidentally slipped into her underwear before coming back to MY apartment?" I yell, poking him in the sternum so hard my finger hurts.

"Uhh… I…" he stutters again.

"Oh, and while you're at it, go ahead and explain how you *accidentally* made plans with her tomorrow, when you were supposed to be whisking me away on some grand romantic weekend?" I haven't stopped pushing, now I am taking tiny steps forward forcing him to walk backward towards the bedroom door.

"You wanna explain how many times you've cheated on me?" I challenge.

"Listen, babe.." He starts, but I don't give him the chance.

"You are disgusting. Get out, Ross. Take your hair gel and your crappy figurines and get your douchey, cheating, stupid face out of my life!" I scream.

"I need to get dressed," he says, gesturing down to his bare chest and feet.

"It's all in there," I say, more calm this time handing him the box. "Goodbye, Ross."

He must get dressed in the stairwell because much to my disappointment he doesn't reach his car as shamefully naked as I had hoped. Once I see his car pulling out and driving away out of my window it all hits me. Hard. I slowly climb back under my comforter and the second my head touches the pillow the floodgates open. I just cry until I am sure I've run completely out of tears. Then I fall back to sleep, alone.

~

Someone knocking on the door wakes me up. Rubbing my eyes I see it's light outside so I know it is morning. I try to check the time on my phone but it's dead. I never plugged it in last night.

I almost pull the cover over my head, but I hear Chad hollering from the other side of the door.

"Room service. Rise and shine love birds!"

I drag myself out of bed and catch a glance of myself in the mirror on my way to the door. There's mascara caked under my eyes in big black smudges. My hair is in a loose frizzy braid, laid over my shoulder and I am still in my sweats.

I look like crap.

"Sorry. I forgot you were coming to work on the sink," I say letting him in.

"Wow, you look…Well, you've looked better," Chad says looking over me.

He's never been one to sugarcoat things. Meddle and stick his nose where it doesn't belong? Absolutely. But he doesn't try to spare your feelings just to be on your side. That, I can appreciate.

I walk into the kitchen and start making coffee.

"Thanks. You too, bud. It's the sink in the bathroom."

Ross had suggested it was Benny's job as the landlord to have the sink fixed, but I felt like he had done more than enough in offering me the space.

"Yeah, I remember. I just figured I'd wait for Lover Boy to finish up in there before I go barging in." Chad tells me, obviously amused with himself.

"Oh, you don't have to worry about him. He's not here and he's not coming back." I tell him.

"Trouble in paradise?" He lifts his eyebrow.

"Liquid hot magma *scorching* paradise," I reply, trying to sound more nonchalant than I feel.

"Well, that explains…this," Chad says waving his hand over my general disheveled appearance.

"I don't really want to get into it before coffee," I tell him, rubbing my face.

"Okay. Can you at least tell me how serious it is? Like we're fighting and flowers will fix it? Or totally broken up?" Chad pries, as he pulls out his phone and starts messing with it.

I take it that he's just trying to seem like he's not too interested to take the pressure off of me. He's smart like that about getting his gossip. I know it won't take long for word to spread though, so I decide to give him the basic details.

"Like, we are never getting back together."

"Like ever?" Chad jokes.

"Never," I say locking eyes with him so he knows I mean it, and I am not ready to laugh about it yet.

"Got it. Get your coffee and I'll start working on the sink." He says putting his phone in his pocket. Then he grabs his toolbox and heads down the hall.

There's another knock at the door before I can even grab my mug from the cabinet. I slink back to the door, taking my time because part of me worries it might be Ross, here to try and apologize. I don't want to get into it with him this early. I check the peephole and to my relief, it's just Mel. I open the door and step back to let her in.

"Is he here?" She whispers making her way over to the kitchen to unload the yellow donut box she carried in from our town's favorite donut shop.

"No. I kicked him out last night" I tell her, walking back to the coffee maker to finally fill my mug.

"Then, I was right to bring wallowing donuts! Tell me everything!" She squeaks.

"Oh no! I am NOT wallowing." I snap back at her.

Mel holds up her hands defensively at my snappy tone. "Not wallowing. Got it."

"He doesn't deserve wallowing," I say, pouring my creamer into my coffee, trying for a more believable nonchalant tone than the one I used with Chad.

I don't know why I am bothering. They both obviously see right through it.

"Right. So tell me, what happened when he got back?" Mel pries, staring at me with her light blue eyes.

Her Weasley-colored red hair in a perfectly styled bob reminds me that I still look like a dumpster fire. She looks effortlessly stunning in her green top and white shorts. Mel has never had trouble attracting men. Keeping them around, is another story entirely. She has more breakup experience than the rest of our friends combined, and it's seldom them pushing her away.

"He came back and went right into the shower," I tell her, finally taking a seat next to her with my coffee.

"Didn't he shower right before he left for 'guys night?'" she asks, doing air quotes as she says the last part.

"Yup." I put my feet on the rails on the bottom of

Mel's stool. "I pretended to still be asleep then started packing all his crap up."

"After what we saw before he left, I can't believe you even let him leave without tearing his head off." she interrupts.

I take this opportunity to finally take my first warm sip of coffee. It's just the thing I needed, now more than most mornings.

"As I was saying," I continue, "right when I grabbed his phone to put it in the box, Leah messaged him. *Again.*"

"SHUT UP!" Mel screams grabbing my arm and spilling some of my precious coffee onto my hand and my lap.

"What did it say?"

"Everything okay out there?" Chad calls, poking his head out of the hallway.

He was clearly eavesdropping.

"It would be better if I could just drink my coffee," I say pointedly.

"Sorry." Mel apologizes, already dabbing me with the hand towel she grabbed off the counter.

After a deep breath, I decide it's best to muscle through the details quickly. Just pull the band-aid and be done with it.

"The notification said 'Can't wait for tomorrow.'"

"He cheated on you?" Chad blurts out. "With Leah?"

"So, when he got out of the shower," I continue. "I shoved the box into his chest and told him to beat it."

"Did he try to cover his tracks?" Mel asks.

"Now I understand the liquid magma comment." Chad nods to himself.

"What are you going on about?" Mel asks him, cocking her head to the side.

"It doesn't matter," I say waving my hands like somehow that's going to get us back on track so I can be done with this conversation as quickly as possible.

"Get this. The jackass had the nerve right before I gave him the box to say 'Let me explain'."

"He didn't!" Mel squeals again, this time refraining from spilling my coffee.

"Want me to kick his ass?" Chad offers.

I'm sure it's not even a real offer just something he's saying to be supportive. On the off chance I ever saw him mad enough to hit someone, I'm not sure he could even go through with it. I don't think I have ever seen him mad enough to throw a punch.

"I doubt that will be necessary. Thanks, bud." I say forcing a small smile his way.

"Let me know if you change your mind." He smiles grabbing a sprinkled donut from the box.

"Yeah because between you and Samantha, you're the one Ross will fear the most," Mel laughs in Chad's direction. "Keep dreaming bud".

Chapter 3

Jess

Chad: *Get to Sammy's ASAP. Fixing her sink and forgot my pipe wrench. Bring one.*

I had just gotten done changing the oil in my truck when I got the message from Chad to come to Samantha's apartment to help him fix her bathroom sink.

Why the heck isn't Ross fixing her sink for her? I think to myself, even though I am not surprised. I mean honestly, the guy probably pays someone to change the oil and brakes on his car. I don't know what Samantha sees in him. Hell, she could change her own oil, and yet she's wasted the last year and a half with some guy whose only real skill seems to be paying other people to be skilled. Apparently, I have spent too much time in the garage this morning. I reason that must be why I am inexplicably fixating on the topic of who can and can't change oil.

Samantha's apartment is right in downtown Glenbrook, on top of Benny's diner. I have to park in the alley and go through the back door to get up the stairs. I have only been here a handful of times since the night we all helped her move out of Leah's. *Another thing Ross couldn't be bothered to help her with.* I knock on the door, wrench in hand, and wait. After some muffled conversation behind the door, I hear Chad finally say "It's just Jess." Then, he opens the door.

"Jess?" Samantha leans out from her stool by the kitchen counter confirming Chad's announcement of my arrival. "What are you doing here?"

"I needed his help" Chad casually answers as I look between them trying to figure out why my arrival is a surprise.

"You didn't tell her I was coming?" I cock my head at him, not bothering to hide the irritation in my tone.

I didn't even want to be here around that douchebag Samantha calls a boyfriend. Now I am butting in uninvited? *Great.*

"You have never needed an invitation to come over, Jess," Samantha reassures me, drawing my attention away from Chad.

It's then that I really look at her and notice how disheveled she is. Not that I haven't seen her in casual clothes like her sweats in the several years we've been friends, or even her hair all messy and frizzy like it is in her loose braid that's draped over her shoulder. What stands out are the raccoon-like rings of mascara under her bright, honey-brown, almond-shaped eyes.

"What happened to you?" I ask her. "Pretty Boy keep you out all night? You look hungover."

Instead of her usual snappy comebacks, I am met with silence as Samantha looks down and fidgets with the drawstrings of her sweatpants.

"She dumped him," Mel blurts out from further in the kitchen with a mouthful of donut.

I hadn't even noticed her there before.

"You what?" I say, looking back to Samantha.

Again, she doesn't say anything. She only looks up a

little, not enough to meet my eyes, and offers me a half hearted shrug.

"He was cheating on her with Leah," Chad explains while Samantha reaches for the coffee sitting before her and pulls it closer.

Shit. She wasn't hungover. *She's been crying*. I realize, now noting the slight puffiness camouflaged beneath her mascara mask.

"Doll, I'm sorry," I say, trying to remove the foot I just put in my mouth. "What the hell is wrong with him?"

My hand tightens around the wrench, as I attempt to channel my anger towards Ross into squeezing the cool metal.

"Besides being a pretty boy?" She attempts a joke but her smile doesn't reach her eyes. "I know you were never his biggest fan," she says, looking down again sheepishly.

Before I know what I am doing, the twist in my gut at seeing her like this has me taking large steps to close the space between us. My hand reaches out with a mind of its own lifting her chin until she finally meets my eyes with hers. Then with all the sincerity I can muster I say to her, "That's because he was never worthy of you for a second and he's just proved it. This is on him. Okay? It has nothing to do with you".

I'll be damned if I let her walk around doubting herself because some entitled prick can't keep it in his pants.

"Ehem…" Chad clears his throat from behind me, reminding me that he and Mel are here.

I take a step back as Samantha looks from me to Chad and Mel who are now staring at us. I almost regret it, knowing that Chad will give me shit about it, and wondering if I made Samantha uncomfortable. Not what I said. I meant every word. I just hope I didn't make things awkward.

"So, we will just get this sink fixed up and turn the water back on. Then we can get out of your hair so you can shower and do whatever it is girls do after a breakup." Chad gestures his thumb over his shoulder back towards the hallway.

"Right," Samantha says, putting her face in her hands with her elbows on the counter. "I look like an emo panda."

"It's not that bad," Mel reassures her in her typical supportive fashion. Samantha isn't buying it though.

"Yeah," I interject. "Pandas are way too big. I'd say you look like more of an emo raccoon."

That earns me a small chuckle from her, which I return before taking my leave to help Chad.

"Well, that was intense," Chad says once we're out of earshot of the girls.

"Yeah. What a prick." I reply. "I can't believe that dickhead cheated on her with the same girl who was so creepy that Samantha had to move out."

"Sure. That's what I meant." Chad snorts.

"You want the damn wrench or not?" I say, avoiding that my childhood best friend is trying to point out that my reaction to the news was probably just as awkward as I was worried about.

"Yeah, about that," he says smiling mischievously. "Turns out after I texted you, I found mine. I just need to turn the water back on."

"And you couldn't be bothered to let me know you didn't need me to come all the way out here? You know I don't like running into that jerk." I grumble.

"Ah, but you see, there is no jerk to run into," he says smiling and nudging me with his elbow.

Of course. I think. *Meddlesome Chad, always butting in where he doesn't belong.* I have half a mind to walk out right now and leave.

"Cut it out, man. I don't know how many times I have to tell you to quit playing around. Samantha and I are just friends." I say rubbing a hand behind my neck while he packs his tools away.

"Yeah yeah, she's more like a brother to you because she doesn't even seem like a girl and she has cooties. Blah. Blah. Blah." he mocks, obviously amused by himself.

"I only said that once, to be fair." I retort, pointing a finger at him. *Because I felt like a complete moron as soon as it came out of my mouth.*

"One time too many." Chad laughs over his shoulder while he cleans up his tools.

"You really wanna be giving me shit right now?" I challenge him raising my eyebrow.

He knows exactly what I am talking about. My best friend hasn't exactly been making an effort with the ladies recently either. Not after getting his heart broken last year, he has no room to give me crap.

"Truce." Chad offers with his hands raised.

I sigh, shaking my head as I walk away from the bathroom. I go down the short hallway and back to where Samantha and Mel have made their way to the sectional sofa in the living room.

"All fixed up," I say, feeling like a fraud for not helping to fix anything, and not wanting the ladies to catch onto that fact.

"Great!" Mel squeals.

"Now you go take a shower. Then you'll have time for

a quick nap to get rid of the headache I know you have because crying always equals a headache, and then you'll have plenty of time to get ready."

"Ready for what?" I ask.

"Ready to go out on the town! Nothin' gets you over a man faster than being under another one." Mel says, winking at Samantha.

What the hell?

My mouth falls open and my eyes go wide, surprised by Mel's statement. I know it's none of my business, but that does nothing to help me hide the look of disapproval on my face. *Under another man?* That's the last thing Samantha needs right now. I put my hands in my pockets to hide my balled fists and tell myself that I am just being protective over her as a friend.

"Yeah… I um.. think I'm gonna have to take a pass on the last part of that plan." Samantha says. "But I don't really want to spend the night alone either. The last thing I need is for Ross to show up and it look like I'm alone sulking."

"Why don't you come over to my place?" I offer, for some unknown reason.

"And do what? Practice being grumpy and changing oil? Pass." Mel says, brushing me off.

"You don't have to come." I jab back at her.

"Of course, I am coming. She's just been through a breakup, you caveman."

Ignoring Mel, I bring my attention back to Samantha who is trying not to laugh at our bickering.

"Well, what do you say, Doll?"

"I guess it beats hanging around here with Mel's wallowing donuts." Samantha gives Mel a look as if she asking her to not put up a fight.

"Fine." Mel concedes. "But I'm inviting some friends."

"I didn't say 'let's throw a party'." *I'm not even sure I invited you to begin with,* I don't say.

"Cool your jets, Grandpa. I was just going to invite a few people, like Matt."

Before I can protest Chad is already coming out of the hallways with his ears perked up. "What are we doing?"

"Having a little get-together at Grumpypuss's." Mel smiles proudly.

"Get together sounds too much like a party." I protest.

"Aw, come on Grumpypuss." Samantha faux-pouts playfully. The little spark of joy in her puffy mascara puppy dog eyes makes me cave.

"See you around five?" I say trying to hold back a smile, completely ignoring that Mel is celebrating out of the corner of my eye.

"Yeah, I'll be the raccoon disguised as a girl." Samantha sniggers.

"So, nothing new," I jest, backing toward the door before she can change her mind.

I wave a quick goodbye to Chad who doesn't see because he's on his phone.

Once I'm back out by my truck I can't hold back the stupid smile spreading across my face. I know I should probably be more empathetic, but I can't help it. I am just excited that Ross is out of our hair for good.

I decide I'm going to make the most out of Mel's "social gathering" tonight. Maybe I should make food, and I should get wine too? I have beer at the house but Samantha doesn't like beer. I reason with myself that getting wine for

Samantha who just had a breakup is nothing to read into. If Chad had a breakup I'd get him that weird hipster beer he likes, wouldn't I?

Yeah, that's what friends do.

~

I'm gonna kill Mel.

It's after six at night, and there is no sign of Samantha yet. I am rushing around the kitchen, putting the finishing touches on the food. *Not that there will be enough at the rate that people keep showing up.* I made way too much for the six people I thought were going to be here, but it seems we're up to about a dozen now.

Every few minutes Mel takes it upon herself to play hostess and open the door to more expected guests. It seems that since we didn't want to go to a bar, she decided to bring the bar to my house. Each person who showed up seems to have received the same BYOB memo. They all have drinks in hand and my fridge has been reorganized to fit various six-packs and such.

"How many more people are you expecting?" I grumble at Mel as she reaches into my fridge for a beer.

"Just a few." She shrugs.

"Seriously Mel. The only reason I agreed to this was to make Samantha feel better, and she isn't even here."

"She's on her way big guy. Don't worry." Mel pats my arm dismissively.

"I'm not.." I start to argue back right as the door behind me opens and Mel's face turns to a shit-eating *I told you so* grin.

"Right on time."

Mel takes her leave, beer in hand as I turn to find Samantha walking in. The tension from my shoulders lessens a bit. I am relieved to see that she looks better than how we left her this morning. Her black mascara rings are gone around her eyes. Her sunshine and honey-colored hair is pulled back away from her face, with the bottom of it left down in trusses that hang down over her tight fitted shirt. I clear my throat and take a step forward to greet her. The feeling of a little sting of guilt for letting my eyes roam over her curves twists below my ribs. It's quickly forgotten when my eyes find her waist and follow the hand on it to someone coming in the door behind her.

What the hell is she doing with Carlos?

Chapter 4

Samantha

My phone keeps buzzing where I left it plugged in on the nightstand. I haven't bothered to look at it since last night. Even after my friends left this morning, I couldn't bring myself to look at my phone. So I just left it there. A Schrodinger's box of whether or not Ross has called or texted. Until I decide to look at it I won't have to know if the notifications were from my friends checking on me or, God forbid, from Ross.

He could have sent me a hundred groveling texts, begging me to forgive him. He could have called and left so many voicemails that my mailbox was full. *Preferably of him crying.* There could be texts gaslighting me into believing that nothing happened and I overreacted. Or, if I was lucky he could have left me completely alone, like I'd asked him to.

I wasn't ready to open that box though. So right after everyone left, I spent the first half of an entirely too-long shower replaying last night in my mind. Going over the more clever things I wish I had said, re-imagining the more satisfying things I could've done. My personal favorite, (and biggest regret that I didn't do last night) would've been if I had packed all of his belongings before he got back and dropped it all out of the window in front of him and never let him up.

I was blindsided though, so I stupidly let him walk right into my apartment and into my shower. The disgust of Ross being in this same shower after just sleeping with Leah, was etching irritation to my skin no matter how much I tried to scrub it away. After I got out of the shower I sat down on my bed, still wrapped in my towel, and thought about the thing that was bothering me the most.

I'm not sad. I should be, I spent the last chunk of my life with Ross. Still. I feel betrayed. I feel angry, but for whatever reason, I don't feel sad. Instead, where I should feel pain, longing, and sorrow, I feel relief. The realization twisted in my gut as I just laid there for a while contemplating what that says about me.

At some point, I must've fallen asleep. I have no idea what time it is now, but it feels like I've been asleep for half the day. It must have been a long time because my thick hair is nearly dry, something that typically takes hours if I leave it to air dry. I know I am going to have to look at my phone to check the time, but I decide that can wait for me to get dressed. I drag myself out of bed, adjust the towel around myself, and head straight to the kitchen to start a cup of coffee. While it brews I head back to my closet to pick out something to wear.

By the time I am caffeinated and dressed it feels like another half hour must have passed. Standing in front of the mirror on my large dresser, I take a moment to appreciate my reflection. My face no longer looks swollen from crying, with the little bit of makeup I've applied and my mascara rings gone. I left my hair half down to show off some of the length but pulled the top back in a clip to flatter my face. In place of my sweats, (since I reminded myself that I am in fact NOT wallowing) I have picked out a great pair of jeans and a fitted tank top that flatters my bust. I know that it's only going to be a couple of us hanging out, but I told myself that I would feel better if I didn't dress like a depressed swamp rat.

Satisfied that I am sufficiently ready to go out into the world, I decide that I have put off looking at my phone for as long as I can. It's been overcast all day so it's hard to judge the time but I am hoping I may have some time to go to the bookstore a few buildings down before I leave. After throwing in a pair of earrings as a last effort of procrastination, I grab the phone and steady myself with a deep breath before turning the screen on.

It seems that with being up half the night and sleeping the day away my internal clock was way off because the first thing I see is that it's already half past five in the evening. Under the time are a series of texts. Starting with several from Mel asking why I am late. I scroll through the notifications, some emails, and social media updates, but nothing from Ross. I'm not sure if the feeling in my gut is relief or disappointment. I clear my notifications and put the phone in my pocket, refusing to allow my thoughts to linger on it too long.

~

It's after six by the time I finally get to Jess's house. I would have arrived sooner but for some reason, my Jeep wouldn't start. I tried looking under the hood, before deciding it could wait until tomorrow.

I called Mel for a ride. She was relieved to hear I was ready to go and not hiding away for the night. She told me to be ready to go in ten minutes, which is why I was surprised when Carlos showed up instead of her. Which brings me to now.

I don't ask Carlos why Mel sent him instead of coming herself. I'm afraid after her earlier advice on how to get over a breakup, I may already know the answer. Instead, I spend the drive trying to decipher between the small talk if he's simply being polite or if this act of chivalry has an undertone of flirtation. *I am so not ready for that.* No matter how charming he may be, and there's no telling what Mel may have said to get him to come pick me up.

Carlos is Jess's right hand at Adam's auto. I've heard nothing but good things about him since Jess promoted him a while back. Other than that, I don't know much about him. I have only met him a few times, all in passing and with limited conversation. His 1970's mustard yellow Datsun 510 tells me more about him than I have learned in our few meetings. Unlike Ross, who drives his shiny new Audi as a symbol of status,*(and makes sure everyone sees it)* Carlos's car shows something about him. Not just that he is a car guy, which is a given working at a shop, but one with personality. It reminds me of Jess's old truck. I wonder if being too stubborn to give up on the carbureted world is what brought them together.

When we finally pull down the long dirt driveway and park between the back of the house and the detached garage, I'm surprised to see there must be more than a half dozen cars already here.

No doubt Mel's handy work.

I don't let Carlos get around the front of the car before opening the door for myself and getting out. I don't want to feed into whatever wrong impression Mel may have fed him to get him to come pick me up. Nonetheless, he greets me by the passenger side of his car. Before I make it two steps I feel his hand on my lower back escorting me toward the back door. When I look up at him in surprise I am only met with a kind smile, reaching up to his mocha brown eyes in a way that's both comforting and confident. I don't say anything, not wanting to embarrass myself if it really is an innocent gesture, but I make a mental note to not give him the wrong impression.

"Sorry, we're late," I say, before we're all the way through the door.

I find Jess and Mel in the kitchen. Jess's face is scrunched no doubt in frustration at Mel for turning a quiet night into a social event. Mel as usual can't be bothered to look the least bit apologetic, instead, she just gives me a wolfish grin as a way of greeting. She mumbles something to Jess that I don't hear. Then she winks at me before strutting out of the room for some sort of dramatic exit, clearly amused with herself for whatever clever thing she likely just said.

I watch as Jess's frustrated expression at Mel changes to one of confusion when he turns to greet me and his eyes find Carlos's hand at my waist, leading me into the room. His eyes lock there for a heartbeat, just long enough for me to worry that more than just Carlos might be getting the wrong impression. I take a step toward him, offering him an apologetic smile, still waiting for a greeting, but Carlos steps in sync, his hand unbudging. Jess shakes his head slightly, as if to compose himself and slides his hands into his pockets in an attempt to look less annoyed.

"What are you doing here?" Jess nods to Carlos over my shoulder, still not greeting me.

"Sammy needed a ride." Carlo's hand tightens the

slightest bit on my waist, the gesture solidifying my suspicions about his intentions.

Jess's eyebrows shoot up, then his eyes dart again from his employee's hand to my face and he finally addresses me. "Is that so?"

A wave of embarrassment crashes over me as I realize how this must look. I step out of Carlos's reach, this time taking larger steps to ensure space between us and shrug. I want to put some distance between us before anyone else sees, so I keep walking to the other side of the kitchen and lean against the counter.

I feel gross, even though I haven't actually done anything wrong, just because I don't like the way I know this *could* make me look. I am less than 24 hours out of a breakup that half the people here probably know nothing about and I show up with a guy's hands on me.

Jess straightens, his shoulders relaxing some, having noticed my shift away from Carlos and he clears his throat a second time.

"Well, you want a drink, Doll?"

"Depends on what you have," I say.

Not drinking beer usually leaves me with limited choices at these sorts of gatherings. I remember being told after tasting my first beer that it was an acquired taste and deciding that I had no interest in acquiring it. Luckily for me, I'm not much of a drinker so other than the occasional cocktail or a few glasses of wine at social events here and there, I don't find myself to be missing out on anything.

"Crane's Ridge, Sweet Red?" Jess gives me a knowing smile, already busying himself with grabbing a glass.

My face lights up and I do a little happy dance in place

that would embarrass most people. It's my favorite wine from a local winery right here in town. It was one of the first wines I tried that didn't make me heave like I'd just drank cough medicine. Though I have a broader taste in wine now than when I first tried it, it remains my favorite.

"You really didn't have to do that," I say, my words of gratitude a cool contrast to the measure of excitement I've just shown with my happy dance.

"Yeah, right. This one can be pretty picky." Jess says over my shoulder, by way of explanation to Carlos, who I realize seems to be waiting on me.

"Hey, I resent that." I half-heartedly defend myself.

"More like *resemble* it." He offers me the now-filled glass with a playful grin.

"I'm afraid I don't know much about wine," Carlos admits, directing his response to me even though I didn't start the conversation.

"Neither do I," Jess tells him, with his arctic blue eyes still on me. "I just know what Samantha likes."

I take a sip of my wine, watching Carlos's Adam's apple roll up and down. The two men say nothing. The silence lingers long enough that I start wondering if something is going on between them at work or if Jess is merely being overprotective of me given recent events. Or maybe he has picked up on the fact that I am not interested and is trying to help me keep Carlos at arm's length.

"I think I am gonna go see where Mel ran off to." I excuse myself, taking the assist, whether intentional or not.

I find Mel in the living room, sitting among several familiar faces. The most familiar of them being Chad and Matt, who Mel promised would be here. Across from her,

Chad sits next to Matt, who used to have a long time helpless crush on Mel. Much to Matt's dismay, she's always just regarded it as an innocent schoolboy crush.

Matt is sweet, he's a few years younger than the rest of us and only fell into the outskirts of our friend group because he is Benny's son. His tawny brown skin and chestnut eyes are the only resemblance he has to his Dad. Benny has been balding and a jolly sort of round around the middle for as long as I have known him, whereas Matt has a full head of curls and a more athletic build.

Matt was always around growing up, pretty much a cousin to me with the way our dads spent most weekends together. It was no surprise when he developed a crush on my best friend, honestly the only way it would have been more predictable would have been if we were siblings. He doesn't get all giggly and strange around her anymore, so either he outgrew his crush or got better at hiding it with age.

"I thought you were coming to get me," I say pointedly to Mel, who raises her glass to me in response.

"Sorry, didn't want to drink and drive you know." Her excuse falls short of believability with the way she loses the battle to hold her mischievous smile in.

"Next time I'll call an Uber." There's just enough lightness contrasting my sarcastic tone to let her know that I'm not mad about her little stunt.

If I'm honest with myself, the attention from Carlos does give a little boost to my wounded ego, which I am sure was her plan all along. Still, it's not something I have the intention of leading into.

I make my way to plop down next to Mel on the couch and put my feet up on the coffee table. Matt and Chad are talking about fishing which is sufficiently boring enough for me to tune out. Don't get me wrong, I have no issue baiting my own hook and casting a line. Growing up in Central Florida and spending summers on the lakes made sure of that. It's just not a hobby I find interesting enough to go on about like they are, so I take the opportunity to sit in silence for a minute. My new plan to get through the night may be just to enjoy my wine and let everyone else do the talking.

Carlos makes his way in, and Mel moves to a recliner nearby to give him a spot next to me. *Traitor.* I give her my best *what the hell* face which she responds to with a suggestive eyebrow raise before Carlos smiles at me and I take another sip of my wine.

At this rate, my glass is already half empty. I haven't eaten all day either. For some people that might be fine, but for me,(*the world's jolliest lightweight*) means I'll likely be lilting out compliments all too soon if I don't get some food. Thankfully, I am a kind and flattering drunk, not an angry drunk. Even so, I usually stay on top of keeping myself in check, not wanting to be anything like my mother.

The relief I get when Carlos joins in on the fishing topic with Chad and Matt is interrupted when I feel my phone buzz in my pocket.

Mel: *I think he wants to give you a ride home too ;)*
Samantha: *I hate you*

Mel only laughs at that and sticks her tongue out at me, knowing I could never mean it.

After a minute Jess joins the boys. I do my best to stay out of it, not wanting to encourage Carlos, despite my best friend's *not-so-subtle* oggling and pulling me back into the conversation. Over the next ten minutes or so I wait for someone to bring up Ross and Leah, to ask about the breakup I know that they're all aware of, but no one lets on. The longer I sit there, the more I am convinced that they've conspired not to draw attention to it, to spare my feelings. It's as if they're walking on eggshells and going out of their way to avoid the elephant of gossip that arrived tattooed across my face. I'm not sure why, but it makes me feel worse. Pathetic, even.

The conversation moves on from fishing to cars, another topic that I could easily keep up with if I felt the desire. I learned a lot about cars as a child, trying to make my Dad proud and to be included in what he was always doing. I listen to them talk about the Mustang Jess bought. I haven't seen it yet, but I don't have to see it or pay attention to know that he got the V8 and it'll take a whole 2 minutes before they start talking about supercharging it if it doesn't already have one.

"As long as it has the backseat intact, I'll love it." Chad pokes at Jess, very amused with his inside joke.

"And seat belts," I add with a meager laugh, now nearing the bottom of my wine glass.

"Seat belts?" Carlos's head cocks to the side, his question directed at me.

I can feel the wine creeping up on me with the way my cheekbones reach my eyes when I smile at the memory.

"When we met, Jess had this horrible Camaro. Awful catfish looking thing. And teeny-bopper Jess thought he could make it faster by making it lighter," I say, my voice laced with nostalgia.

I feel a little brighter as I raise my hands in air quotes around "lighter". At least enough to put on a mask and try to be a part of this conversational shift.

"My ass hurts just thinking about it," Chad adds in, and another ripple of laughter spreads among us.

Mel, zones out on her phone for a minute, disinterested. She wasn't around much the summer I met Chad and Jess, but she has heard this story several times.

"Set the stage," I say, spreading my hands out to open an imaginary set of curtains. "Teenage Samantha gets a text from her new friend Chad asking if she wants to hang out. I tell my Dad that I am going to stay the night at Tabitha's house, a house that I have *NEVER* seen in my life, and go meet this bozo at the end of the road."

My nod towards Chad is met with a proud smile claiming the title of said bozo.

"Which happens to be a cemetery." Jess cuts in.

"Shhh, I was getting there." I continue. "So here I am, in the middle of nowhere, it's starting to get dark out and this black crapbox pulls up."

Jess rolls his eyes, but that doesn't hide the amusement in the creases that fan the corner of his eyes.

"At a cemetery?" Carlos asks, confirming Jess's addition to the story. His face is a combination of intrigue and uncertainty.

"At the cemetery." I beam.

"It wasn't that bad. You should've seen it when I first got that car." Jess's hands raise defensively. The story goes that it was beautiful when his parents gifted him his first car, but it got damaged, and then he took some less-than-artistic liberties.

"But I didn't. I saw it when it was a creepy crap box." We all laugh, and I turn back the Carlos who is hanging on to every word. "He had roller-painted the car a flat black. A two-year-old could've done a better job."

"What happened to Chad's ass?" Carlos asks, looking equal parts confused and amused. "Or don't I want to know?"

"*Sammy* happened to my ass." Chad raises his beer to me.

I hold up the last sip of my wine glass in an invisible *cheers*. "Always the gentleman."

I down the last sip and continue, "As if the outside of the car wasn't scaring girls away fast enough, Jess stripped the whole inside of it. He had a steering wheel, a shifter, and two front seats. That's it. No backseat, carpets gone and he must've gotten a whole extra horsepower from the seat belts being removed. Which meant Chad sat on the hot back floor, tanning his buns over the muffler so that I could have the seat up front."

Chad smiles proudly at his act of chivalry. "I never should have introduced them. I spent the rest of that summer burning my ass in the back of that car."

Jess makes a half-hearted effort to roll his eyes. "You didn't introduce us."

"Yeah, I did." Chad protests.

Jess takes a sip of his beer. "Hmm, must be my mistake."

But it's not. We met a few weeks before when he was delivering parts from his Dad's shop (at the time). I don't know why he doesn't say how we actually met, it's not like it was anything interesting. But for whatever reason there's a playful bit of camaraderie behind his smile, which I return in a silent agreement to keep it to ourselves.

The guys move on talking about other vehicles they've

each had, which I take as my out to go to the kitchen and find some water and maybe something to eat.

Chapter 5

Samantha

The kitchen smells so good I don't know how I didn't notice it when I walked in earlier. I hadn't even realized there would be food. There is a spread on the island of assorted taco fixings. I scan the room to find the source of the delicious smell while I grab a glass from the cabinet near the fridge and fill it with water.

A glass of water per drink.

I mentally commend myself. I'm not an alcoholic or anything, I know that's what someone would think if I explained my rule. I only drink on occasion, and when I do I am extra vigilant about not getting too drunk. I have seen my mother, too many times too drunk or high out of her mind to push my own boundaries. *When she bothered to come around.* So, when I have a glass of wine, I make sure to have water before a second glass and I never drink on an empty stomach. Except for tonight, which I am attempting to remedy now.

Of course, no one ever notices my extra precautions or how I drink less than everyone else. They just chalk it up to me being a frangible lightweight, *which is accurate,* and proactive protectiveness against hangovers. Again, accurate but not the whole reason. I also will not allow myself to be seen not handling my alcohol right after a breakup. From moving out of Leah's to her taking a wrecking ball to my relationship, I really don't want to add any more pathetic elements to my public image.

They're already treating you like you're breakable.

"You stealing some food?" Jess's deep voice pulls me from my thoughts.

"I haven't eaten all day, these smell delicious," I say, not looking up from my plate as I pile on the food. "Who brought the food?"

"That'd be me," Jess says, hopping up to sit on the counter and make himself a taco with no plate like he's still the teenage boy I remember.

"Wait. YOU cooked tacos?" The look I give him is mixed with equal parts skepticism and surprise.

"Not just any tacos," Jess takes in a big whiff, stirring the Crockpot. "My super top secret special tacos. I am a man of many talents, you know."

His half smile is meant to portray playful cockiness but it doesn't quite cover the humility underneath.

"Ah yes, our very own *Jess of all trades*," I respond brightly. It's true though, if there is something he can't build or fix I haven't seen it yet.

Over the next couple of minutes, we sit quietly together as we eat, occasionally laughing at some of the noises coming from our friends in the living room. These tacos are surprisingly delicious, which makes me wonder what else has changed with Jess while I wasn't paying attention.

Outside of adjusting to my first year of teaching, I have basically buried my head in the sand of a relationship that turned out to be a waste of time. Mel has been getting used to teaching right alongside me, but I have missed a lot of what's been going on with everyone else. Including most of whatever is going on with Chad, who seems to be around a lot less.

"Seems like I have missed so much this past year." The thought escapes, even though I didn't mean to say it aloud.

"Not that much has changed, Doll." He offers me a reassuring smile, but it falls short.

"Oh, you definitely have," I reply looking him over.

I hadn't even noticed really, the changes that happened so subtly over time. He's not as smaller framed as he was a few years ago. His shoulders and chest are broader, making him look more like the strong, salt-of-the-earth man that he has grown into. His young goatee has matured into a fuller beard that he keeps cleanly cut short. It's black, like his hair making his eyes pop even more than they always have because of their bright contrast to the rest of his rugged features.

"Maybe that's the problem, maybe I haven't changed enough." I go on because he's busy stuffing his face and I feel the need to fill the silence.

"I mean look at you. You've morphed into a full-grown man, you're doing great with the business and I'm over here starting from scratch. *Again*. I've got issues piling up so high it's no wonder Ross wasn't content with someone like me." I stop, surprised by the thought I hadn't even realized I had.

Even though I'm not heartbroken about Ross being out of my life, I couldn't help the sting in my gut that felt like he had cheated because I wasn't good enough. Maybe deep down, I was only with Ross because I thought somehow it added some sort of validation to my self-worth. Because he wasn't from a world with broken and dead parents and hadn't grown up struggling the way I had. *Maybe* part of me just liked that someone who wasn't broken found me worthy.

Until I wasn't.

"The guy is a piece of shit Samantha. That's all there is to it."

I try to hide my shock at his sharp words, keeping my only response to a small shrug as I take another bite of my food.

"I mean it. Don't make me drag you out to a bar with Mel just to show you that every damn guy there would be lining up to buy you a drink."

"Yeah, right." I roll my eyes, and my self-deprecation seems to fuel Jess's frustration.

"He's lucky I don't knock his damn teeth out."

"These are delicious," I say with a mouthful of taco. "I can't believe you made them."

It only takes a heartbeat for him to read my abrupt shift for what it is, and oblige in changing the topic.

"I've been working on perfecting these for a while. I throw them in the pressure cooker in the morning, then it turns on low automatically for the rest of the day it just softens and soaks up all the flavors. I have been using Chad as my taco guinea pig for months now, while I worked out the kinks."

"Months?" I say dramatically like he's wounded me terribly. "You've been keeping tacos from me? For months?"

"Yeah well, Ross didn't seem like he really wanted to eat tacos with me anytime soon." Jess looks down as if it's his turn to regret blurting before thinking.

Guilt washes over me in a wave that I try and fail to hide from my face because I know he's right. I have pushed our friendship aside for my relationship, *and what for*? I hate that the conversation keeps coming back to Ross, but at least Jess isn't treating me like I am breakable like the others.

"Yeah, I guess that's fair," I say, now fidgeting with my water glass.

"Well, you ready to get back in there?" Jess nods towards the living room filled with people and starts to stand.

"No." The bluntness of my answer surprises us both, but I can't take it back now.

I know I agreed to come over, but that was before I knew how many people would be here. I am still debating if the tacos make up for the drain in my social battery.

"Okay. Let's go." His response surprises me even more.

Jess is already opening the door, looking back for me to follow him when I ask, "Where are we going exactly?"

My question is just a formality, I'd suddenly rather be anywhere but here.

"To introduce you to Sally."

His new car.

I follow him out to the garage and we spend a few minutes looking at *Sally*. He shows me some of the cool features but doesn't drone on about it. I am fairly certain he doesn't expect me to be too enthused by the car, and that he really just used it as an excuse to give me a break from everyone in the house. *One that I am very grateful for.* When I have given Sally a sufficient amount of attention I take a seat on the four-wheeler sitting off to the side, not ready to go back in just yet.

Jess gives me a knowing look, seeming to understand this and instead of ushering me back into the house asks, "You wanna go for a ride?"

"In the car?" I ask.

With his hands in his pockets, he shakes his head. Then he is walking closer to where I sit on his old four-wheeler. "Move back."

I do. Then Jess climbs between me and the handlebars and starts the engine. He looks back at me over his shoulder, giving me an out that I don't want to take. I'd much rather be riding in the silence behind him than go back in with everyone else.

"Let's go." I ready myself, grabbing the back of his shirt to hold onto and Jess doesn't hesitate to start pulling out of the open garage door.

Before anyone has a chance to notice, we are down the long dirt driveway. In a matter of minutes, we've ridden down the side of the road, towards a familiar red clay road. Once the tires hit the clay I know better than to hold on by the back of his shirt anymore. This is, after all, the road Jess crashed that old Camaro into several little trees drifting around the corners one night. Thankfully they were little trees, and no one was hurt, it was actually a fun night as far as adventures go. I smile to myself at the memory as I wrap my arms around Jess's stomach to hold on.

As soon as my hand wraps around my wrist to hold on tightly Jess accelerates. The slight breeze of our cruising speed turns into a rushing wind, blowing my hair back behind me. Orange dust trails behind us as we go, and the smell of the orange blossoms grows stronger as we get closer to the groves that I know we are headed for.

A familiar contentment wraps around me, like a warm embrace soothing away all of the recent turmoil. I hold on tighter the faster we go. The more we pick up speed, the calmer I feel, the less I remember Ross, and Leah and the house full of people dancing around not bringing up the breakup. Until it's just peace and the wind.

Jess brakes just enough as we turn off the clay road onto a trail leading into the orange groves and then punches it as he straightens out, causing me to hold on tighter. We haven't done this in so long that it's hard not to notice how much he has changed since the last time I rode with him. His broader chest and shoulders reflect the labor he has poured into the shop, making it harder to watch where we are going over his shoulders. *Being this short doesn't help.* I don't need to see where we are going though to feel safe with him, he's always been an adept (if a little reckless) driver.

We come to a stop where the orange grove borders the woods near a small lake or maybe it's a large pond. It's not one of the larger lakes that all connect together, where it's always abuzz with boaters and skiers. It's one of the few places you can still go in the area where the growth of people moving into the state hasn't touched.

Beautiful, calm.

I don't realize I am still holding onto Jess with my head resting against his back until he turns off the four-wheeler. The engine sounds are replaced with the sounds of crickets and wind in the trees. We just sit there for a moment in a silence that I am grateful for, one I hadn't known I needed until I feel weird that I am still sitting with my legs around him and get off.

I walk a few steps closer to the lake and look at the ombre of oranges and reds painted in the clouds behind the trees on the other side. It's breathtaking. The sunset coupled with the orange blossoms on the breeze and the soothing sounds of nature around us spark a warmth in my chest. I wonder if it's the wine briefly, but with the water and food I know that's not the source.

"You doin' alright?" Jess breaks the silence from where he stands beside me. It doesn't escape my notice that he is the first person to actually ask me that.

"I think so." I slowly nod, not sure if I am trying to convince him or myself more. "I was just thinking about your driving."

"Don't tell me I scared you, Doll?" he pokes me playfully and I swat at his hands laughing.

"Don't flatter yourself."

"Alright, I'll bite. What about my driving?"

"I was just thinking about that time that my Dad called and said it takes 20 minutes to get home from anywhere in Glenbrook."

Jess straightens up a little, but the surprise in his expression fades just as quickly as it came, into a nostalgic smile. "I remember that, weren't we down near Tampa for some reason?"

"I have no idea why we were there, but yeah." I take a seat in the sand and Jess follows suit.

"We made it, though." His proud smirk reaches his eyes.

"That has to be the fastest I've ever gone." My head goes up and down subtly as I remember zooming through traffic on I-4.

I can still vividly see us, in that Camaro, with Jess shifting lanes between every other car and semi-truck. It was as if no matter how many cars were ahead of him, he'd needed to beat them all. To be the fastest, to get to the front, but there were always more to pass. Until we weren't on the road anymore and we made it back to see my Dad waiting outside. His stern fatherly mask, not quite able to hide his knowing smile behind his fu manchu.

"I swear, I don't know why he liked you." I laugh, shaking my head at the memory. "He chased a boy in a pickup truck away for giving me a ride home one time, you know?"

"I can totally see that." Jess nods thoughtfully.

"He was a sweet boy too, I think he even called him sir."

"That's probably why Karl scared him off."

"Right. And here you are, in your trashy sports car, driving his daughter around at warp speed and keeping me out at all hours of the night."

"You think he knew? When you said you slept at girl's houses but we really just drove around and did nothing all night?"

"Oh, he knew." I turn more towards Jess, "One time you dropped me off about a half hour before he got up for work and he came in my room, called me out for pretending to be asleep already, and said 'Did you have fun with Jess?'"

Jess's mouth drops open in a shocked smile. "He did? You never told me that."

"Yeah," I say, my head yet again in a thoughtful up and down motion. "He just told me to leave a note next time."

"I've missed this," Jess says softly after another quiet moment.

"Me too," I almost whisper, watching the brightness in the sky across the water fade.

"I don't think Ross really liked me being around you.

So unless it was everyone around, I just stopped trying to make plans with you." I can hear hurt in his tone. It's subtle, but it's there.

Crap. I take a deep breath and steal myself, trying to decide if I want to tell him why Ross didn't want him around. It seems tonight is filled with walks down memory lane, so I decide one more can't hurt at this point.

"Do you remember that night when we had to go get Chad to drive him home because he drank so much?" I ask him, not looking away from the sky.

I can hear the deep swallowing noise his throat makes before he clears his throat and answers me.

"Uh.. yeah, Chad decided it was a good idea to do shots at the bar every time his team scored. And they had one heck of a game." He recalls, steering around the elephant in the conversation.

"Right. When you called you kind of interrupted Ross asking me to be his girlfriend. Officially." I admit.

"Wait." His eyes shoot open in amusement. "So you just took my call, gave him a 'that sounds fine' and left to come get Chad with me?"

"I didn't answer him. I just took the out and left."

"You what?" Jess guffaws, looking dumbfounded.

"Yeah well, after we dropped Chad off and assumed that he was safely tucked into bed… he may have texted Ross," I say slowly, hardly looking to gauge his reaction.

"I didn't know this at the time. Ross didn't tell me until months later, but I guess Chad drunkenly texted him warning him to back off because, according to Chad, you had feelings for me as *'more than a brother'* and he was in the way of that. Or at least that's what Chad said." I explain, now feeling nervous and slightly embarrassed about bringing up the whole conversation.

What if he thinks I am fishing for him to confess to liking me?

I feel like I have to keep explaining. "Anyhow, like I said, Ross didn't tell me until way after the fact. I remembered Chad bringing that up that night, and how you shut him down, and how silly the whole thing was. I didn't wanna bring it up to you again because it was already a settled matter but, that was Ross's issue. I left our date to go somewhere with you. Then Chad puts that out there for him to worry about and it made him jealous. Which is ironic right? Because he was the one who couldn't be trusted." I end my rant with a self pitying laugh to cover how absolutely stupid I feel for trusting a man who cheated on me.

"Chad really did that?" He asks, rubbing his face in embarrassment.

"Yeah," I shrug. "But it's Chad. You can't stay mad at him. Besides, he probably doesn't even remember it, he was so drunk."

"Right." Jess agrees, shaking his head. "Drunken Chad, a treasured, meddlesome pastime."

A mosquito lands on my arm, and even though they aren't swarming around us like they would this time of day in the summer, we decide it's time to head back before more of them come along. Jess drives a little slower on the way back. I'm not sure if he's taking longer for my benefit or his own, but I don't complain. Even with the air getting a little more chilly against my arms, wrapped around his stomach.

~

Carlos offered me a ride home not long after we got

back, but I told him I was going to have Mel drive me, which she reluctantly did. He also offered to come by in the morning and take a look at my Jeep, which Jess overheard and insisted on taking care of it himself. Carlos looked like he wanted to object, but thought better of it, thankfully.

Chapter 6

Jess

I decide to swing by a drive-through and pick up a latte on my way to Samantha's apartment. I don't drink coffee, so I opted for a chai tea, trying not to look like I went out of my way. I am holding the drink holder in one hand and fidgeting with my hat while I wait for her to answer the door. I can't decide if I should have it on backward or with the bill facing forward, which I realize is a stupid thing to be worried about. I am just here to give my friend a hand with her car.

Backward it is since that's the way it is facing when she swings the door open.

"Mornin', Doll," I say, holding the latte out to her.

Her face lights up as she takes the cup from me and steps back, letting me into the apartment.

"Jess, you shouldn't have." She smiles, greedily taking the warm to-go cup in both hands.

"Just figured you could use the pick me up." I try for casual indifference.

"I'll take all the coffee I can today, thanks." She says pointing to the mess on the coffee table.

"What's all this?" I ask.

She lets out a big sigh and plops herself onto the sofa before explaining. "It's all of the grading I have to get done before grades are due this week. Mel and I barely put a dent in it Friday night before everything happened. Then yesterday got away from me. Meaning, I still have approximately one truckload of papers to finish grading before the deadline."

"Looks fun," I say dryly. "Well, I took a look under the hood before I came up and it looks like the starter wire was the issue."

"Oh, was it eroded?" Samantha asks then takes a sip from her coffee. That distracts me for a moment, as a small satisfied moan hums in her throat.

"No," I clear the huskiness from my throat before I continue. "Looks like something with sharp teeth gnawed right through it in one bite. Maybe a rat or something."

"Okay, so can we splice it until a new one comes in?"

"Already done, just need your keys to test it out."

Samantha stays upstairs with her mountain of papers while I go back out to test start her Jeep. Thankfully, it starts up right away, it should last her until a new part comes in. I make a note on my phone to order it the next time I go into the shop. Usually, I would just text Carlos and have him do it, but I don't want to bring up Samantha with him right now.

He's a good guy, don't get me wrong. He's a hell of a hard worker and I like having him around. I just don't like his style with women. He's known around the shop as a bit of a player. Whether or not that's true, I am not sure, but it's a reputation he built for himself, and I don't want to hear him talking to guys in the shop about her like he does with other women. *If those stories are even true.*

When I get back upstairs Samantha is diligently focused on her grading. So concentrated that I don't know if she hears me tell her I got it started. I don't know what comes over me, or why, but I just start gathering up the papers, trying my best not to mix the piles. I stack them on the laptop she has sitting on the table.

"What are you doing?" Samantha asks me.

"You need to get this done," I say *like she doesn't already know that*. "And you said yesterday that you didn't wanna be here alone. So we'll work on it at my place. Do you have a bag you want to put this in?"

Samantha gapes at me with her mouth half open as she watches me pick things up. To my surprise, she doesn't argue with me though. Instead, she stands up, coffee and red pen still in hand, and starts walking towards the door.

"Can we get pizza?" she requests, slipping on her sandals and grabbing her purse from the hook near the door.

"We can get whatever you want, Doll," I tell her, the stack of papers and computer in hand.

She never answered me about a bag so I just opt to carry them. I open the passenger door of my new Mustang for her and she climbs in, minding to keep her sun dress from coming up.

Before we pull out onto the road she has put the radio on and started singing along. It's such a Samantha thing to do, which makes me smile. She looks more like herself today, bright and bubbly.

She's always been an infectiously happy and kind person. One of those people who brightens the whole room the moment they enter it, and makes everyone feel like she can relate to them. One time I saw her talking to a kid who told her that his mom was in jail and her response was just *"That's okay, sometimes mine is too"*. I think her candidness surprised the boy as much as it did me. But I'll never forget how he looked at her like he was grateful for someone who understood. Teaching was the perfect job for her. No one was going to care about those kids the way that she could.

We are pulling down my long drive before Samantha actually says anything directed at me. She's just been singing along to the radio and channel surfing.

"You don't have to keep coming to my rescue, you know," Samantha says, nudging me in the arm as I down-shift.

"Easy on the driver, Doll." I laugh.

That's exactly what she looks like today too, a Doll. Big honey brown eyes, little freckles forming a triangle beside her nose, her dirty blonde hair in a low bun on the back of her head, even a floral sun dress like the one she wore the day I first called her that name. I shake my head, trying to clear my thoughts as I shift the car into neutral and pull the e-brake, then reluctantly get out. She follows me into the house and starts to make herself at home as I call up the pizza place to get our order in.

To my surprise, she hands me a red pen, and a stack of papers with an answer key to work on. Since she is actually letting me help, we have a few of the stacks done before the pizza gets here. We eat and chat while we work. I do my best not to drip pizza sauce on the tests that she says have to be sent home for the parents to see once they are graded. Once we get down to the last stack, Samantha lets me check them over so she can start putting the grades into her laptop.

"Miss Bunting," I say, trying to make my voice higher. "Can I have a sticker for being such a good helper?"

"That was a terrible impression." She bursts out laughing at my stupid joke. *At least she is smiling.*

"Seriously, thank you, Jess. I don't know how I would have gotten all of this done in time without you."

"Yeah, good thing I showed up when I did." I joke. "No way Mel would've gotten it done this quickly."

"True, but to be fair Mel is usually grading her *own* classwork when we do this," Samantha says folding her laptop closed and placing it on the coffee table.

"We should celebrate," I say, standing to stretch.

"I can't," she says looking up at me. "I have to be up for work in the morning."

"How about Friday then, after work?" I try again, attempting to mask the disappointment in my tone. "We can do it up big, whatever you want."

A big smile spreads across her face before she jumps up and wraps her arms around me. "That sounds amazing. Thank you, Jess, for everything."

"You don't have to keep thanking me, Doll." I sigh wrapping my arms around her.

She is just small enough to fit right under my chin when she hugs me like this. I try to focus on that and not the feel of her breasts pressing against me. Just like I tried not to think about them pressing against my back last night while she held onto me on the back of the four-wheeler.

"You've got a few days to decide what you want to do. Make sure you choose wisely."

Chapter 7

Samantha

I have just dropped my class off at art, so I have a break. Sitting down at my desk, I pull my phone out and open our group chat. Anytime Mel or I have a student say or do something really funny we usually share it in the chat with Chad and Jess.

Samantha: 6. That is the number of times one of my students has said "Aww biscuits" today.
Chad: Biscuits? As in gravy?
Samantha: Yup. Apparently, things that prompt such a response can include (but are not limited to) breaking your pencil, your shoe being untied, and it not being time for recess ten minutes after the day has started.
Mel: How precious!
Jess: Come on, Doll, let the poor girl have recess!
Samantha: Traitor! You're supposed to be on my side.

I have gotten all of the grades in, on time thanks to Jess's help. We haven't really talked since he helped me on Sunday. He was such a lifesaver this weekend. Between fixing my Jeep, helping with papers, and let's not forget the coffee. I mean the man shows up on my doorstep with a latte in hand that he clearly went out of his way to get because he doesn't even drink coffee. If it were any other man, my knees would've buckled on the spot. And then there's his vague invitation to hang out on Friday.

Saturday I was pretty sure he was just looking out for me with Carlos and getting me away for a minute. Then Sunday when I got home I wasn't so sure. It was almost like Jess was flirting with me. Nothing he did on its own was out of the norm but added together in succession, I wasn't sure. Which gave me huge knots in my stomach, left trying to decide if he thinks our Friday plans are a date.

That's stupid, right?

To add to my confusion I feel a hint of guilt for thinking about anything like this so soon after my break up. Don't get me wrong, it's not like I owe anything to Ross after he cheated on me. I just feel guilty that I don't *actually* feel bad. Past the first 24 hours, I have barely thought of Ross. Which tells me that maybe I was never really in love with him, solidifying my thought that maybe I was just with him because I thought it validated me somehow. Now having time to look back, it seems like I was just making a lot of compromises and excuses for him, and now that he's gone I just feel relief.

Now that it's Wednesday and I haven't heard from Jess, (outside of the group chat) I am starting to think I imagined the whole thing. Normally I would talk to Mel about this sort of thing but after her stunt with Carlos, that is not gonna happen.

Besides, Jess is one of our closest friends, part of "the gang". I don't think I can talk to her about this unless I am ready for the entire dynamic to shift. *If* he is indeed flirting with me and things go wrong it could not only mess with our friendship but draw a line for Chad and Mel as they have to choose sides. On the other hand, this is probably just all in my head, and bringing it up would be a major embarrassment and create an uncomfortable situation for everyone. I am on my own with this one.

I am checking my work emails on the computer when another text comes through. This one is not in the group chat.

Jess: *You decide what you wanna do Friday?*

Samantha: *Not yet, unlimited possibilities puts too much pressure on a girl.*

Jess: *You've got two days left to decide, Doll.*

Jess: *Insert Jeopardy theme song*

Samantha: *Any suggestions?*

Maybe getting him to help choose will give me a hint as to what he is thinking.

He doesn't reply immediately so I put the phone in my pocket and make my way over to the art room to walk my students back to my classroom.

I am approaching the Art classroom when I do a double take, confirming that I see Leah walking out of a classroom. My blood boils at the site of her.

"Leah? What are you doing here?" I ask, trying to keep a professional tone in case anyone hears.

"I'm working." She says, mirroring my professional tone and stance, but there is a challenge in her eyes as she continues. "As a substitute teacher."

I silently kick myself, knowing that I let my mask slip and allowed her to see how shocked I am. She never mentioned applying when we were living together and I know the process takes months to get through before you are in a classroom. I subbed while I was in school, as much as I could.

"Oh," I say. "I didn't know you applied."

"Yeah. Well, I think we're learning there's a lot you don't know." Her low secretive tone gives me instant chills despite the warm day.

"I think I know enough," I tell her, trying for indifference.

"We'll see about that." Leah smiles, then walks away towards the cafeteria.

Like hell am I letting her near my students.

~

I tell Mel about running into Leah later at lunch. Since we teach the same grade we usually get to have our lunches and recess time together. She hadn't heard about Leah getting hired either. It's annoying but as usual, it's not really something I can say anything about. I push it aside and by the end of math, I am able to get her out of my mind. It is the end of the school day by the time I have the chance to check my phone again.

Jess: *I know the perfect thing.*
Samantha: *Perfect, you say? Do tell.*
Jess: *One word…Karaoke*

A huge smile spreads across my face, Leah forgotten completely.

I love karaoke.

I mean, I am not the best singer, or even a good singer but there is no stopping me. My dad used to joke that God forgot to install the embarrassment feature on me when I was born. I will sing in the shower, in the car, when I am cleaning, anytime. Jess knows me well, just like I know that he isn't going to do karaoke. Singing with me and the radio sure, but only when it's just us there. He picked something he knew *I* would enjoy. Which, brings me full circle in wondering if this is a date.

Samantha: *You were right. It's Perfect.*

Chapter 8

Jess

I'm at the shop when Chad pulls up, midday on Friday. His truck was overheating this morning so I told him to bring it by. After a quick look under the hood, I am pretty sure Chad's self-diagnosis was right. It's just the water pump, an easy enough fix. I let Carlos know we need to get one ordered before I take Chad to lunch in my truck.

"Looks like I need a ride for tonight if my truck's gonna be down," Chad tells me as the waitress fills our glasses from her pitcher of sweet tea.

"Where you goin' tonight?" I ask him, leaving out that I have plans of my own.

"Karaoke with Sammy and Mel." He cocks his head in a question, looking up from his menu. "I thought you were going too?"

It takes me a heartbeat to realize that Samantha must have invited them, and another to readjust my face to hide my disappointment. *It's not like I told her it was a date.* Though, I had hoped it would just be the two of us.

"Yeah, I uh.." I clear my throat, "I just didn't realize you were too."

"Should I not be?" Chad asks raising an eyebrow.

Of course, I don't want him and Mel tagging along. It *was* going to be my chance to change the way Samantha looks at me. Historically I have no issues talking to girls, but it's always been more difficult with Samantha. Every time I have gotten close I have shoved my foot so far in my mouth I could still kick my own ass with it.

You're more like a brother to me.

The thought mocks me. How am I supposed to get closer to her with our friends hanging around all night? I pretend to look at the menu, like I don't always get the same thing, instead of answering him. Clearly, I'm doing a poor job of using a convincing tone.

"Oh. I see what's going on here. Mel wasn't invited either. Was she?" Chad speculates.

At least he's doing me the small kindness of not saying it outright. He's always suspected my feelings for Samantha, no matter how much I denied them. Hell, I'd offered to put the backseat back in the Camaro when she started hanging out with us when we were younger. He refused, claiming that she'd probably sit in the back instead of by me if I did.

"No." That's all I need to say.

One word and Chad knows that I wanted to be alone with Samantha tonight. I grit my teeth and try not to crumple the aging menu, waiting for the jabs I'm sure are about to come. To my surprise, Chad gives me an understanding nod. Then after a moment of uncomfortable silence he says, "You know I would offer to stay home, but then you're gonna have Mel at her side all night and you won't get a word in edgewise."

My shoulders relax, if only slightly, at my best friend's casual response.

"It's alright man. You should come." I tell him as the

waitress, Maude, arrives with our food.

Maude is Leah's aunt, so she's familiar with our friends. From what I remember, Leah was pretty much raised by Maude after her mom ran off, or something like that. I wonder how much she knows about what's been going on between Samantha and Leah. I decide not to bring it up just in case. We haven't actually ordered yet, but we don't have to. Maude knows our regular orders and half the time she just brings them out without bothering to ask what we want.

"You'd better clean up and wear something nicer than that *Adams Auto* t-shirt if you think you got a shot of getting out of the friend zone," Maude tells me.

Evidently, she has been eavesdropping, and at least knows Samantha and Ross broke up.

"Here I thought I was supposed to be the one tipping you," I respond dryly as Maude walks away.

"I'm making an idiot out of myself, aren't I?" I ask Chad when she is out of earshot. "Who am I kidding? You know. Ross knew. Maude even knows. There is no way she doesn't know how I feel. She probably had Mel weasel her way in on purpose." I take a bite of my fries, ending my rant and feeling sufficiently pathetic.

"I don't know man." Chad starts cautiously. "How is she supposed to know when you've never had the guts to come out and tell her?"

"I fixed her car, man. I made her the tacos. I took her a coffee. What more am I supposed to do?" I say hanging my head in defeat.

"I mean that's a good step. Smart thinking, really. Doing all the crap Ross would probably be too good to do for her. Showing her you can take better care of her." He says winking at me.

"It's not like that. I'm not competing with that jackass. I just feel like…" I take a deep breath trying to find the right words. "I feel like I am up against myself man. I wasted so much time, denying anytime someone brought it up. Hell, we've been talking about it this whole time and I still haven't actually admitted it out loud."

"Sounds like it's time for you to get out of your own way," Chad says with an empathetic smile. "Look, I will still come tonight. I'm gonna text Mel and ask her for a ride. I'll run interference with her, help you get some alone time, and lay some groundwork with Sammy."

"You don't have to do that man," I tell him out of a mixture of politeness and self-doubt.

"It's already settled, man. Just don't get all in your head about it. Think of tonight as a pre-date. Go lay on the charm, get her to start thinking of you as a real option, and keep showing up man. You got this."

It's not the worst plan, I hate to admit. *This could work.*

"You're a good friend, bud," I say.

"Gotta earn my friends and family discount at the shop somehow." He claps me on the shoulder and we both laugh.

~

After work, I went over to the barber shop for a fresh haircut. I had them clean up my beard, keeping it short but still full. Samantha's last boyfriend was a pompous pretty boy with a baby face. But I overheard her telling Mel one time that she liked beards when they were talking about a guy Mel was considering a date with, so I decided not to shave it off. It makes me laugh a little as I look in the bathroom mirror. Then I pull my phone out to shoot her a message while the shower warms up.

Jess: Pick you up at 7 Doll
Samantha: I don't know if Mel needs a ride
Jess: She's giving Chad a ride. His truck's in my shop.
Samantha: 7 is perfect then. I'll be ready.

Thank you, Chad.

With that settled, I head into my shower with a huge grin on my face. I change my shirt twice, before deciding the original shirt I put on was the better choice. I pair it with some dark jeans and my favorite watch, then spray on some cologne Samantha gave me as a gift last year. She said it reminded her of me when she smelled it at the store. I don't know what that means. But if she picked it out she must like it, and that is reason enough for me to wear it. I check my watch and it is still too early for me to leave. I am too anxious to keep sitting around here though, so I get in the truck anyway.

I drive past Samantha's apartment and Benny's restaurant, deciding I don't want to look pathetic showing up too early. Turning at the next light, I see the coffee shop and remember the smile on Samantha's face when I brought her the coffee last weekend. Would it be just as pathetic to show up with another coffee as it would be if I'd show up early? Without a doubt. But only one of those options has the chance of making her smile like that again.

Fifteen minutes later I knock on Samantha's door, another latte in hand. I hear Samantha shout from somewhere in the apartment, "The door is open." So I turn the knob and walk in.

"You know, you really should lock your door," I call out.

She must still be in her room or bathroom getting ready so I take a seat on the couch.

"I just unlocked it when I saw your truck pull up." She calls back.

That makes me feel a little better.

Was she looking for me?

"You almost ready?" I call again fiddling with the cold to-go cup.

This time I brought an iced coffee which felt like a risk. Iced coffee has way too many options. I did my best to make something up based on things I knew she liked. None of the fussy milk alternatives, I've never heard her order something like that but I know she likes caramel and I had them add some of that fancy foam on the top that I saw on the menu photo for good measure.

"Yeah, I just need some help with my zipper," Samantha says right behind me. I turn from where I look out the window to see her coming up the hallway.

When I turn around I swear my mouth hangs open like that stupid cartoon wolf. *So much for playing it cool.* She is stunning. Her hair is curled and pulled over one shoulder. She's holding her dress closed behind her back. Even unzipped, her emerald dress is already hugging her curves in all the right places before flowing out at the waste so it moves as she does.

"Wow, Doll." That's all I manage to say.

"Is that for me?" she asks, pointing to the iced latte I'm still holding.

"Um, yeah. I didn't want you to get tired too early." I tell her as she takes it and spins for me to zip her up.

I think she stiffens slightly when I place one hand on her waist, holding the fabric in place. I can't be sure though, considering that I am putting all of the effort I have into not making an ass out of myself right now and keeping my hands from shaking.

"Wouldn't want that." She smiles back over her shoulder at me.

I may bring her coffee every day if she keeps looking at me like that.

Chapter 9

Samantha

"Is that for me?" I ask, looking at the iced coffee in Jess's hand.

"Um yeah. I didn't want you to get tired too early." He tells me handing me the cup before I turn around for him to zip up my dress.

He went out of his way to bring me a coffee.

Again.

I can't remember even a single time when he got a coffee for Mel or Chad.

"Wouldn't want that." I smile back at him over my shoulder before turning to get a good look at him.

Jess is wearing a black button-up shirt, with the sleeves rolled up to his forearms. It's a refreshing change from his usual "Adam's Auto" shirts I am so used to seeing him in after leaving the mechanic shop that bears his family's name. When I finally look up past my eye level I realize his hair is freshly cut, along with his beard. It's still full, still contrasting his bright blue eyes, but it's definitely been cleaned up. He looks, and smells for that matter, *really* good. Another hint that makes me regret letting Mel worm her way into our plans tonight.

I didn't invite her intentionally. She just sort of invited herself when I told her that I already had plans with Jess on Friday. I didn't know how to tell her that she couldn't come just in case *maybe* the guy who has said a thousand times that he has zero interest in me *might* have changed his mind a week after a break up that I am not heartbroken over. At least not without sounding… how that sounds.

"You ready, Doll?" Jess asks.

"I hope so," I answer honestly.

The nerves in my stomach twist as Jess places his hand on the small of my back and leads me toward the door. I might have called the feeling butterflies if I were more sure of how to feel. He keeps his hand there until we reach the small parking lot behind Benny's. I am surprised to see his truck, rather than his new car. But I don't mention it, and he opens the driver-side door gesturing for me to climb in.

The driver's side. I note that he intentionally brought me to this side of the truck, and decide not to wait for any more subtle hints before deciding what I want. The worst thing that can happen is I make an absolute fool out of myself.

I smile up at him through my eyelashes and climb across the driver's seat, stopping at the middle seat. There's no subtlety to the blush on my cheeks or his coquettish grin, acknowledging the gesture. My stomach is swirling like a whirlpool as his leg presses against mine and he turns the key.

This is it. I am pretty sure I am on a date with Jess Adams.

There is no karaoke bar in Glenbrook so we have to drive into the city. Jess's arm is draped over my leg, his hand on the shifter, just as it has been many times before. Only, tonight I am hyper-aware of each subtle movement his arm makes over my leg.

Every glance my way or time he leans into me as we turn seems amplified. The way his muscles in his arm tighten when he shifts gears, shifting the fabric of my dress on my thigh right along with it. Neither of us says much, I think we are both too nervous, the delicious tension of the drive and our closeness making us both more aware of each other as the drive goes on.

One thing about living in Central Florida is that there are lakes everywhere. In almost every established town you can find a road going around a lake, and nine out of ten times it's called Lakeshore Drive. We are almost to Glenbrook's Lakeshore Drive, still both avoiding saying anything when Jess breaks the silence. We are coming to the end of Brookhill Road, another side road that ends in a three-way stop on Lakeshore, so we are going downhill to the three-way stop.

"Oh no!" He pumps his leg on the brake pedal. "Looks like we have no brakes!"

I roll my eyes as Jess flashes me a playful smirk. We both burst out laughing as the truck comes to a stop at the intersection and we look out at the lake in front of us.

My dad used to make the same joke every time we came down that hill growing up, which was a lot. I smile, feeling a warmth in my stomach at Jess making one of his cheesy dad jokes. Then that warmth is replaced with a feeling of worry. If this is what I think it is and it doesn't work out, I could be risking one of the few people in my life who remembers my dad that way. On the other hand, it's nice to be able to talk to Jess and not have to explain. Ross tried to be sympathetic about me missing my dad at times, but I always knew he couldn't really understand.

We end up talking more for the rest of the drive. Mostly

about little things like school, and the guy he's got managing the shop. It's so natural, that I forget about my reservations.

I don't forget about Jess's arm across my thigh. It's almost impossible not to be distracted by the material of my dress sliding between my thigh and the strong weight of his arm. I don't know how Jess is managing to be aloof right now. I wonder if he's just as flustered as I am. If so, he's certainly better at hiding it.

As soon as Jess parks the truck he turns towards me, moving his hand from the shifter to behind me on the seat.

"I need to ask you something." He says with soft sincerity looking out the window behind him, rather than right at me.

"Yes, the rumors are true." I tease, trying to lighten the mood. If only to lessen my own nerves. "I did win the pie eating contest at the fair in eighth grade."

"Did you really?" he asks skeptically, softening a little.

"Of course, why do you think I can't eat apple pie anymore?" I say.

Once he laughs a little, I feel safe enough to steer us back on topic. "What was it you wanted to ask me?"

"Did you invite Mel and Chad on purpose?"

Shit. My stomach falls into my lap.

Now Jess is looking right into my eyes like the weight of my answer changes the meaning of this whole night. Maybe it does, if we let it.

I take a deep breath to prepare myself for what I am about to admit.

Matching the sincerity in his tone, I tell him, "I didn't invite Mel or Chad."

"Good" His shoulders relax as he says it, and my nerves spike again, feeling like a beehive in my chest.

"Good."

"I called ahead and put you down for a song, but it's a surprise."

"If it was a surprise, why did you just tell me?" I ask, thankful for the topic shift.

"The song you get to sing is the surprise." He tells me, "I picked it out myself. So don't go running off, disappearing on me."

He looks at me seriously when he says that last part, so I place my hand on his forearm in a reassuring gesture.

"I'm not going anywhere, Jess."

Jess looks into my eyes for a moment, almost like he is trying to see right into my mind. Like he's trying to figure out if I am as nervous as he is, or if we are on the same page. Then with a heavy sigh, he breaks his gaze, nods, and says, "Alright. Let's get in there."

There is no sign of Mel or Chad yet, which is almost a relief. Jess leads me with his large hand on the small of my back to a high-top table where he helps me onto my stool. Then he grabs the stool from the other side of the table and moves it around next to mine before taking his seat on it. All of his motions and gestures are subtly more intimate tonight, including something about the way he looks at me.

When the waitress comes by he orders an old fashioned for himself and a rum runner for me.

"How was your week?" He asks me, leaning in so I can hear him over the crowd and music.

"Well, let's see." I start trying to recall highlights of my week that are not too boring. "Yesterday I looked out my window and saw four students carrying a girl across the playground. Each with a wrist or ankle in their hands."

Jess's eyebrows shoot up. "What did you do?"

I can't help but giggle at his alarmed tone before I give him a nonchalant shrug.

"Nothing."

"Nothing?" I am not sure if he is going to laugh or if he's repulsed.

Either way, this is fun.

"She looked like she was enjoying it," I explain. "Their teacher told them to put her down before I could get out to do anything. Don't worry, she walked away laughing with all four limbs intact."

Jess actually sighs in relief.

It's adorable. He is supposed to be this grumpy, serious, masculine guy. At least that's how everyone else sees him, and I guess in some ways he is. But here he is worrying about a little girl he doesn't even know, in a situation that wouldn't make most teachers so much as blink.

"At least there was a happy ending." He says as the waitress appears with our drinks and a bowl of nuts.

"Then one of the little boys asked me if we could play 'CandyHang'."

"What is that?"

"It's what first graders say when they can't remember what Hangman is called."

"Cute." Jess laughs which warms the smile I have had this whole conversation.

"Let me see what else," I say taking a sip of my drink. "Oh, and I just found out who the new substitute the school hired is."

"Anyone I know?" he asks.

"It's Leah."

"Shit."

"You can say that again," I sigh.

"Don't let her get to you, Doll," Jess says putting his calloused hand over mine on the table.

"I know I shouldn't," I say as he starts to rub little circles on my hand with his thumb.

I try to act like it's normal. I don't want him to stop if I draw attention to it.

"It's just so weird that she would choose to come work at my school after the whole 'I hate you because I wish I had your life' thing. She would have had to start the application months ago."

Jess doesn't say anything so I keep rambling. "I mean sure, you like your friend's dress, so you get one too. But my Jeep? Copying my haircut? And I don't even care about the Ross thing, but *my school*? I know I probably sound paranoid but it's just weird. She doesn't even like kids."

"You aren't paranoid. She's jealous of you. We could all see it the whole time you were roommates." He tells me.

"Jealous of what?" I scoff, rolling my eyes at how ridiculous that sounds.

"Samantha, have you not seen yourself?"

The look he gives me burns a blush across my cheeks.

"How could she not be jealous?"

I feel my stomach doing somersaults. My heart is racing and either this is one strong drink that I have only had two sips of, or Jess has just shattered the friend zone with a sledgehammer and sauntered right over to the other side.

Before I have the chance to say anything, Mel appears and

squeezes between us. I am both disappointed, because Jess pulls his hand off of mine in a smooth movement to pick up his drink, and grateful because I need to catch my breath. I can see Chad trying to catch up behind her. It almost looks like he gives Jess an apologetic smile.

"I thought this was a celebration, why do you guys look so serious?" Mel says, looking between us. "Party pooping already, Adams?"

Jess's jaw clenches in annoyance.

"Hey guys, what did I miss?" Chad greets us.

"Leave Jess alone," I tell my best friend.

"Oh, come on," Mel shrugs, "We all know he's a big fuddy duddy."

"Sorry. I may have let her pre-game a little before driving her here." Chad explains.

She is usually a little quippy when she's been drinking. Maybe that's what Chad's face was trying to convey.

"As long as you're driving her home," Jess tells Chad.

We have always taken turns being sober drivers. It's something we take pretty seriously.

"It's fine. And he is not a fuddy duddy. In fact, Jess was just taking me to dance. Weren't you, Jess?" I say, brightly reaching out my hand.

"I sure was, Doll." Jess smiles, taking the lead and steering me towards the dance floor.

I can't see over his shoulder or around him as he leads me through the crowd to the dance floor. So I am looking at the way his hand engulfs mine, noting how strong his hands are compared to my own small ones. When someone bumps into Jess, he stops to apologize and I run into his back. Then he mumbles a curse as he sees who it is and I step around him to get a better look.

Leah. Of course.

"What are you doing here?" Jess asks her.

Leah looks at my hand in Jess's and smirks. She's probably celebrating in her head about Ross and I breaking up but I don't care. It's honestly been a relief not having him around.

"I heard Mel in the cafeteria talking about this place. It sounded fun." She smiles at Jess, twirling her hair.

Seriously?

I roll my eyes and mentally curse my big mouthed best friend.

"Well, you'll have to excuse us," Jess says, effectively blowing her off and winning more points in my book. "We are going to dance."

Once we reach the dance floor he places a hand on my hip and leans in to say something in my ear over the roar of voices around us.

"I am probably gonna step on your toes." He warns with a grin.

His voice and closeness are already cooling the boiling rage I had towards Leah being here.

"As long as you carry me out of here if I can't walk." I laugh back.

In response, Jess flashes me the most flirtatious smile I think I may have ever been on the receiving end of and then spins me by the arm. When he pulls me back from the spin, to his chest, he glances from my mouth to my eyes. I can feel his bright eyes, trying to read me again, getting ever so closer. I am sure he is thinking about kissing me but before we get any closer I hear my name from behind me.

Jess looks up past me and his expression shifts, whiplashing from flirtatious to pissed, much angrier than it was with Leah. Jess wraps his hand around my arm and pulls me to his side as I turn to be surprised by another unfriendly face.

This is not my day.

"Ross," Jess says more warning than greeting.

"Sammy, you need to come with me," Ross says, ignoring Jess, even though his eyes track Jess's hands on me.

"Like *hell,* she does, pretty boy." Jess snips, taking a protective step forward.

"I mean it, Sammy. I don't want to make a scene in here." Ross says.

His words don't sound like a warning though. Somehow it sounds like a plea. Like he has something to say that's really urgent, and the part of me that cared for him is picking up on whatever he isn't saying.

"What's going on?" I feel a sting of guilt at Jess's shock when I pull out of his grasp.

"Just one minute. *Please.*" Ross gestures for me to follow him and starts walking towards the exit.

"Doll, don't," Jess says.

Then I can't explain why, but I tell Jess "I'm sorry."

Then, despite the rock sinking in my gut, I follow Ross out the door.

Maybe I'm expecting him to apologize, and hoping to use some of the brilliant one-liners I came up with in the shower the other day. Or maybe I really believe he had some imperative emergency that I might need to actually hear about. Whatever it was, I hope it won't keep me long. I am already regretting the look of betrayal I'd put on Jess's face.

As soon as we make it out the door I stop, feeling like the wind was knocked out of me by an invisible wall. Leaning against his car, is the last person I expected to see. The last person I would want to see. I would rather go back inside with Leah at this point and watch her and Ross make out.

I stand there in shock, looking between my ex-boyfriend and the woman walking towards me in confusion. I had thought maybe he was here with Leah, but now I'm not sure what's going on. *Why is she with him? Why do people keep showing up? Why would he bring her here? How did they know where I was?*

"What the hell is going on here?" I blurt out.

"Oh, wow. You look great, sweetie." My mother finally says trying to wrap her arms around me. My arms instantly come up to my chest in a defensive position to push her away.

This can't be happening. Not tonight.

And she got Ross of all people to bring her to me. Jess must be fuming, but I can't think about him right now. I need to get to the bottom of whatever this is and figure out how to get her out of here as quickly as possible.

"What are you doing here, Carol?" I say, refusing to call the woman who abandoned me every chance she got *"Mom"*.

"I just wanted to see you, sweetie. How have you been?" Carol says.

"What are you doing bringing her here?" I shout at Ross, knowing my mother won't admit what really brought her here.

"How did you know where I was?"

"She said Leah sent her to my office to find you. I guess she didn't know we broke up, or that you moved." Ross explains. "I didn't think you'd take my call, so I checked Mel's story and she posted about coming here. Not too long of a shot to guess you'd be here with her."

"Dammit, Mel," I grumble, rubbing my face with frustration.

Why does it seem that all of the invaders of my evening stem from my friend's big mouth?

"Oh, honey. Ladies really shouldn't swear." Carol says.

"Don't mother me, Carol," I snap at her.

Like she knows what a fucking lady would do.

She always does this. Shows up out of the blue, tries to mother me into a connection, asks for money, or steals it, and then disappears on another bender. I don't know that I have ever seen her for more than twenty straight days. At least not once I was old enough to remember. This time it's been just under a year since I saw her last. That time, she showed up and crashed on my couch for a week before stealing my TV, which I had to buy back from the local pawnshop. But what am I supposed to do, make her sleep outside?

"Okay, I get it," Carol says raising her hands defensively. "I haven't been back enough, I'm sorry."

"I'd prefer if you were back less," I say hoping my words feel as sharp to her as her presence does to me.

Ross, clearly uncomfortable being stuck in the middle of this, clears his throat.

"Did you drive here, Sammy?" he asks.

"No, I rode with Jess," I say.

He looks wounded by that, if only for a second, but seems to push it down before saying. "Okay, well I'll give you two a ride in the Audi. That way you don't have to hash this out in a bar parking lot."

I let out a frustrated sigh, knowing he is right, and tell

Carol to get in the backseat. Once she is in with the door closed, I look back over my shoulder at the bar, wondering if I should go back in and talk to Jess before I go. But I know that if I go in there, Carol will follow. Being the award-winning mother that she is, she won't resist getting wasted and causing a scene. Then I'll never get her out, and whatever tonight was supposed to be between us, will be a giant red flag reminding Jess that with me, comes Carol. I can't go back in, and at least Jess has Chad and Mel still here. I will talk to him in the morning.

Jess will understand.

Chapter 10

Jess

I am standing alone in the middle of the dance floor watching Samantha follow Ross out the door when Chad finds me.

I am still trying to figure out how she went from being in my arms, so close that I could feel her breath across my lips, to walking out the door.

I barely hear it when Chad asks, "What was that about?"

We make our way over to the bar and I explain to him the little that I know.

"Pretty boy showed up and asked her to leave. Then she did," I tell him holding my hand up to get the bartender's attention. "Whiskey, neat, keep 'em coming."

"I'm sorry, bud." Chad pats me on the back. "I know that's not how you wanted tonight to go.

"I must be a complete dumb-ass. I thought she was into me. Or maybe she could be, at least. She was the one who pulled me out there." I say pointing back to the dance floor. "This was a stupid idea."

"Maybe she just went out there to tell him to get lost," Chad reassures me.

"You think?' I ask, trying not to sound too hopeful.

"Only one way to find out." He nods towards the door.

Maybe he is right.

Maybe Samantha is out there trying to get Ross to just leave her alone. Maybe he is ruining her night just as much as mine. I didn't think she had talked to him since the breakup, maybe she needed closure. But then, how did he know where to find her? If this was a date I should probably go check on her. So that's what I decide to do.

I feel worse when I step outside just in time to see Samantha tucking her head into Ross's car and shutting the door. Then they just drive away, and I feel like an idiot, watching his taillights pull out of the parking lot.

Maybe this was too soon for her. I thought we both understood the unspoken agreement of what tonight meant. Clearly, she didn't, she wouldn't have just gotten into her ex's car and rode away if what was going on with us meant that much to her. No goodbye, no reason, just gone.

When I get back to Chad at the bar, the bartender brings over my drink. It disappears just as quickly as it appeared in front of me and I gesture for another.

"Didn't you drive here?' Chad asks pointing to the empty glass in front of me as a new one takes its place.

I dig in my pocket for my keys and hand them to my friend. "Yeah, but I'm not drivin' home."

"Sammy wasn't out there?" he guesses, sensing my mood.

"She's driving off in an Audi." I throw the next drink back as Leah appears on my other side.

"What, no Sammy?" Leah asks.

The freaking viper must've seen her leave from the dance floor.

"I guess not," I say trying not to sound as pathetic as I feel.

"Why don't you come try that spin move on me then?" Leah says, shamelessly flirting with me. She walks toward the dance floor swaying her hips dramatically, looking back for me to follow. And even though I can't stand Leah, even though I know I shouldn't, I am just hurt enough that I swing back my third drink and stand to follow her.

"You sure you wanna do that?" Chad asks, grabbing my arm to stop me.

"Why wouldn't I?" I say, knowing very well the answer, but being too pissed off to care.

"Sam." He says.

He's right, she would hate this, date or not. But…

"Isn't here, is she?" I pull away and follow Leah onto the dance floor where Samantha left me.

~

My head hurts.

My mouth is dry.

The sun is too bright.

I drank too much last night. I fumble to pick up my phone on the nightstand. I have several missed calls and messages.

3 Missed Calls from Samantha

1 Missed Call from Carlos

Chad: Dude, where'd you go?

Chad: Tell me you didn't leave here with her.

Chad: At least let me know you got home safe jackass.

* * *

Leave there with who? Chad didn't give me a ride here? I get out of bed and walk towards the kitchen, looking out by the garage to where I normally park my truck. It's not there, but there is a blue Jeep in its place. That's when I smell the coffee that must've just been made and then I hear the shower start in the bathroom.

Samantha came back? Did she drive me home?

She left with Ross, didn't she?

Why is she getting in my shower?

Please, Lord above, tell me I didn't spend the night with Samantha and have no memory of it because I drank too much. (My last thought turns into an actual prayer).

I pour a cup of coffee and sit down on the couch. Normally I don't like coffee but I hope it will help my hangover. I only keep the coffee pot around for my friends and guests. I'm surprised I even had some coffee in the cabinet. It tastes just as awful as I remembered, but I keep drinking it anyway. Maybe once my head stops throbbing I can remember what happened. In the meantime maybe there are more clues in the other texts.

Carlos: Chad's truck will be ready by lunch.

Samantha: Sorry I had to go. I'll explain later.

Samantha: I really am sorry, I didn't want to leave. Call you when I get home?

Samantha: Please don't be mad.

So there was an explanation.

I never even saw that she must have sent the first message right after she left. It looks like Samantha came back and explained herself and somehow ended up here, in my shower.

I don't get it. I rub my face, trying to make things make sense. Why did she leave with him? How did she explain that? Did she come back to the bar and drive me here? Did Chad call her? He is always meddling, so that's not a stretch.

Did she see me with Leah? My gut sinks at the thought.

I am typing out a message to let Chad know about his truck when I hear tires coming down the driveway. He probably got a ride to get his truck already and is coming to check on me. I decide to grab some aspirin before he gets in here. That should help the coffee wear down this migraine and brain fog. Then hopefully he can help fill in the gaps before she gets out of the shower.

I am standing at the sink, looking out the window for him to pull around while I fill my glass to take the aspirin. I put the pills in my mouth, along with a mouthful of water, all of which are spit out, when I see another Jeep pass the window and park by the first.

Both Jeeps are the same Chief Blue that Samantha loved when I went with her to test drive hers. I take a good look and notice the "Tuna, no crust" bumper sticker on the Jeep that just arrived. Then realization hits me. Hard.

Samantha is not in my shower.

Which means Leah is. Her ex-roommate who obsesses over her, swooped in the moment she saw Samantha leave, and… Shit. I don't remember what happened but it can't be good. I have Samantha's sworn enemy in here, naked, in my shower.

Knock. Knock. Knock.

I opt to come outside to greet her, careful not to open the door too wide behind me before closing it.

"I'm sorry." Samantha sighs, looking more tired and

upset than the morning after she and Ross broke up.

I step out the back door and close the door behind me, not wanting her to hear the shower.

"You don't have to apologize. It's not like you owe me anything." I say quickly. I need to rush her out of here before Leah comes out.

"Don't be like that, let me explain. Please, Jess." Samantha pleads.

Even though I don't want her to see Leah here, I am still pissed that she ran off with Ross last night.

"I don't know what you mean," I deflect.

"Come on." She tries reaching for my arm, but I pull back.

"No, I mean it. It's not like we were on a date or anything right? Why stick around to ride home with me, when you have pretty boy in his fancy car, ready to ride you off into the sunset." *Yeah, that didn't sound jealous.*

"It wasn't like that, Jess."

"Oh, you don't have to defend yourself, just don't come back crying to me when he doesn't keep it in his pants again," I say, hating myself as the words come out, but knowing that I can't take them back now.

"You don't have to rip my head off. If you would just let me explain…" Samantha starts. That's as far as she gets though because the damnable door opens. Out comes Leah, holding the mug I left on the coffee table, with her hair in a towel. Thankfully she has clothes on, unfortunately, they're the same ones she wore last night. This doesn't look good.

"Hey, thought you might want your coffee," Leah says looking from Samantha to me and giving me a peck on the cheek. *Gross.* What is she marking me as her territory? If I hadn't been twelve rounds past sober last night there's no way I would give her the time of day. She probably only came onto me to piss off Samantha, anyway, which is enough to make me feel sick without the hangover.

I really regret not putting on a shirt. Samantha looks from me to Leah, then to Leah's jeep, and back to me again like she can't make sense of what she is seeing. An invisible knife twists in my stomach, at the hurt in her eyes. *I am an absolute idiot.* Of all of the people in the world for her to find here, it had to be fucking Leah. I think I see tears start to fill her eyes, and all she says is, "Oh."

"Samantha, it's not what it looks like," I try to lie. But even if I don't remember it, how could it be anything else?

"It wasn't a date right?" her voice cracks as she turns and heads back to her jeep.

"So, breakfast?" Leah asks, with a smug smile like she came out on top of whatever just happened here.

"You need to go," I tell Leah. Whatever happened between Samantha and Ross, this just made it worse. I grab my phone to text Chad while Leah gets her things.

Jess: *I think I messed up*

Chad: *You did. Sammy just started a new group chat without you.*

Jess: *So she could talk crap about me sleeping with Leah? Like she didn't just spend the night with Ross.*

Chad: *Worse. She isn't talking about you at all. Which means you must've ticked her off enough for her to shut you out.*

Jess: *What the hell gives her the right to be mad after she ran off with Ross?*

Chad: *She isn't back with him.*

Jess: *Then why did she leave with him?*

Chad: *That's what the new group chat is about. You should talk to her. It's not my place to say.*

Jess: *She just showed up trying to talk to me and saw Leah coming out of the shower.*

Chad: *You messed up man. Big time.*

Fuck.

Chapter 11

Samantha

Chad: Is this a new group chat?

Mel: Did you actually leave last night with Ross?

Samantha: Yes, but I didn't have a choice. He showed up with Carol.

Mel: Carol's back?

Chad: He brought her to the bar?

Samantha: Carol showed up at his work. Mel posted that we would be there and he saw it. I didn't want to go back in to explain and have her follow me into the bar.

Mel: Good call, you'd never get her out.

Chad: Where is she now?

Samantha: My place. She hasn't fessed up about why she is here this time.

Mel: Hide your wallet. And the TV

Samantha: How am I supposed to hide a TV?

Chad: Mel has a point. Just keep an eye on her.

Samantha: Hopefully I can get her out of here today.

I have been sitting in my Jeep in the alley parking lot drinking my latte, while I message Mel and Chad. I am not ready to face Carol. She was asleep when I left this morning. I was too worried about Jess being upset with me for leaving last night to sleep. I just wanted to apologize and explain. I don't know how I missed Leah's Jeep when I pulled up. I am chalking it up to being focused on what I would say to Jess.

I knew Jess would be upset about me leaving, but I also thought he would understand once I could explain. What I didn't count on, was getting the chance to explain. I mean, of all people… did it have to be Leah? She never so much as batted an eye his way until she saw us together last night. I am trying really hard to convince myself that she's not going out of her way to spite me. Then again, she's not the one I am crying over. Which is why I am still in my Jeep, instead of upstairs in my apartment.

I can handle being upset about Carol being back. I'll figure out what she's up to eventually. I can even handle the mixture of emotions towards Jess and this whole situation. Somehow I will handle still acting friendly, for the sake of our friends until I get over it. What I can NOT do, is walk in there and let my mother see me upset. She will see it as an excuse to give me advice, bond, or Heaven forbid… hug me. Maybe it's some Freudian response or something, I don't know, but Carol touching me gives me panic attacks. Not spiders, alligators, or anything else, just *her*.

World's best mom.

I silently laugh off the thought as I flip down my visor to check my face in the mirror. I wipe away last night's mascara that has smudged from crying and decide this will have to do. It's not like Carol knows what I usually look like in the morning anyway. If I can get up there and get rid of her, at least all the bad could be contained to one day. I just want to get this whole day over with.

When I walk into my apartment, to my surprise, Carol is

sweeping the floor. It's odd. Carol is known for leaving messes, not cleaning them. I expected to walk in and find her riffling through my belongings, or to not find her at all. I never would've bet on her cleaning my apartment. But then I never would've thought Jess would sleep with Leah, or that him sleeping with anyone would make me feel this way.

What do I know?

"Hey, baby girl," Carol says, turning off the vacuum.

Goosebumps crawl across my skin at the sound of her pet name for me. As always, I try to ignore them and focus on the bizarre scene in front of me.

"What's with this?" I ask pointing from the vacuum to the bucket of cleaning products on the counter.

"Heartache calls for help." My mother says so empathetically, you'd think she regularly does this sort of thing.

In actuality, this is a first. She wasn't even around when my Dad died to comfort me, yet here she is acting like some supportive super mom. It's another tactic of hers, pretend to be cleaned up, reach out constantly, love bomb, try to worm her way back in. I can't say I have never fallen for it, but I have learned not to fall for it again. The thought irritates me but I try to keep my frustration out of my tone when I deflect.

"I am fine, thank you."

"I saw you through the window. I'm sorry about Ross," she says.

"I'm not upset about Ross. You shouldn't have gone to him," I tell her, not letting on more than I have to.

"I didn't know how to find you," Carol says.

"Did you go to Leah's?" I ask, remembering Ross's words from the night before.

"Yes, she told me you moved so I assumed you moved in with Ross. She didn't know where his apartment was so I went to his work."

"Of course," I reply rubbing my face. I didn't tell Leah where I was moving to when I moved out. But it doesn't make sense for her to send my Mother to Ross's work. She would have known that we had broken up. I can't exactly blame her for the breakup, Ross is the one who cheated. Even still, she was a key player, so why would she act like she had no clue and send Carol to his work looking for me?

"What are you doing here, Carol?" I finally ask her, losing the battle to keep my tone polite.

"I just wanted to see you." She says, looking at the floor while she starts her familiar speech. "I've been sober, going to meetings, even snagged myself a sponsor."

She fidgets with the chord on the vacuum before pushing on, "I came to make amends, apologize for my part."

Great, yet again I get to be guilt-tripped into not becoming a trigger for her relapses.

"Sober how long?" I ask her.

This isn't the first time she's gotten "sober". I have gotten involved and been let down by her more times than I can count.

"Not long enough. Sammy, I am sorry. I should have been here with you after your Dad's accident." She isn't finished but I cut her off.

"Don't. Do *not* try to use him to bond with me." I feel a bit of guilt rise up with the anger, as I snap at my mother.

Why the hell am I always trying to protect her feelings? Even at the expense of my own comfort.

Not this time.

"What do you want from me? To forgive you? You're forgiven. Now please leave."

"I understand. You have every right to be upset, take the time you need. Ricky is on his way to get me."

Damn right, I have the right to be upset.

"Who is Ricky?" I ask. I never know who is a boyfriend, sponsor for the week, or sometimes drug dealer. I am not sure I want him to come to my apartment.

"Don't worry, I told him to meet me at the bookstore on the next block," Carol says as if reading my mind. "I didn't take anything either."

I snicker in response, which causes Carol to pause until a guilty expression covers her face.

"I realize a normal Mom wouldn't have to say that, but I didn't."

"Thanks, I'd hate to have to buy *my own* TV back again," I say, too tired for the eye roll the situation calls for.

"Can I ask you something before I go?" *Predictable.*

"I don't have any cash," I tell her, rubbing my eyes while I sit down.

"It's not that. Actually, I have a job. So I was able to get a phone. I was just wondering if I could call you and check in sometime? Or maybe text?"

I almost crack, almost give in. But, I remind myself what it looks like to go down that road and steel my resolve against the habitual feeling of guilt in my sternum.

"I don't know if that's a good idea," I say hesitantly.

She tries to hide her look of disappointment by turning up the corners of her mouth. It doesn't really work though. I'd almost feel bad for her if it was my first time being faced with a *new and improved Carol..* Or even the twelfth time. But it's not, and I have learned that the only way to survive being her daughter is to guard my heart from letting her be my mother.

"Number's on the table if you change your mind," Carol says.

Then she walks out and closes the door behind her, leaving the vacuum and cleaning supplies for me to put away.

I take the note with her phone number off the counter and slide it into the junk drawer in the kitchen along with some batteries, scissors, and other things I keep out of sight. Maybe I should throw it away, but I don't. I tell myself I might need it sometime, it's not that little remnant of familial guilt that makes me decide to keep it.

I want to call Mel, but I don't know what I'd even say. If she and Chad know what happened they are avoiding talking about it, and if they don't, then I'm not going to be the one to bring it up. I know I should be focused on why Carol was here and what she possibly took this time, but seeing Leah on Jess's porch is the only thing that keeps coming to mind. It's ridiculous.

It wasn't even officially a date.

He can't even admit to having feelings for me.

My inner cynic has a point, but then I have another thought that stings worse.

What if he was just trying to get laid?

Chapter 12

Samantha

It's been a week since Carol showed up at the bar with Ross. I've been trying to keep myself busy, staying late at school and working on projects for the kids. I told myself if I just gave it a few days, everything would go back to normal. In some ways I was right. I convinced myself that Mel and Chad had no clue what was going on between me and Jess. Mel came over to grade papers like she usually does, and thankfully she didn't bring Jess up at all. She obviously knew to avoid the topic because he'd be a shitty friend to sleep with my ex-roommate. If she had an inkling of anything deeper than that, she didn't let on. We did talk about Carol and the whole Ross showing up thing, but that was about it.

Did Jess even know there was something going on between us?

I roll my eyes at myself. It was a little bit of flirting when I just got out of a relationship, nothing more. I can't keep sulking about it, and I really can't let it mess with our friend group. I need to get out of my head and out of this apartment to get my mind off of things.

I think about taking a walk, but I grab a large tote bag from my closet and stuff my laptop with my Kindle, chargers, and clothes instead. I don't know where I am going, I just need to get out of here. I can't talk to my friends about this. I certainly cannot sit here in my head about it. Forget a walk. I am just gonna drive until I hit the ocean, maybe stay in a hotel, get a massage. Then I realize that would upset Mel since that's something she's been asking to do together. I can't run off to do it by myself without hurting her feelings.

Maybe not the beach.

I'll just drive until I figure it out.

~

I have been driving for about an hour when my phone rings over the radio speakers. My heartbeat picks up speed, not expecting to see Jess's name on the caller ID. Out of panic, I send it to voice mail. This is the first time he's tried to contact me since I left his house that day. I don't know what I would even say to him. Technically speaking he doesn't owe me any loyalty, there was no spoken reason he shouldn't have slept with Leah that night, *besides being my friend and knowing our very recent history.* I can't expect an explanation from him either. I left what I am sure we both thought was a date with my ex-boyfriend without explaining first.

I am an idiot.

I should have gone back in and talked to him. Even better, I should have asked him to come outside with me in the first place, but I wasn't sure I wanted him to see me rip into Ross the way I'd hoped the encounter would go. I did this. I made Jess feel like I chose Ross ... so he chose Leah. Only I didn't choose Ross and I can't unsee Leah kissing Jess when she brought him out coffee, which he doesn't even drink, just to rub it in my face. I was just coming to terms with things, or starting to anyway, and now his call has me spiraling.

Did it have to be Leah?

It's hard not to think about it, to keep telling myself all of the coincidences aren't revolving around myself.

My hair and clothes.

My Jeep, and my school.

Ross...ol Jess.

Would she have wanted any of these things if I didn't have them first? Was she obsessing over me for some reason? I instantly feel like the big-headed idiot that I am for thinking that. It's not like I think of myself as someone people are often jealous of. Something tells me there is too much of a pattern to keep thinking of it as a coincidence. But then, it probably is a little far-fetched to assume she really does that many things with me in mind.

No matter how many times I change the station I can't seem to shake my train of thought. I have gone over the night from last weekend several times in my head by the time I reach my destination. It doesn't escape my notice that I have sulked more over Leah taking Jess from me than I did when it was Ross. Just like it doesn't get past me how ridiculous it is because I never really *had* Jess. Nevertheless, that's where my mind keeps going back to.

I don't remember deciding where I was going, almost driving on autopilot. I honestly can't remember if I stopped at any red lights, or bothered to check them at all. I know I must have though, because here I am. I drove myself to Gramma's house, without meaning to. I guess it makes sense. There's always been refuge for me here.

Gramma is my favorite person, she is who I want to be when I grow up. She is funny, and comforting, hard as nails when she needs to be, but gracious and forgiving like no one

I've ever met. She's seen her share of joy and a bigger share of heartache, but nothing seems to ever break her. She is the kind of grandmother who you don't swear in front of, but you could tell her anything and she wouldn't make you feel judged.

As usual, Grandma's front door is left open, only her clear storm door is closed. I can see her through the storm door in her favorite chair. She is always sitting there when I get here. Usually, she is expecting me so I just walk in, but I haven't told her I was coming. I don't want to startle her so I announce myself before opening the door.

"Hello, Beautiful!" I call through the glass.

Gramma looks over and a surprised sort of delight covers her face.

"Oh, Samantha! I wasn't expecting you. C'mon in, mind the stairs."

I feel better already, walking in and taking my shoes off by the door like I have my whole life. Something about her house, her, and the same greetings and stories each time I see her brings me peace.

This is just what I needed.

Gramma takes no time disappearing into the kitchen as I follow her through the living room. "I'll start a pot of coffee. Then we can sit down and you can tell me what brings you all this way."

In a few short minutes, I am sitting across from my grandmother at her cozy dining table with my legs folded in my lap. The chairs are soft and cushioned, another comfort along with the warm mug of coffee that I now have in between my hands.

"Lucky you, I keep creamer here for our game nights with

the ladies," Gramma tells me. She lives in your typical senior Florida neighborhood. She has several neighbors who have been here since they turned 55, just like her back in the 90's. I love that they all get together and look out for one another.

"Well?" she pries.

"I was just in the area?" I say, but it comes out as more of a question. Almost as if I am asking if she would accept that excuse and let me not talk about it.

"Nice try," Gramma says, cooly. "Now, try again."

She waits patiently while I take a deep breath and squeeze the warm mug in my hand, thinking of where to begin.

"Okay. You know that Ross and I broke up." I'd already told her during one of our many phone calls.

"I do," She answers simply.

"Well, something happened. Or a series of things happened really." I pause and take a sip of my coffee. "I don't know if I was as upset about the break up as I should have been. I didn't feel sad at all I just… felt relieved."

"Well, you know what? You didn't love him." Gramma says with casual indifference as if she'd known all along that Ross wasn't the one for me. "You don't need to burden yourself for *not* being upset about a man who cheated on you. It's a blessing that you aren't in more pain because of him"

"I thought I loved him." I think out loud. "At the time."

"Then, you're here to sulk about Ross?" she calls me out.

"No," I say, but she already knew that somehow.

"Then you weren't *really* in love with him." Her matter-of-fact declaration eases some of my guilt.

"You're right." I sigh.

"But, there's more?" Gramma guesses correctly.

"Yes. There is."

"Are you seeing him again?" she asks cautiously.

"No. But I think Jess thinks I am."

I know if I had said yes she would've held her tongue and supported me. Even so, there's no hiding the relief in her dropping shoulders when I shake my head.

"Jess?" Gramma asks, surprised by the shift in topic.

"Would Jess have reason to mind if you were seeing Ross again?"

Eighty-two years old and she is still sharp as a tack.

"I don't know," I admit. "We have been spending more time together. He helped me with my Jeep. He has brought me coffee a few times. He helped me finish grading my papers on time. All of which I realize is nothing to write home about."

"But?" Gramma says urging me to say more.

"But he found little excuses to be close to me, or he sat beside me instead of across from me. It was little things that I was sure I was picking up. I thought he was flirting with me. Then he said we needed to celebrate getting my grades in on time which seemed like just an excuse for wanting to spend time together. I thought it was a date. I was sure he thought it was a date."

"So, then what happened?"

"Mel and Chad crashed our 'date' if that's what you wanna call it. Neither of us ever said it was a date technically, but it felt like one."

"Did you want it to be a date?" she asks.

I nod, finally admitting it to myself, and then take another sip. "I really did. Everything got so screwed up though. Mel told everyone who would listen that we were going to the karaoke bar in Orlando, so not long after we got there, Leah showed up."

"Oh, that's not good," Gramma says leaning across the table. As if that will get her the details faster.

"She flirted with Jess and he blew her off. He led me out to the dance floor and made a show of twirling me, it was wonderful. For a second I forgot that Leah was there, and then Ross showed up."

"That's a lot of surprises," Gramma says.

I laugh, knowing she hasn't heard the half of it.

"Ross tells me he needs me to come outside with him, makes it out to be some big emergency or something so I told Jess I was sorry and I followed him out. Maybe I should have had Jess come with me, I don't know. But I followed Ross out to his car where Carol was waiting for me."

Gramma freezes, just as surprised as I was about Carol showing up out of the blue. Gramma is my Dad's mom. She was always kind to my mother, but she never really trusted her. I think it's part of why she and I are so close. Gramma had to fill that role for me a lot growing up.

"What did she want?" Gramma asks.

"She said she was sober and just wanted to apologize. You know, her regular spiel. But I couldn't risk taking her back into the bar, so Ross gave us a ride back to my apartment. She left the next morning."

"Well, good. I hope she gets it together this time." Gramma says, as always the picture of grace.

"Anyhow I went to Jess's. He wasn't answering his phone and I thought if I could explain he would understand that I didn't run off with Ross. At least, not like *that*."

"Did he? Understand?" she asks.

"I didn't get the chance to talk to him. When he answered the door Leah came out with her hair in a towel and kissed him. So I just left." I say.

An invisible weight lifts from my shoulders, relieved to finally be finished with the story.

"He slept with Leah?" Gramma clarifies.

I nod. "He thought I left with Ross, which technically I did. So he slept with Leah."

"So, what now?"

"I don't know, I was thinking I would hide out the rest of the weekend and avoid everyone and everything. There's no school Monday because of Presidents' Day."

"I don't think that will help," Gramma says. Then she pulls the mug out of my hand and stands to take it to the sink.

"Why are you taking my coffee?" I ask, pouting.

"There's a five-dollar bill there on the counter. You can get one on your way home."

"My way home? Are you kicking me out?" I ask, my tone laced with offense and shock.

"I would never 'kick you out'." Gramma rolls her eyes. "But you can't hide out here and expect anything to solve itself. Go home, keep a close eye to make sure Carol isn't coming back again right away. Take a shower, read a book, and when you are ready. Talk to Jess."

"I don't want to talk to him," I pout. "I feel worse about him sleeping with Leah than I did about Ross cheating on me with her. I feel mad and hurt and like crying which is stupid because I have no claim over him and until recently I was in a relationship with someone else, not even looking at him that way."

"Until recently, you were both scared to ever admit how well you complement each other," Gramma says. "It hurts more because you care more for Jess. Lord knows I have watched him pining over you long enough to know he feels just as bad as you do right now."

"He has not been *pining* over me." I protest.

"Sammy-Belle, he has been. I know it, your friends know it, Benny knows it, your dad knew it. I just don't think he's ever dared to admit it."

She gives me her *you know I'm right* look when she says that, but I don't know it. It doesn't make any sense.

"That's ridiculous. Jess has dated plenty of girls. He certainly wasn't afraid to take Leah home. He has no problem talking to women." I roll my eyes.

"Talking to women you don't know well, who are shallow and easy to win over, like Leah is a lot easier than admitting to being head over heels for someone who already knows you, and hoping they want you the way you are." She says, like some wise old fortune teller.

"I don't know. I just said I thought it was a date. I don't think he has liked me all this time." I say.

"If you say so," Gramma says as she practically herds me towards the door. "Drive safe, text me when you get home."

Gramma grabs my left cheek and pulls me towards her until our right cheeks press together and she says "Mwuah." Without actually kissing me. It is her signature goodbye, another familiar comfort that I will never grow tired of.

"Thanks for the coffee," I tell her, taking my purse that she carried to the door.

On the way home, I am fishing in my bag for my wallet in

the drive-thru line, when I find the five-dollar bill that I purposely didn't take from the counter. It makes me smile. *Predictable Gramma*

Samantha: *You little sneak. Thank you, in the drive-thru now before hitting the highway.*

Gramma: *You are welcome. Don't text and drive.*

Chapter 13

Jess

You've reached Samantha, I'll call you back.

Voice mail. *Of course.*

I don't even know what I thought I was going to say. I opened my phone to text her every day this last weekend and couldn't come up with a single thing to say.

Sorry, I slept with someone else.

Nope. That sounds like I think we were in a relationship. Which, I have been too chicken shit to tell Samantha that I want. One that I don't even know if she wants.

What really happened if you aren't back with Ross?

No. That would tell her that Chad has been talking to me and she would stop trusting him.

Hell, for all I know she was just flirting with me to make herself feel better after Ross cheated on her. I tell myself that she wouldn't be upset enough to avoid me if she was just using me to get over her shitty ex, but it's more complicated than that.

It just had to be Leah, you dumbass.

I still can't remember anything after the bar. I had no intention of sleeping with her that night, I know that much. I was pissed enough to dance with Leah, then we got another drink, and after that…Blank. For the life of me, I can't figure out how it got as far as it did.

I put my phone down and give up for the umpteenth time on trying to fix what happened last weekend. The whole situation is screwed. I need to find something to do. I walk around for a minute straightening things up before I remember that Chad's truck is still at the shop. The parts we ordered got delivered to the wrong address so we have been waiting for them to be reshipped. That could keep me busy if the parts are in.

Jess: The parts in for Chad's truck yet? I can come put them in if so.

Carlos: No need Boss. It's already taken care of. He can pick it up tomorrow.

I should have known, Carlos is yet again annoyingly on top of things. I should probably give him a raise, even if I was irritated to see him show up here with Samantha. I'm pretty sure she spent the rest of the night trying to avoid him. That hasn't stopped him from asking about her or bringing her up in conversation since Mel told him she was single, which is especially grating while I am trying to keep my mind off of her.

I don't have anything I can do around here, so I decide to go into the shop anyway and do payroll. It's not really time to do it yet but I need *something* to keep me busy. While I am there I can talk to Carlos about his raise and give Chad an update on his truck.

~

"I told you, Boss, I am taking good care of Chad's truck,"

Carlos says as soon as I walk in. "You don't need to worry."

"I know you are," I say patting Carlos on the shoulder. "I came in to do payroll."

"On the weekend?"

Part of the point of promoting Carlos was so I wouldn't have to work weekends. He knows that. But I don't want to get into why I am really working on a Saturday. I especially don't want to talk to him about Samantha.

"Yeah man, listen when you get a minute come see me, okay?" I say gesturing towards my office on the side of the shop.

"Alright Boss," Carlos says, then a small part of me is relieved to see him making his way back over to Chad's truck.

This is moronic. I tell myself mentally. Being annoyed at my best employee, who I'd even consider a friend, because he paid attention to someone who wants less than nothing to do with me. *Yep, Moronic.*

I only have six employees including Carlos, which means it shouldn't take me long to do payroll. This is a task that usually takes me less than half an hour a week. Not today though. I keep running over what happened between picking up Samantha and her knocking on my door Saturday in my mind. Chad says Samantha isn't back with Ross, but I can't figure out a good reason she would have left with him. Even if she has a great reason I really screwed things over. Chad told me as much in his text.

You messed up man. Big time.

I have been half-assed working on this for more than an hour when Carlos knocks on my office door.

"You wanted to see me, Boss?"

"Yeah, come on in man," I tell him gesturing at the chair

in front of my desk.

"What's going on?"

"I've been having a problem since you started managing the shop. I've been thinking it over and there is only one solution I keep coming back to." I tell him. Maybe it's petty, but it is fun to watch him squirm a little.

Carlos shifts in his seat like he's trying to keep his nerves together and asks, "Can we talk about it? What seems to be the issue?"

"It's about time management," I say keeping my face and voice serious.

Now that he's reacting I can't help but mess with him a little more.

"Every car has been getting back to customers on time, haven't they? I don't understand." He tells me, but he's definitely squirming.

"That is correct. I am facing a different time management issue." I explain.

This is the only fun thing I've done all week so I am ready to really drag it out. But I think he is already actually sweating from nerves so I decide to take it easy on him.

"Since you started, I keep coming in to run the shop, only to find myself useless here." I give him a half smile.

Carlos relaxes noticeably when he realizes he isn't in trouble.

"You've really stepped up here Carlos. You've been great with the customers and other mechanics. I wanted to thank you."

"Thanks, Boss," Carlos smiles. "It means a lot that you noticed."

"So pizza party Friday?" my tone is more playful and

sarcastic, knowing it takes more than that to keep good employees around.

"Thanks, Jess. That sounds great." Carlos says and then stands to leave.

"I am messing with you, Carlos," I say to stop him. "I'm not thanking you with pizza that'll be gone in five minutes. I am giving you a raise."

He actually looks surprised, and then he cocks his head to the side as if considering his options.

"Can I have the raise *and* the pizza?"

"Sure." I nod, knowing he has more than earned it.

"I don't want to push my luck…" his voice shifts to a more cautious tone and I note that he is trying not to fidget with his hands.

"Yeah?"

His next words come fast like he's trying to get them out before he loses the nerve. "Do you think you can ask Sammy if I can have her number?"

My chest twists, and my mask of composure must have slipped in the few seconds that I panic, trying to decide how to respond.

"Or not. The pizza's great. I love pizza." Carlos shifts to a more defensive position, hands up in surrender as if trying to rid himself of the implications of his question. It's as if my face told Carlos in that small blip of time more about how I feel than I ever told Samantha directly. Before I can try to say something nonchalant and cover my tracks, he is backing out of my office door.

I spend the next hour and a half finishing the payroll, just so I don't have to see him again before the end of the day. It nearly takes me that long too, still not able to keep my mind focused. Then I shoot Chad a text to update him on his truck.

Jess: You can pick up your truck tomorrow.

Chad: *I'll need a ride.*

Jess: No problem.

~

Once the shop has quieted and I am sure Carlos is gone for the day I take off, deciding that I can't take sitting still anymore. I need to talk to Samantha if only to be able to clear her from my mind so I can function without making an ass of myself around here. Since I can't think of anything to say over text and she isn't answering her phone that leaves me only one, pitiable option.

Knock. Knock. Knock.

"Samantha, it's Jess," I call through the door.

Only silence meets me on the other side.

I saw her Jeep parallel parked out front of Benny's diner when I pulled up. Samantha usually parks out back unless she is just popping back in quickly. Either she is inside ignoring me, or she is in the diner, possibly about to leave. I rush down the stairs, skipping every other one, and try my best to not look out of breath when I make it around the front of the building. The blue Jeep I saw when I arrived is still parked out front, but I am not fooled so easily this time. It's Leah's Jeep.

"Oh hey, handsome." Leah smiles up at me as I walk into the diner.

"What are you doing here?"

Maybe I'm an asshole. For sleeping with her and not

remembering, or for feeling defensive towards her being here on Samantha's behalf. If so, that's fine because regardless of whatever happened last weekend every internal alarm I have is going off at the site of her here. Or maybe I'm just worried that if Samantha does see her here it will fuel her anger longer.

"Getting lunch. Wanna join me?" she says scooting further into the booth.

"I mean why are you in this building? Are you trying to mess with Samantha?" I make sure to lace my tone with disinterest and suspicion, and Leah notes it.

"Why should she care where I eat?" Leah cocks her head to the side, eyes roaming over me. Reading me.

"I think what Jess here means to say is that Samantha eats here a lot because I was close with her dad," Benny says slapping me on my shoulder.

I stiffen under his hand, with realization. Thank God for the interruption, I forgot that Samantha made a point of not telling Leah where she moved. My big mouth almost just drew her a map up the back stairs. However, something in her tone makes me suspect that she may already know Samantha lives here.

"Okay…" Leah says. "So she gets her own part of town now?"

"Of course not." I roll my eyes at her self-deprecating show.

"I think you seem to be forgetting the part where I was the one in your bed most recently." Leah reminds me. *Asshole is right.*

Benny looks between us with uncomfortable surprise and then awkwardly turns to walk back to the kitchen without a word.

"I am sorry Leah, that was a mistake." I try for sincerity. Truthfully it was a mistake, but my gritted molars make the delivery fall short.

"Oh save it. We were using each other for the same thing and we both know it." Leah snaps at me. "You don't owe me any apologies. We both won."

"I didn't mean to make you feel used. I was really drunk and I honestly don't remember the whole thing." I tell her, only half listening as I take a seat and rub my hands over my face.

"It worked for me." Leah shrugs.

I am not even sure what that means.

"Wait, win what?" her words finally register.

"Sammy won't forgive you, you know. This whole *will they or won't they* thing you've been doing… I hope you realize that's over. A consolation prize really." Leah boasts.

"That's ridiculous, I only slept with you because I thought she left there with Ross." I don't bother denying my feelings for Samantha. Everyone else knows by now. *Except Samantha.* I shake the thought away, hoping she isn't right that I blew it for good.

"Yeah, that took a minute to set up." She chuckles to herself, picking at her food.

"What do you mean set up? Is this some sick game to you?"

"If it was, all I did was just give a few pawns a light *nudge.*" Her smug pride and the realization of what she means sends invisible spiders crawling up the veins in my arms.

"Ross?" the sinister glimmer in her eye is enough to

confirm it. "You being there? Sleeping with me was part of some sick plan? What the *hell*, Leah?"

I stand up suddenly and take a step back, suddenly needing to be farther from her.

"Yes, yes, and no." She says, counting the yeses on her fingers. "I didn't sleep with you. You wouldn't even kiss me. I just gave you a ride home and once you passed out I figured you wouldn't remember if we did it or not. I hoped Sammy would be over that night to explain, but the morning after was worth waiting around for."

"You need help." I don't bother hiding my disgust. "Stay away from me and stay the *fuck* away from Samantha."

That sinister sparkle in her eye only grows, fueled as she delights in getting a rise out of me.

"She won't give you the time of day now, you know."

"Why?" I ask, slapping my hand harder than I meant to on the table. "What is your obsession with her?"

"Everyone thinks she is *so* perfect. Let's see how much you still like your little *Doll* when she cracks." Leah snarls standing up, leaving the table.

She doesn't leave any money to cover her food, so I take my wallet out and throw forty bucks on the table. It's not Benny's job to be handing out free food, not when he's already forgoing the extra money he could get renting the upstairs apartment to someone else. I know I should be pissed right now, but I am too relieved to focus on that. I quickly give Benny an update so he won't let her in here again, then head out the door.

I didn't sleep with her.

"Thank you, God, I didn't screw up as bad as I thought I did," I say into the clouds, as I make my way to the back parking lot.

I pull out my phone to try calling Samantha again. I don't feel as nervous to talk to her now that I know I didn't sleep with Leah. She doesn't answer though, which stings enough to remind me that she still doesn't know that. When I reach the alley where I parked my car, Samantha's Jeep is now parked beside it. The second I see it parked in her usual spot with the telltale sticker on the back I bolt up the stairs in the back entry and bang on the door.

I have to see her.

I have to tell her what Leah did.

What I didn't do.

"Doll, it's Jess. Let me in please," I yell over my fist pounding on the door.

Chapter 14

Samantha

Jess's car is sitting in one of the alley parking spots when I pull behind my apartment. For a moment I thought I might just keep driving. I could go to Mel's for the night, or just drive around until he left. *I don't think that will help.* I deflate as I hear Gramma's voice in my mind, and I decide that she is probably right. *As usual.*

After checking to see if he was waiting at my door, I walked around to the front of the building. Halfway around the building I feel my steps slow down, weighed with hesitation. There's a very real chance that he may not be here to see me at all. I need to manage my expectations. He might be helping Benny with another project, I tell myself. *Go in quietly, and if he's using any power tools I'll have my answer and slink back out.*

Pathetic, but at least I have a plan. Instead, I am surprised, yet again, by Leah's clone of a Jeep parallel parked front in center. It gives me the creeps, way more now than when she first got it. Too many things have happened these past few months to brush it off. But that's not nearly as bad as what I see through the diner window. Jess is sitting at a table with the girl he took home last Friday night, right under my apartment.

They're on a fucking date.

My reflection in the glass pales as the blood rushes out of my face. Gramma was wrong. Jess doesn't want me, he wants Leah. There is literally no one around me, and I still feel as if I've been humiliated in front of a crowd. I am frozen in time, trying to wrap my head around the reality of what I am seeing until the movement of Jess standing up has me ricocheting back around the corner. *I can't let them see me watching their date.*

I turn around quickly and start to hurry back to the alley entrance for my apartment. I don't really have anywhere else to disappear to, not in this state of upset. So up the stairs I go, wondering how every hero in the stories I read manages to take them two at a time, when my short stature works against me and then ultimately betrays me near the top. I fall with a thunderous thud that I hope is not echoing through the restaurant below as I cry out.

"Gah." I try to muffle my pained groan, not wanting to cause more ruckus, and have Benny come to check on me.

It really hurts but thankfully I didn't hear a snap. I don't bother checking it for swelling and redness in the dark stairwell, it's probably too soon to tell anyway. I hobble up the last few stairs and lock the door behind me once I am inside. Tossing my bag into Dad's chair, which Jess put by the front living room window, I plop down on the sofa and grab my remote. In pain, out of breath, and humiliated to be in my own company. *I am at an all-time low.* I'm sulking over a guy who doesn't want me, and clumsily hurting myself literally running away from them. I can't change my mind and go anywhere else because of the ankle I hurt, which I need to drive.

Defeated, and out of energy I decide to just put on my comfort show, the show I have watched every episode of more than I can count. Gilmore Girls.

I think Dad used to watch this with me because he thought somehow it would be good for me. He was always watching girly things with me like that. Most of which I didn't realize until I got older. We watched a lot of action movies and things most other teen girls probably would've hated too, now that I think of it. Most teen girls probably didn't go with their dads to every Fast and the Furious movie. I loved it though. Movies and shows were sort of our thing, even if I didn't realize it at the time. But he always made an extra effort to watch "chick flicks" with me, probably so I wouldn't miss having a female influence that he didn't know how to give me. As if the only way the burly biker could think to make up for the mother that was Carol, was to put female role models on the screen for me. I didn't need them though, I may have worn the pretty dresses and loved my Barbies, but I was always my dad's right-hand man.

Knock. Knock.

"Doll, it's Jess. Let me in please." Jess bangs on the door, disrupting my walk down memory lane.

I think about not answering it, but he would have seen my Jeep. He knows I am home. I stand up and carefully put pressure on the ankle I rolled. It hurts, but it can hold weight. I just need to take it slow. The extra time it takes to cross the living room, buys me just a bit longer to compose myself, leaving me grateful for each pained step. There is another single knock before I swing the door open to Jess's fist nearly knocking into my face. Thankfully, he is alone.

"Doll," Jess says with a heavy sigh like he's surprised I opened the door at all.

Did he see me running away downstairs?

Kill me now.

"Jess," I respond cooly, trying not to show too much embarrassment or rage, though I am feeling plenty of both.

"I have so much to tell you. So much has happened." Jess says urgently.

"I saw, you got a new girlfriend," I say putting on a fake smile that doesn't reach my eyes. "Congrats."

Then guilt stings in my gut as I think about Mel and Chad, who know nothing about what happened, *or didn't*, between us. I can't let this tear apart our entire friend group. I have to act like everything is fine. If I was fine, I would let my friend in, so I back away unblocking the doorway, and start to limp back over to the sofa.

"That's not what I was… Wait, are you limping?" Jess cuts himself off, shifting his attention to my leg.

"I rolled my ankle on the stairs, it'll be fine." I try to reassure him without giving away my shame.

"Let me help you." Jess offers, wrapping his arm around my waist.

He helps me back to my seat then picks up the squirrel throw pillow I found at a thrift shop from the other end of the sofa, and carefully puts it under my ankle. "This looks swollen. Do you have ice?"

"I might have frozen peas," I tell him, thankful for the second time for my hurt ankle, so I don't have to talk to him about his new relationship.

"Stay here, don't move." Jess orders, rounding the counter to rummage through the kitchen.

A moment later he reappears, with a bag of frozen blueberries. He sits down by my feet on the sofa and wraps a dish towel around the bag before putting it on my ankle.

"You didn't have peas, only frozen blueberries," Jess says gently, still looking down at my ankle.

Act normal.

"Same thing, small colored balls," I joke, trying to ease the tension.

"One is a vegetable." Jess laughs looking up to me.

"You say tomato, I say potato."

This feels so natural, our ridiculous banter, almost like nothing has changed. But it only lasts for a moment before he pulls us back on topic.

"Listen, about Leah…" Jess's voice is laced with trepidation.

"I'm happy for you." I lie, cutting him off.

I don't want to hear about it.

"Happy for me?" Jess asks, his eyebrows crinkling in confusion. "You don't think I am with her, do you?"

"Aren't you? I mean she was in your shower and then you two were clearly on a date at Benny's just now. You don't need to be here taking care of me. I am fine. Leah probably wouldn't want you around me anyway. She can get very jealous." I ramble.

Jess lets me finish my rant before he says more.

"I am *not* with Leah." His eyes lock on mine, begging me to believe him. "She gave me a ride home. We did *not* sleep together."

"You didn't?" my breathy response fails to hide how much relief it would give me to believe him.

"No." He shakes his head. "We weren't on a date. I was confronting her. Leah is the one who sent Ross to the bar."

"Yeah, kind of. Carol said Leah thought that I moved in with Ross." I remember out loud. "Which, even if she did think that when I moved out, she of all people should know we broke up."

"Carol?" confusion knits together in his brow.

"Yeah, that's why I left that night. Ross showed up with Carol. I knew if I went back inside she would follow me in and cause a scene." I explain.

"I saw you getting in his car?"

"I didn't have a car there, so Ross gave us a ride back here. Carol was in the backseat. That was all."

I can see the same relief wash over Jess that I felt hearing he didn't sleep with Leah. This whole thing has been an unnecessary mess.

"She knows where you moved."

"Carol? She does now."

"No." He cuts me off. "Leah. She knew you broke up with Ross, and she knew that we would be at the bar together. It was a setup."

"I thought I was the paranoid one," I tell him. "You really think she orchestrated my mother, Ross, and herself all showing up at the bar? Why would she do that?"

"She told me she did. She flat out admitted it." Jess says, urging me with his eyes to believe him. "You're right about her being jealous, but it's not about me. It's about you."

Jealous of me? Yeah, that makes sense. My inner cynic mocks me until I hear Jess's words from the other night in my mind.

"How could she not be jealous?" he had said.

"Why would she go through all that just to mess with me?" I say, trying to separate my conflicting feelings from the topic at hand.

Jess takes a deep breath as if he is deep in thought or trying to decide if he should tell me something. My ankle is throbbing, but I try not to draw attention to it so he doesn't change the topic.

"Maude is Leah's aunt right?" The question is so random it throws me off. I don't see what Maude has to do with any of this.

"Yeah, why?"

"I took Chad out to lunch before we all went out. Maude was our waitress."

"Okay? Is there some connection here, Sherlock?" I ask, growing impatient. The pain in my ankle coupled with the rush of confusion is making me irritable.

"I was talking to Chad about you. Maude was eavesdropping, I know because she came over and put her two cents in on the conversation." Jess elaborates. "I think she talked to Leah about it, and Leah saw it as an opportunity."

"You were talking about me to Chad?" I can't hide my intrigue. "What about?"

"You know what about, Doll," Jess says.

The knot in my stomach begs me to press him, but I don't. It's the closest he has ever been to admitting he has feelings for me. But he is practically begging me with his eyes not to push him into confessing it out loud. So I don't.

"What did Carol want?" Jess changes the subject.

"I don't know, it was weird. She just showed up and didn't say much or ask for anything. She said she got a job and she wanted to know if she could call me sometime." I say.

"She didn't ask for anything? Didn't take anything?" Jess asks suspiciously.

"No, she said she was sober and she just wanted to apologize."

"But now she knows where you live." Jess clarifies. "She shows up and finds out where you live right before Leah comes to Benny's diner downstairs for the first time since you moved out."

"You think Carol told Leah where I moved to?" I ask.

"That's exactly what I think, she never knew you and Leah were on the outs. Carols probably saw no reason not to tell her." He says. "I don't know how to explain it but there was something about Leah downstairs. It's like a switch flipped and she's gone from jealous to… obsessed."

"With me?" I ask pointing to myself in disbelief. "I thought she was just jealous because she wanted Ross."

"Unfortunately." Jess places his hand on my unhurt leg and gives it a reassuring squeeze. "I think if that was all about Ross, she would have moved on by now."

Jess is right. She got what she wanted, breaking us up, so why the run around at the bar? Now that I think of it, Ross didn't even bother talking to her at the bar. I assumed they started dating when we broke up. But it didn't seem like it at the bar. This is too much to make sense of.

"Listen I don't like the idea of you staying here alone tonight." He says. "Why don't you come stay with me tonight?"

"I don't know," I say, unsure about where this whole situation has left us.

"Or, if it makes you feel better I'll crash on the couch." He offers.

"I don't know if I can make it down the stairs tonight, and I don't love the idea of leaving the apartment empty for Carol," I say. "I can just ask Mel to come over."

"You don't need Mel. I'll stay on the couch." Jess says matter-of-factly.

"You don't have to do that." I protest, not sure where we even stand right now.

It's no use though. He doesn't even justify that with an answer. Jess has already kicked off his sneakers and made himself at home on the other end of the sectional.

"What are we watching, Doll?" he asks, gesturing towards the TV that I never paused.

"Gilmore Girls," I tell him, deciding I don't have the energy to put up a fight.

"Gilmore Girls?" He gives me an *Are you serious* look but to my surprise settles in further without a word.

~

We have watched about 4 episodes of the show. Jess has been asking me questions about the characters and what's going to happen next. I keep telling him I won't give him any spoilers. If he wants to find out he will have to watch. We just paused it when Benny knocks on the door with food for us. I hadn't realized that I didn't eat anything but coffee all day until my stomach rumbled. Jess immediately ran downstairs to get dinner for us from the diner and Benny told him that he'd bring it up when it was ready. I think it was Benny's way of checking in on me, even if he didn't stay long.

"I am just saying, I am team Jess." He smirks at me.

"Of course you would say that." I roll my eyes. "It's

literally your name."

"Oh, so you prefer the tall guy?" Jess challenges me.

"I am not saying that." I defend myself. "I am just saying you can't pick a team in season two."

"Fair enough," Jess says, spreading out the food on the coffee table before us.

"Hey Doll," his voice turns a little more serious. "Can I ask you something?"

I sit up straighter and turn to face him, careful to be gentle with my ankle as I place it down.

"Of course you can."

His hesitation matches my own but he pushes the words out. "Are we good?"

I don't think I have ever seen him look like this. I can't tell if he is nervous, shy, or worried. I just know I have this strong desire to make him feel better as he holds my gaze, waiting for me to respond.

"Yeah, Jess, we're good." I give him a half smile and watch him relax.

"Good." Jess nods, but I am not sure he looks convinced.

"I was worried for a minute."

"It's been a weird week. Let's just try to forget about it." I suggest.

I don't want to think about Leah, Carol, or Ross for a very long time. I just hope this stunt of Leah's was the last.

"Right. We'll just forget about it." Jess says. Then he hits play on the TV and we keep watching the show while we eat.

Chapter 15

Jess

I wake up with the smell of fruit and sunshine covering my face, Samantha's hair. She fell asleep on the sectional last night watching TV after refusing my offer to help her into her room to go to bed. I didn't want to sleep with my feet in her face, so I opted to sleep with my head by hers on the other side of the sectional after I put a blanket over her. It took me a lot longer to fall asleep than it did for her. I just stayed up watching her show and looking over at her, as if I was going to wake up today at home having dreamt of making up with her.

I am still trying to wrap my head around everything that has happened since last Friday. Yesterday I thought Samantha might never want to talk to me again. This morning I am waking up in her apartment, grateful that I didn't screw up as bad as I thought. Though, I'm not sure she will want to pick up right where we left off. She told me last night she wants to pretend the last few days never happened. I am not sure what she means by that. Does she mean she wants to pretend nothing was happening between us? Or is she just talking about Leah and all the drama she concocted?

Even though I am relieved that we aren't fighting, I'm still bothered that she left with Ross. I understand now, why she went with him after seeing Carol there. I just can't wrap my mind around why she went outside with him, to begin with. She told me right before going into the bar that she wouldn't run off, and then she did anyway.

Before I can give it more thought Samantha wakes up, in the most dramatic slow stretch and yawn combination I have ever seen. It's adorable. Her hair is a mess and she still has yesterday's clothes on, just some black leggings and a loose T-shirt, but I can't look away.

"AHH!" Samantha screams when she sees me out of the corner of her eye before she seems to remember why I am here. "Holy cow, you scared me half to death."

"It's just me." Shoulders shaking with laughter.

"Oh you find that funny, do you?" She throws the squirrel shaped pillow at my head and I catch it before it can land the blow.

"A little," I admit still laughing, as I toss the pillow back at her. "How's the ankle this morning, Doll?"

She rolls her ankle around testing it out, and then stands slowly before giving me her answer.

"Much better Doc, I'll take two M&M's and call you in the morning." Samantha jokes.

I recognize that line as one of Karl's old dad jokes. Sometimes I think she tells them, even though they're terrible because he can't anymore.

"Good, now let's pack your things," I say, then start heading down the hall towards her room.

"Pack my things?" Samantha repeats following behind me.

"You said you couldn't handle the stairs last night, so I stayed here." I remind her. "Your ankle is feeling better, clearly it can handle some walking now, so you can stay with me tonight."

"Why do I need to stay with you?" She asks, grabbing my forearm and turning me to face her.

"Because you have a crazy, stalker ex-roommate and I don't want you staying here alone," I say, stepping closer.

And because I don't want to be away from you.

"Leah knows where you live too, you know." Samantha challenges me. "And I don't think I need to be afraid of her."

"True, but I don't have any clean clothes here. I need to go home and take a shower and I am not leaving you." I retort, trying to ignore the sting of guilt for bringing Leah back to my place. I don't comment on the last part. Mostly because Samantha didn't see the dark side of Leah that I did last night, and while it was enough to scare me, I don't want to upset her.

"Well, I need a shower and my clothes are here," Samantha says, stepping closer so now there are only a few inches between us. I can see in her eyes that she is only fighting against coming with me for the fun of seeing who will win. This girl loves to win a fight, even if it's not a real one. She's always been incredibly smart and quick-witted, it's one of the things that makes being around her so fun. The determination barely cloaks the whimsy in her honey-brown eyes as they look up at me. Those eyes and the mention of her in the shower have my mind racing.

"You can bring your clothes to my house." I counter, mirroring her step forward so I am towering over her. We could touch if either of us took a deep enough breath. "The water pressure is better."

And the shower is bigger.

"I have to work in the morning." She looks up at me through those thick eyelashes and it takes every ounce of my willpower not to close the gap.

"I live closer to the school than you do."

I can't stop looking from her eyes to her mouth. If she is feeling the same things I am right now she doesn't let on. But that's no surprise, she's always had a hell of a poker face. Having her this close is only making this last week's confusion worse. My heart is thumping so hard, I think it might start floating up my throat.

"Seems like there really is no changing your mind," Samantha says, not breaking her gaze and taking one final step so I can feel her against my chest.

I wrap my fingers in hers and I swear I could jump start a car with the electricity running through me. When she doesn't pull away a giant grin spreads across my face that I couldn't stop if I tried. I need every moment I can buy to be near her to get things back to where they were before Leah's bullshit. Even passed that.

"I am not leaving here without you, Doll."

"Do you really think she is dangerous?" Samantha asks, bringing the conversation full circle.

The worry in her voice wipes the smile off my face. Truthfully, I don't know. So far Leah's antics don't seem necessarily dangerous, but it's not a risk I want to take. Not after seeing her fish around downstairs. I don't want to find out why she was so close to Samantha's apartment.

"I don't know," I say sliding both my hands up her arms. "But I don't want to find out."

She nods and then wraps her arms around my back. I hate that she is scared. I hate that I played a part in Leah's plan against her. I want to fix everything, but all I can do right now is wrap my arms around her and comfort her. So that's what I do.

"I am sorry, Samantha," I say squeezing her, selfishly feeling glad to have her in my arms.

"Thank you for staying." She sighs in my chest, letting more of her weight lean on me.

"I'll stay as long as you let me, Doll. If you really wanna stay here I can have Chad bring me some clothes."

"No, that's okay, you're right." She says pulling back enough for me to see the playful smile she makes appear. "Your shower is probably better."

~

I followed Samantha back to my place, staring at the sticker on the back of her Jeep. *Tuna, no crust.* Helping her car shop had been one of the last times we'd hung out, just the two of us before she started seeing Ross.

The image of her throwing her head back in a carefree laugh when she read the sticker I'd chosen for her fills my mind. I can still see her bright smile so vividly, glowing with a warmth that no one around her could replicate, though they'd tried. There's an authenticity about Samantha that outshines every bit of sadness she'd ever faced. As if she couldn't be bothered to care that her laugh was too loud, or her dancing was uncoordinated. She was just grateful to dance or to smile. That smile… no, her *joy* is infectious and contagious, and being the one to bring it out at that moment, I'd almost been brave enough to tell her how I felt. *Almost.*

I push the memory aside as my phone rings over the car

stereo. Chad's name on the screen is a welcome interruption. I know he's been waiting to hear about his truck, so I expect that's what he wants.

"You gonna come give me a ride to my truck?" He says before I can greet him.

"Well, hello to you too," I say, calling out his lack of proper greeting.

"I am sorry, you're right," Chad says, his words so laced with sarcasm that I can practically hear his eyes roll. "Hello dearest friend, how are you? When can I expect you?"

"I need you to see if Mel can take you."

"Why? I can literally hear that you're in your car right now." Chad argues. "Where are you going?"

"Home," I say, unsure how much I should say. I need to talk to Samantha and see how much she wants to tell him and Mel.

"Home? In the morning? I swear if you tell me you are driving home from Leah's my head is going to explode." Chad scolds me.

"I am not coming home from Leah's. I never actually slept with her, it turns out." I say, still relishing the relief of that realization. "Listen I have some stuff to take care of. I might need you and Mel to come over later to explain. For now, please just see if she can take you to get your truck, okay?"

"Is everything okay man?" Chad asks. I can hear the worry in his tone because I am being so vague, but I won't say anymore before I talk to Samantha.

"Yeah Bud, don't worry. Everything is gonna be fine. I'll text you in a bit and let you know when to come by."

"Alright," Chad says hesitantly, and then he hangs up without saying goodbye.

He needs to work on his phone etiquette.

~

When we arrive at my house I help Samantha bring her things in and take them straight to my room. The guest room, if that's what you want to call it, is really used more as storage so it doesn't have a bed in it. There is also a third bedroom technically but that one is set up as my home office which also doesn't see much use.

"Why are you putting my stuff in your room?" Samantha asks following behind me.

I knew she would protest, always the first to support everyone else and never wanting to put anyone out. She can really dig her heels in, trying to resist help, but I can be a lot more stubborn than her. Plus bantering with her is always half of the fun.

"You'll be sleeping in here tonight, Doll," I tell her, readying myself for pushback.

Samantha looks from my bed to me, biting her lip, and to my surprise only asks. "You want me to sleep in here…with you?"

Absolutely.

That's not the gentlemanly thing to say though. I clear my throat trying to refocus my thoughts.

"I was offering to sleep on the couch," I say hooking my thumb over my shoulder in the direction of the living room.

A faint blush rolls over her cheeks. A subtle whisper of embarrassment alluding to what she thought I was insinuating before she schools her features.

"You can't sleep on the couch for me. It's your house."

"If you want me to stay in here with you just say so," I say with a wink, only half joking.

The rosiness of her cheeks deepens, the only reaction she lets me see.

"I am not going to take your room," Samantha says trying for intimidation with her tone and stance.

Game on I tell her with the raise of my brow and half smile. I take a step towards her, and from the roll of her throat, I know I am not the only one thinking of how close we were in her apartment earlier.

"Well, you aren't sleeping on the couch," I tell her, booping her nose with my finger.

It takes all I have to turn away without watching her shocked reaction. I walk into the bathroom and turn the shower on leaving the door open behind me.

"So I am just supposed to stay in your room while you shower with the door open?" Samantha calls through the doorway.

"I was warming the shower up for you. It can be tricky."

She's sitting on my bed with her legs folded when I lean against the door frame.

"Oh. Thanks."

I could get used to seeing her there.

The flush on her cheeks and the site of her on my bed is a teasing combination. Just enough that I slide my hands into my pockets to hide the effect she is having. Not enough to humiliate me with a solid erection, thankfully, but enough that I hope she doesn't notice. *Hell, I could get used to seeing her in my shower too.* My cock responds to the thought of the water and suds sliding over her peaks and curves and I know I need to either sit down or leave the room to keep it concealed.

"So, I talked to Chad on the way over," I tell her, hoping the change of topic will help as I take a seat on the other side of the bed. "I told him to have Mel take him to get his truck. I wasn't sure how much you wanted to tell them, so I just said I would talk to him later."

Yup, the conversation shift is helping.

"Oh, they should probably know everything," Samantha says immediately, which doesn't surprise me. She's always been an open book. She's the most candid person I know. Which makes me wonder.

"Everything as in..?" I prompt her, unsure if she means to include whatever has been going on between us. Only the gaze in her eyes seems to recoil, if only slightly when she realizes what I mean.

"Everything about Leah and Carol." She clarifies.

"Alright." I nod, not daring to push the subliminal subject.

The tension already feels like a rubber band, ready to snap against my sternum if we say anymore.

"How about you go take your shower, and I can ask them to come by in a bit."

"Perfect. Thanks, Jess." She smiles and then heads into the bathroom.

I go out into the living room, that way Samantha has privacy in my room to get dressed when she gets out of the shower. I decide to send a text to the group chat instead of calling Chad again. This way hopefully he will ask fewer questions.

Jess: *I need everyone to meet at my house. Samantha is here. She is okay but we need to tell you guys some stuff.*

Mel: *Last time we got a text like this we had to go move Sammy to a new apartment in one day. Is everything okay?*

Jess: I don't think that will be necessary, everyone is okay.
Chad: Is this a food thing? We can bring takeout.
Jess: Good idea.
Mel: Samantha? Are you alive? Why aren't you saying anything?
Jess: She's in the shower smart ass.

~

"You told them I was in the shower?!" Samantha yells, coming out of my room in nothing but a towel.

Good gracious, she looks hot. I have seen her in bathing suits before throughout the years, but this feels different. Samantha is standing in my living room naked. I mean, she has a towel covering herself, but she is naked and wet. I have to look away from having a repeat of the incident in the bedroom since clearly, my body seems to respond to her like a hormone addled teenager. It takes me so long to compose myself that I almost forgot she'd be expecting a response.

"I um…" I start to speak but fumble over my words. I can't think with her standing there with beads of water rolling down her collarbone. *What did she say?*

"I need you to put some clothes on." The words are out before I can take them back and watch her recoil with surprise.

"I have a towel on Jess. Be a grown up." Samantha says, waving a hand over her towel as if I hadn't noticed it.

"Doll, if you want me to speak in coherent sentences you need to be wearing a lot more than a towel," I admit.

I instantly regret blurting that out, until I see Samantha's face. Her cheeks turn a reddish pink, blushing as she looks down at her towel like she's assessing if she's really worth the reaction. Then, without a word she turns on a dime to walk back into my room. *Was she flattered? Does she want me to look at her like that?* I hope so because I can't seem to help myself anymore.

"There, clothes. Happy?" Samantha says reappearing in a pair of jean shorts and a tank top… with no bra. She can't possibly think I wouldn't notice her not wearing a bra, right? She has to be doing that on purpose. My nerves start to jump as I try not to read too far into it, and fail. Chad and Mel need to hurry up before I make an ass out of myself. It's a lot easier to control my feelings with a buffer around. I don't say anything, I just stare at her and hope that my thoughts aren't plastered across my face.

"You told them I was in the shower!" Samantha says again, breaking the trance her tank top now holds on me.

"You were," I say, dragging my eyes back up to her face.

"Yeah, but they have no context. To them, it looks like we are sleeping together." She says, crossing her arms.

I hadn't thought about it that way. But then I really wouldn't care if the whole world thought we were sleeping together. I wouldn't mind if it was true, either.

"Jeez. Don't say it like it's the most outrageous possibility." I say, failing to hide the offense I took.

"That's not what I mean Jess." Samantha huffs. "The last thing they knew. You took Leah home. Now it looks like you slept with Leah and I just let you sleep with me too."

Damn, she's right. That doesn't paint her in a very self-respecting light. I did tell Chad that I didn't sleep with Leah, but no one really knows the whole story yet. As far as I know,

Mel probably knows less than what I've told Chad. I'm not sure Samantha told Mel we've been… whatever we've been.

"I am sorry, Doll." I apologize as she takes a seat next to me. "I didn't mean to make you look bad. I'll explain everything to them as soon as they get here."

"You will?" She lets some of the tension fall from her shoulders.

"Of course. I shall defend you honor *Milady*," I jest, trying to lighten the mood.

It works because Samantha smiles and shoves me playfully.

"Okay, smartass. I need to text Mel and see if they can swing by and grab my work laptop. She has a key." Samantha tells me, pulling her phone from her back pocket.

Chapter 16

Samantha

Mel: What the hell is going on guys?

Samantha: It has to do with Leah. We will explain everything when you get here I promise.

Mel: Yeah you will. This is freaky Sam.

Chad: Jess, don't let her out of your sight.

Jess: What happened? Is there something wrong with her apartment?

Mel: I'm sending a picture but it's taking a while to load hang on.

Mel: We are on our way now. Order pizza or something because I am not waiting for food to talk about this.

"What do you think it is?" I ask Jess.

My stomach is in knots. It's not unlike Mel to be dramatic, but this feels different.

"I don't know, but I have a feeling that it wasn't good. Otherwise, Mel wouldn't be so freaked." Jess says empathetically.

He is right. Mel has been around for years of Carol drama. Plus she has had her own share of messed up family growing up. She doesn't scare easily, but those messages sounded freaked out. I don't know what to expect.

"The picture isn't coming through on my phone. Do you have it yet?" I ask Jess, pacing the living room.

After giving me a worried look he checks his phone and shakes his head. The look of defeat on his face would've been enough to tell me he doesn't have it yet either. I am starting to surpass anxious and venture into a restless panic.

"I need something to do while we wait. Keep me busy." I blurt out. My pacing gets a little quicker as more time passes.

"We should probably order that pizza," Jess suggests. "It sounds stupid, but I don't know what else to do."

"No that's a good idea. I need to chew something." I tell him, trying not to chew on my nails that I haven't bitten in years. "Get a regular pepperoni for me and Mel and meat lovers for you and Chad."

"Okay. Any drinks?" Jess asks looking at the pizza app on his phone.

"Unless they have something hard enough to calm my nerves, I'm gonna pass," I say, knowing that even if he did I wouldn't drink right now. The need to keep myself the polar opposite of my mother prohibits me from letting myself use stress as a reason for alcohol.

Both of our phones buzz at the same time and we hurry to check the message from Mel. Jess watches me as I open the picture. I drop my phone as soon as I see it, and then Jess finally looks down at the phone in his hand. In our group chat is a picture of the four of us plus Ross last summer, stuck to my apartment door with a knife. The blood rushed from my face so fast that I must be as pale as a ghost. Ross and Jess's faces have been crossed out with red sharpie, with the question "Who will be next?" written in the sand at the bottom.

What. The. Hell.

I feel goosebumps crawl from my skull down my spine and cover my arms. My mind races as I try to process what it could mean. It's clear who left it there, but what does she stand to get from it? *Is this a threat?* The red X's across Ross and Jess's faces make me feel like throwing up, but at least they don't seem to symbolize hurting them. It's more like they symbolize hurting me, or separation from me maybe, since she likely doesn't know Jess and I have made up yet.

Does she want to replace me?

"Why would she do this?" I ask, my voice shaking.

"Come here, Doll," Jess says hastily wrapping his arms around me.

The instant my face presses against his strong chest muscles I start sobbing into his shirt.

What does she want?

The question washes over my brain like a wave, flowing away and then crashing back against me with each sob.

What does she want?

I grip his shirt as tightly as possible like it's the only thing keeping me safe.

What does she want?

"I got you Doll," Jess promises, pressing a kiss to the top of my head.

"We, we were *just* there." I stammer, trying to push away the thought of what she planned to do with that knife if I was home.

If Jess hadn't insisted on me staying with him…

"I won't let anything happen to you." He squeezes me tighter as if he knows what I am thinking. "I got you Doll."

I don't move, or say anything. I just stand there in his arms and cry.

What does she want?

Was that a threat?

Why is she doing this?

What did I do to her?

My mind races with questions but I don't say a word, I can't.

"Come on, let's get you to the couch," Jess says.

When I don't move he picks me up and carries me the short distance to the couch. He doesn't let go of me as he sits down so I am half on the cushions with my top half still wrapped in his strong, comforting arms. My head is laid against his chest, and I can hear his heart thundering as fast as mine, even though he's showing no signs of fear or worry outwardly. The weight of either his chin or the side of his face pressed against the top of my head is comforting enough that I don't pull away.

"Why me?" I whisper.

I don't expect Jess to have an answer. I'm not really sure if he could hear me. He doesn't say anything, he just squeezes me tighter. We stay like that until we can hear a vehicle coming up the driveway which I realize must be however long it took for Mel and Chad to fly across town to get here. Then Jess lets go of me and gets up to check who it is from the window.

"It's Mel and Chad." He reassures me, walking to the back kitchen door to let them in.

I wasn't worried about who was here though. I don't feel afraid here with him. More than anything I just feel confused.

"Where is she?" I hear the panic in Mel's voice before she

makes it through the door.

"She's in the living room," Jess tells her. "I think that photo really freaked her out."

"Her and me both," Mel says.

They all make their way into the living room, but I don't look up or say anything. The second I do, I know I am going to start crying again. Jess sits back down beside me and wraps one arm behind me, still trying to comfort me. Mel sits down on the other side of me and Chad sits in the recliner by the window. It's obvious they're all being cautious, not wanting to upset me more. *Just like they always do.*

"I can't take it anymore." Mel outbursts. "Somebody start explaining please."

"I think Leah snapped." Jess starts.

"Leah did this?" Mel's tone is confused, but not one of disbelief.

"That's insane," Chad says. "What's the point?"

"She set it all up," I say quietly, deciding I've taken enough time to compose myself.

Everyone looks at me, almost like they're surprised I said anything at all. That's not me though, no matter how much they have all tried to protect me since my dad died. Like hell am I going to let Leah and her little stunt break me.

"Leah sent Carol to Ross and told them where to find me at the bar. Then she tricked Jess into thinking he slept with her when he really didn't."

"Why would she want Jess to think he slept with her?" Mel asks.

"Shh. Don't interrupt the story." Chad says. The way his eyes shoot to Jess and back to me makes me wonder if he knows the answer, but he doesn't say.

"She got me to bring Carol to my apartment, and I think she convinced Carol to tell her where I live." I continue.

She clearly didn't follow us that night if she was with Jess all night.

"Leah showed up at Benny's diner last night and flaunted the whole scheme in my face like some generic James Bond villain." Jess expands. "She said Samantha wouldn't ever forgive me, now that she thought we'd slept together."

"Wait, so she is trying to get us to turn on Sammy?" Mel asks. "Like she got Ross to cheat on her?"

"Maybe," Jess shrugs. His next words come out as if he can't bear to say them, but needs to all the same. "She said she wanted to watch you break."

Jess gives me an empathetic smile when he says the last part. I try to return it, but goosebumps start to spread all over my body, so I try to rub them away on my arms. Jess clearly notices because he squeezes me tighter, and then he starts to rub his thumb in a smoothing motion over my wrist. It's surprisingly comforting despite his callouses, reminding me of how he did the same thing at the bar.

"Hey," he says lifting my chin with his free hand to look me in the eye. "I will not let her get to you. Do you hear me?"

I nod, locking eyes with him. I know he means it, and I feel so much safer here with him. Even if it's not a very practical promise, I am suddenly very glad that he talked me into staying over at least for tonight.

"What are you gonna do about this?" Chad chimes in.

Jess lets go of my chin but keeps his arm around me when he turns to answer Chad. Our friends' eyes tell me that they notice the closeness, but neither says a word about it. I'm glad they don't because I now find myself worrying that Jess would back away if they did.

"For now, the plan is that Samantha stays here. I have a flexible schedule with Carlos running the shop, I can keep her safe." Jess explains.

"Wait," Mel cuts him off. "Why wouldn't you stay with me?"

Her question makes my stomach drop. I don't have a good answer for it, and I love Mel but… something somewhere inside me feels sad at the thought of not staying here with Jess.

"It was just supposed to be one night before the whole stalker, knife, picture thing," I tell her. "We haven't discussed it more than that."

Jess seems to read my hesitation and the question in my expression.

"Don't be ridiculous, Doll. Until we are sure that Leah isn't a threat I am not leaving your side." Jess says.

"That should be fun to explain to the principal." Mel scoffs.

"I didn't mean at school, smartass." Jess retorts.

"Shit… School." I blurt out. "Leah is a sub. We need to report this. She can't be trusted with the students alone."

"I'll call the Principal," Mel says, already pulling out her phone and walking to the front porch to make the call.

"Has anyone talked to Benny?" Chad asks.

"I told him last night what she said in the diner. He said he won't let her in anymore. But we haven't had a chance to tell him about what you and Mel found." Jess explains.

"Okay, I'll go call Benny and fill him in." Chad offers.

"Thanks, Chad," I say.

"It's the least I can do." He says with his phone already in his ear, walking out to the porch where Mel is on the phone with the principal of our school.

Just like that, they've all banded together for me again. Just like they did when they heard about my dad's accident. We hear more tires coming up the driveway, so I shift toward the window, trying not to worry about who it is. Jess holds his grip on me by his side though, not wavering in the role he assigned himself as my comforter… or maybe bodyguard.

"It's just the pizza, Chad'll get it," Jess assures me.

Pizza. Right, I forgot about the pizza.

"Hey, Principal Clayton wants to know if you need tomorrow off?" Mel asks popping her head inside.

"No, I would rather be at school, and keep myself busy if that's okay with him," I tell her.

"You sure?" Jess asks, not pressuring me, just really checking on me in a way that calms me.

"Yeah, I am." I nod, I have been through a lot worse than Leah and these schemes and petty pranks. "I'll be fine."

"I'll let him know," Mel says and then pops back outside.

A few moments later Chad and Mel come back inside with the pizzas. Chad plops them on the coffee table in front of us, then hunkers down on the couch. I stand to go grab plates from the kitchen and Jess gets up to follow me.

"I have paper plates in the cabinet by the window," Jess tells me. "Do you want a soda or some water maybe?"

"Water is fine," I say. "Thank you."

"I'll take a beer if you're taking orders in there." Chad hollers at Jess.

"Yeah, get up and get it yourself, bonehead." Jess laughs, carrying two glasses of water back to the living room.

Jess starts fiddling with the TV while I pass out the paper plates and we all grab our first slices of pizza. I don't realize what he turned on until Chad and Mel start staring at him like he has eight heads.

"What?" Jess says, stern face challenging them to disagree with his choice of show.

It's a challenge neither of them takes.

I hear the theme song before I see the screen and the first smile I have had in hours covers my face. He put on Gilmore Girls, *for me*. But he started an episode at the beginning of season three.

"How much of this did you watch without me last night?" I say with eyes wide.

"A little, but I figured you've seen them all a hundred times, so no foul right?" Jess's stern face melts into a nonchalant smirk back at me.

My cheeks start to feel flushed with warmth under the smile I can't seem to stop. I would have thought he'd turned it off as soon as I fell asleep. I can't help but find it adorable that he stayed up watching it. It seems odd to be feeling like this, with everything going on, but I can't help it. My mood is lifted entirely.

"What the hell is going on here?" Chad bursts out. "Leah being a creep is one thing, but you're bingeing *Gilmore Girls*?"

"Yeah, that is a little weird," Mel adds, giving Jess a skeptical once over.

"Mind your damn business," Jess says tossing a piece of his crust at Chad, his demeanor falling somewhere between the stern one he bore moments ago and playful.

We all continue to eat pizza and watch the show for the

next hour or so. Mel and I take turns answering the guy's questions about the show. She's seen it, but not as many times as I have, so there are some things she doesn't remember. It's nice, having friends around, eating junk food, and not concentrating on all of the chaos. But it is getting late and most of us have to be up early for work.

"We'd better get going if we are gonna stop by the shop and grab my truck," Chad tells Mel.

They both get up give me hugs and tell Jess to keep a good eye on me before they leave. Jess walks them to the door so he can lock it behind them while I go into his bedroom to find something more comfortable than my jean shorts to sleep in.

"You hanging in there?" Jess asks, leaning against the door frame.

"I think so," I tell him because I'm not sure what else to say.

I have been through worse.

At least no one I loved died today.

"You're amazing, you know that." Jess's words take me by surprise.

"I don't know about that," I say, rejecting the compliment.

"I mean it." Jess insists, walking further into the room to get my full attention, but I turn to my bag and start fussing with my things.

"I have never met anyone who faces shit like this with as much strength as you do."

"I don't feel very strong," I admit, looking down into my bag of clothes for answers that aren't there.

It's true, I don't feel strong, I just sort of feel numb. Tired, confused, and *numb*.

"I'm glad you're here." His soft shift in tone is laced with trepidation. As if his words are trying to convey relief that Leah didn't succeed in tearing us apart. Even if she believes she did. Even if he can't bring himself to say it outright.

"You don't have to be strong tonight either." He says when I don't respond. I can feel the body heat coming off of him as he steps behind me. "You won't let her break you, and that brightness and the bubbly personality that pulls us all in, won't be dulled at all."

"How do you know that?" I ask.

Jess being this close to me is suddenly making my heart race. It's taking more than a little concentration to keep my breathing regular and I don't know if I can keep that up if I turn around. I feel his chest against my back as he leans over my shoulder and I stop breathing, even though I don't mean to, as the warmth of his breath warms my ear. He lifts my left hand and lightly traces his fingers over the tattoo I have on my wrist.

The tattoo says "*Bigger Than The Universe*". I got it a few months after my dad died. When I was little we used to always do that thing where I would say I loved him bigger than something, like a chair. He would come back with something along the lines of I love you bigger than a car, or a horse. No matter the objects we came up with, it always ended with him letting me win with the most obvious trump card a child could come up with. "I love you bigger than the universe." I didn't know if Jess realized on the couch that he was rubbing it with his thumb. I am almost certain that he did now.

"Because I've seen you do it before," Jess says, releasing my arm and stepping back towards the door. "Try and get some sleep, Doll."

As soon as he closes the door behind him I remember to breathe. I rub my face in my hands then plop face down on Jess's bed. I don't know I you can get seasick from contradictory emotions, but I also don't know of another way to describe this feeling.

Chapter 17

Samantha:

I wake up to my phone ringing beside me on Jess's
nightstand. It takes about the same amount of time for my
eyes to clear from the sleepy blur to get my bearings. I don't
recognize the number, it's from a local area code. Benny filed
a police report last night and told me he gave them my
information to reach out. I'm not sure how helpful I will be
since I wasn't even there to see it in person, but I still try to
answer the call quickly in case it is the police.
"Hello?" I answer, my voice still crackling from sleep.
"Miss Bunting?" A deep male voice asks from the other side.
I'm pretty sure from the professionalism in his tone that I
must be correct about who's calling.
I sit up in the bed before he says anything else. It's weird,
waking up in Jess's room, in his bed which smells like him. I
pull one of the pillows to my chest and hug it.
"This is she," I say, trying to stifle a yawn.
"This is Officer Underwood, from the Glenbrook Police
Department. I'm calling to follow up with you about the
incident at your apartment last night."
I nod along as he speaks, even though he can't see me.
"I wasn't actually there at the time. I stayed with a friend," I
tell him, feeling unsure about reporting it at all.

The day after it somehow seems less serious. Like a weird little prank that wasn't worth calling the police. It's just some marker on a photo after all. I'm beginning to feel silly like this whole thing is being blown out of proportion.

And the knife? My inner cynic doesn't allow the fact to slip my mind. *She could have taped it or slid it under the door.*

"That's what your landlord told me." Officer Underwood says.

"Yeah, well I am not sure how much more I can tell you," I say honestly, disappointment lacing my tone.

"That's alright, if it's all the same I'd still like to interview you and your friends who found the threat…" He continues talking, but I don't hear the rest of what he says.

My head started spinning when he said the word *threat*. I remember wondering if that's what it was last night. It sounds more surreal coming from a cop, somehow. More serious. I am going over the photo Mel sent last night in my mind when the Officer's voice snaps me out of my daze.

"Miss Bunting?"

"Oh, I am sorry." I shake my head trying to focus on the conversation. "I um.. Yeah, we can do that."

"Great, 3 o'clock, your apartment." He confirms.

I must've missed the part of the conversation where he asked about time and place, but I agree anyway.

"We will be there. Thank you." I tell him and then hang up.

I stay in the middle of the bed, looking down at the phone in my hand, and clutch the pillow tighter. A *threat.* The officer's word is stuck in my head, waring with the part of me that feels silly about this whole thing, trying to drown it with fear. There is a soft knock, even though the door is wide open, which thankfully snaps me out of it.

"Was that the cops?" Jess asks, standing in the doorway with a hand holding onto the door frame.

"Uh, yeah," I say, shaking away the fear and trying not to stare at the part of his stomach where his shirt is lifted just above his waistband. Though I have to admit, I am grateful for the distraction after that literal wake-up call. *Not that I am supposed to be looking at him that way.*

"Can I come in?" He asks.

"It's your room, you don't have to ask to come in," I say, moving over to make room for him next to me, taking the pillow with me.

"What did they say?"

"He said he wants to interview me, Mel, and Chad," I say reluctantly, the next part comes quieter. "He called it a threat."

"The picture?" Jess clarifies.

"Yeah," I nod, looking down at my hands. "I guess I just didn't think of it as being that serious. I mean, it was upsetting, but I didn't think Leah was dangerous. Or I didn't want to anyway."

I lived with her.

Jess doesn't bother asking if I am okay. He knows me well enough to know that I'm not, so instead he wraps his arm around my shoulder and lets me lean against him. Maybe I am just letting the cop's words get to me. I don't know how this whole thing escalated so quickly. Leah and I were friends, I thought. How does someone go from being one of your closest confidants to completely turning against you in such a short amount of time? After a few minutes of sitting quietly with my head against his broad chest, Jess finally breaks the silence.

"C'mon Doll, I made coffee." He says standing and holding his hand out for me to follow him out of his room.

"You don't like coffee." I point out, cocking my head to the side curiously.

"But you can't live without it." Jess counters, pulling me off the bed by my hand and leading me out to the kitchen.

He made coffee for me.

I can smell it as soon as I pass through his bedroom door. The smell and the gesture both bring me comfort. This is the third time he has gone out of his way to make sure that I have my caffeine fix. It's thoughtful and sweet, but not enough to get me to get my mind off of Leah. The last time I saw her here, she was drinking coffee and bringing some to him just to spite me. An undeserved pang of jealousy wipes the smile off my face. Thinking of him making coffee for her somehow makes it less special.

"So you make coffee for all your overnight lady guests?" My eyes go wide with surprise as words spill out before the thought is fully formed.

Subtle.

It would appear I am not awake enough to hold back my intrusive thoughts yet. I don't know why I said that. I don't want to talk about him with Leah. I don't need to hear about whatever did or didn't happen, even if he says they didn't sleep together. I step past him to grab a cup from the cabinet, hoping to avoid the conversation I just started if I don't make eye contact. Of course that works out about as well as you'd think, which is not at all. When I turn around Jess is standing right in front of me, looking down at me with an agitated look that he usually reserves for the rest of our friends more than for me.

"I didn't make *her* coffee." He retorts, knowing exactly what I was talking about.

 I sigh and look down at the cup in my hand, regretting bringing it up. I already let the worms out of the can though, so now it looks like we are having this conversation.

"Leah brought you coffee when I was here, and since she kissed you I just figured..."

"She kissed my *cheek*. She did it to bother you, Samantha." Jess cuts me off, lifting my chin with his hand so I am forced to make eye contact. The knots in my stomach remind me that this isn't the first time recently that he's made this intimate gesture. It's frustrating how my stomach somersaults when he does that, and it's been happening a lot more lately.

"Let me be perfectly clear." He goes on. "I didn't make Leah coffee. I didn't sleep with her. I didn't kiss her. Hell, up until I saw your Jeep pull up I thought she was *you*."

"You thought she was me?" I recoil, not bothering to mask how offended I am by that.

"I don't remember that night after you left with Ross." Jess starts to explain.

"She was in your shower, Jess." I snap at him, more than I probably have the right to. I just hate the thought that she spent so much time and effort copying all of these aspects of me, and it worked.

"I know. Just let me explain." He rubs his face with frustration.

I can see he's trying to gather his thoughts, so I fight the urge to walk away. I need to hear him out, even if I don't like what I might hear.

"I don't remember her bringing me home. I thought Chad brought me home. When I woke up she was already in the shower. I didn't see her before that. I went into the kitchen and saw a blue Jeep out there and the coffee was already made. I thought…" Jess stops and turns around to face away from me, rubbing his neck with his hand.

"You thought what?" I pry, despite not wanting to hear the answer.

"I thought you came back and I fucked it all up," He says cautiously, then chances a look at me expectantly, like I am supposed to say something. When I don't, he answers my next question for me.

"I was scared that I didn't remember." He explains softly, rubbing his hand over his face again.

I am stunned trying to figure out what he means. *Is he saying he thought we had sex and he forgot?* He looks back at me, trying to read my expression again, probably because it keeps changing. My mouth hangs open, failing to produce words because I'm not sure what to say. I think I get why deer don't move in headlights now. I must be feeling what they feel because I am still standing here like a frozen idiot. *Scared I forgot.* He wasn't upset because he thought he slept with Leah. He was scared he slept with *me,* and couldn't remember it. My heart is beating again but for an entirely different reason.

"Jess…" I start, but he cuts me off again.

"Then I saw you pull up and I felt like an idiot. Because you left with Ross and you didn't come back." He says an undertone of irritation surprises me in his words.

"I'm confused. Were you upset that I was here, or that I wasn't?"

"Both," Jess grumbles.

"I told you what happened." I defend myself.

"But you left *before* you knew." Jess retorts. "I get why you left after you saw Carol, but before we went inside you promised me you wouldn't run off. You knew, Samantha. You had to have known what that night meant and you just left with your ex-boyfriend."

I don't like the feeling I get when he says my name like that. He hasn't called me Doll once, just Samantha. I am blindsided by how quickly the feeling of guilt hits me in the stomach. Jess is right, I knew we were on the verge of something that would change everything. I promised him, and then I left. I can't even remember what it was that made me think I needed to follow Ross out or why I didn't ask Jess to come with me. I'm not the one who gets to be mad here. The truth is even if he had slept with Leah, or anyone else, it would've been because I let him think I chose Ross over him.

You knew, Samantha.

Those words hit the hardest. I feel like I fell flat on my back and had the last bit of denial knocked right out of me, along with my breath.

"Jess, I'm sorry," I say, my voice cracking in an attempt to suppress the urge to cry. "I thought I could just get rid of him quickly and come right back in. I should have asked you to go out with me. Or maybe I shouldn't have gone at all. I didn't mean to"

"But you *did*." He says softly, resting his weight against the counter.

I can see the hurt on his face and I hate that I am the one who put it there.

"Maybe I should go," I say, placing the empty mug on the counter next to him.

Jess doesn't follow me as I walk back to his bedroom to gather my things. When I get in his room I start to pack up the few things I have out of my bag from the night before. I am grabbing my charger from the wall when he comes and stands in the doorway again.

"Just give me a minute and I'll be out of your hair," I say, avoiding looking at him.

I'm starting to feel shaky and like my heart is floating up into my throat as I sling my bag over my shoulder and grab my phone off the nightstand. I keep my eyes low as I walk past him in the doorway and Jess steps back to let me through the door.

Neither of us says anything else as I slide my shoes on by the back door and head out to get in my Jeep. The Jeep that now reminds me, and everyone else apparently of Leah. *God, I hate this Jeep.* I loved it before, really. But now all I see as I get in and slam the door is how easy it is for Leah to take my identity from me. How wearing my hairstyle, and driving the twin of my vehicle, anyone could easily mistake the two of us. She could come and go from our lives and take my place as easily as she has with Ross and Jess.

Just make it out of the driveway, then you can cry.

I just turn over the engine when my driver's door opens, and Jess stands next to me. With one hand on the door and the other on the roof of my Jeep. I brace myself for him to yell, to keep fighting, or to tell me he's done wanting anything to do with me. My fingers wrap around the steering wheel until they turn white. His face is still stuck in that surly grimace that I am not used to being on the receiving end of and looking down, I see he didn't bother to put shoes on.

"You said the cops wanna see you guys today?"

My head draws back, waiting for more bite in his next words.

"Yeah. At my place this afternoon."

"Can I come?" He asks, the smoldering seriousness on his face softening before he says. "Please, I just want to make sure you're safe."

I noticeably relax, letting my kung-fu grip on the steering wheel go, and melt back into my seat. As much as I want to point out the emotional whiplash, I want him there more. I know I won't be alone, but I am also relieved that he's willing to come. Mel and Chad will be there, but it's not the same. Somehow, without even trying, he became who I need around right now, and I'm relieved I haven't ruined that.

"Yeah, you can come." I softly move my head up and down, and my answer seems to give him the same relief.

"Okay, just let me get shoes."

"You are coming with me? Now?" I clarify.

I thought he meant he wanted to come over later for the interview. I didn't realize he wanted to come with me right now after whatever that was, in the kitchen. He doesn't answer me though. He just runs back into the house and quickly reappears in my passenger seat with his shoes on a few minutes later.

Chapter 18

Jess

On the ride over to Samantha's she called Chad and Mel to let them know about the interview with the cop this afternoon. I think she's just trying to avoid talking to me. Honestly, I am grateful for it, though. I don't want to fight with her when I am worried about keeping her safe.

I didn't even mean to argue with her. I probably shouldn't have said anything, she was visibly upset when the cop called Leah a threat. It makes sense that she'd be upset, being reminded of Leah, I guess. I just couldn't take her making me feel like shit for something I didn't do. I needed her to know that I didn't want anyone there but her. Hell, I haven't wanted anyone but her for a while. I just did a shit job of conveying it. Don't get me wrong, I've dated but no one ever really stuck in my head the way that Samantha does. Which is exactly what makes this line were riding so dangerous.

Why the hell did I bring up her leaving with Ross?

This whole morning was a disaster, which resulted in me sitting on the couch while Samantha continued to find excuses to avoid me in her apartment all morning. As soon as Mel and Chad got here Samantha and Mel went into her room, leaving me with Chad. He's waited a whole 7 seconds after her bedroom door closed to start his meddling.

"Sooo?" Chad says as if we were already mid-conversation.

"What?" I grunt.

He's my best friend, and I love the guy, but I am not in the mood today.

"You know." He winks, "How was it?"

Shithead.

"Nothing happened." I dismiss him, shaking my head.

"What do you mean nothing happened?" Chad asks in disbelief. "You had your arm around her all last night?"

"I was comforting her, jackass. She was upset." I roll my eyes.

Not that I wouldn't have wanted something to happen.

"You two spent the last *two* nights together," Chad continues in disbelief. "She's been glued to your side!"

Does he think if he presents enough evidence I am suddenly going to tell him a different story? I'm not sure I would tell him if something did happen, but nothing did. Now I don't even know if we are talking, or fighting. But I think it's safe to say that *something* is definitely continuing to not happen for the foreseeable future.

"I don't know what you want me to say, man." My patience is wearing off and by the way he shifts in his seat, I know he can tell. "Nothing happened. End of story."

Finally, three firm knocks on the door let us know the cop has arrived. Samantha and Mel are making their way up the hallway when I open the door to let him in and shake his hand.

"Good afternoon, I am Officer Underwood." He holds out

his hand and shakes mine. It's a firm handshake, but not one where you can tell the other guy's trying too hard. His hair is brown, in your typical buzz cut for a cop.

"Jess Adams," I say, then nod towards Chad. "Chad Wilkins."

"Nice to meet you," Underwood says to Chad, then turns his attention to the ladies. "Which one of you is Samantha Bunting?"

"That would be me," Samantha says reaching out to shake his hand.

Officer Underwood looks over Samantha as she shakes his hand and says, "Nice to meet you."

"Which leaves me," Mel interjects as she steps out from around Samantha with her arms folded.

"Melissa?" the officer asks, he clearly knows her but he doesn't seem sure that it's her.

"It's Mel." She snaps back at him.

I am beginning to think however they knew each other, it didn't end well. He's a few years too old to have gone to school with her. It's unusual for Mel to know someone well enough to be seething at the site of them and Samantha does not have a clue why, but she looks just as confused as the rest of us. When Underwood notices all eyes on their interaction he clears his throat and steers us back to the reason he is here, refusing to break his professionalism. I'm sure I'm not the only one who's curious about what that was about but we have something more important to handle right now.

"Well, now that the introductions have been made I have a few questions. Is there somewhere we can all sit?" Underwood asks.

"Of course, the living room is over here," Samantha says,

leading him the few short feet to the couch.

In those few short feet, Samantha and Mel seem to have an entire conversation with their eyes. Samantha asks Mel what the hell that was about and Mel not only dodges the inquiry but manages to build a damn wall around the subject just for Samantha to knock it down insistently and for Mel to seemingly cave as if to say she'll talk to her about it later. By the time we've taken our seats the silent discussion has settled and I am the only one who seems to have caught even a glimpse of it.

"Now, Miss Bunting you weren't here last night at the time of the incident. Is that correct?" He asks sitting down in the chair by the window.

Mel hasn't stopped looking at him since he came in. She took the seat on the sectional farthest from him. I sat down right next to Samantha. Even though things were tense today, I need to be by her for this. Chad sits to the right of me on the other end of the couch.

"Correct," Samantha responds. "I was at Jess's. I asked Mel to pick up my laptop before coming to meet us over there."

"How long were you out of the apartment?" He asks, opening his notepad.

"Just long enough to get to Jess's and take a shower," Samantha answers.

Underwood's eyes shift from Samantha to me with that answer. Then back to her before the next.

"And that's when you found the threat, Miss Eddy?" he asks Mel, who looks just about as pleased to be called that as Melissa.

I notice Samantha tense up when he calls it a threat again.

"Yes, when Chad and I came upstairs it was knifed into the door." Mel recounts, not hiding her irritation with him very well.

Samantha starts picking at her fingers. Without thinking I reach over and take her hand in mine. She doesn't look at me while she interlaces her fingers in mine. She's keeping her attention forward, trying not to show emotion. Not sure if she's steeling herself for the interview, against me, or both, I'm just glad she didn't pull away.

"Is that what you think the photo was?" I ask the question everyone else has been avoiding. "A threat?"

Samantha's hand tightens in mine and I think she holds her breath until the cop answers.

"I'm afraid that's the only way the police look at anything left on a door with a knife." The officer says offering a sympathetic shrug.

He must be about my age, I think. Maybe a little older. He seems like a nice enough guy, but I'm still trying to get a read on what it is about him that pisses Mel off. I don't care if he's some Tinder date who never called again, that's her problem. But I do care if it's something that will affect his ability to protect Samantha and handle this case.

"What can you tell me about the person you believe left the note?" He pushes on with his next question.

"Leah," Samantha says quietly.

"Right," Underwood confirms her name looking at his notes, and clicks his pen. "Your landlord, Benny, he didn't know her last name."

"Leah Woods," I answer. "She was Samantha's roommate until about a month or so ago.

"May I ask why you moved out?" Underwood leans

forward, intrigued.

"I don't know how to explain it. It sounds weird." Samantha says, rubbing her eyebrow with her free hand. "It was a hundred little things that meant nothing, unless you noticed them all together, I guess."

"Leah was acting obsessed with Sammy," Mel interjects. "She went from copying her clothes and hair and little stuff to full-out creepiness. She bought the same car as Sammy."

"It's a Jeep," I cut Mel off. I don't want the cop scribbling down that she drives a car in his notes. It's not accurate.

"It's the same color as Samantha's." She goes on.

"I see." He says now looking up from his notes. "Is there anything else you can tell me?"

"Leah slept with her boyfriend," Chad says.

Officer Underwood looks surprised by Chad's statement. He looks at Samantha's hand in mine in confusion, then back to Chad. He must think that Chad meant me because I am holding her hand.

"Not me," I explain. "Her ex, Ross. It happened after Samantha moved out."

"I see." Underwood nods. "Did she ever do anything to make you think she was dangerous when you lived together?"

"No. She always seemed really happy to have me around. I think she felt closer to me than I did to her. She would say we were like sisters." Samantha recalls. "Until I said something about her getting the same Jeep, then something flipped. She said everything we did was a competition. She even got a subbing job at the school I teach at."

"Okay, well I am going to follow up with the school. As soon as the restraining order goes into effect she will have a seriously hard time getting a job around kids in the future as well." Underwood says.

"Restraining order?" Samantha asks. Her hand tightens around mine again.

"I think that is the best course of action from here." Underwood nods. "Can you stay with your boyfriend tonight? Just as an extra precaution?"

Samantha looks down at our hands and then back to the officer. "Oh. Jess isn't.."

"Going to mind at all." I cut her off.

I feel everyone's eyes on us as she looks at me, no doubt trying to figure out why I didn't let her correct him. For one, I really do prefer she stays with me. Even if nothing happens (*much to Chad's dismay*) I will know she is safe. Plus, maybe a small part of me thought he phrased it that way on purpose, trying to see if she was single. I'm not going to give him an in if that's what he was doing. Neither of our friends says anything as they stare. After a few seconds that I'm certain only feels like an eternity, Samantha cocks her head to the side and breaks the silence.

"Are you sure you don't mind?"

"I'm sure, Doll," I say rubbing circles on the tattoo on her wrist with my thumb.

She gives me a small smile and nods.

"Okay then. If you can think of anything else, or something else happens please feel free to give me a call." Underwood says, passing each of us a business card. "In the meantime, I am gonna get started on the restraining order."

"Thank you," Samantha tells him, shaking his hand.

Chapter 19

Samantha

"You okay?" Jess asks me while Mel begrudgingly walks Officer Underwood out.

I'm not exactly sure why she wanted to walk him out. They seem to know each other somehow, which is strange. If Mel knows him, why don't I know who he is? She was practically fuming from the minute that tall, dark, and uniformed strutted in the door. Okay, maybe he's not dark, but he did have a nice tan and brown hair. He looks like one of the cops you'd see on the lake patrolling for life jackets, but I don't think the city cops do that.

"I just wanna go to bed," I tell Jess, even though it isn't night yet.

This has been exhausting. I wasn't expecting Underwood to suggest a restraining order. I'm not even sure how much it will help. Maybe it's just all the cop lingo that's bothering me. I didn't have as much of a hard time with it until Underwood started saying things that made it seem so serious. The one thing keeping me grounded right now is Jess's strong hand intertwined with mine. He makes me feel safe.

"Okay, you should go get your stuff." Jess nods but still doesn't release my hand.

"I'll help you." Mel cuts in.

She nods toward my room, still grimacing. I give Jess an apologetic look as I reluctantly let go of his hand and go with Mel back to my room. I feel his eyes on me until we reach the hallway.

"You wanna tell me again what happened last night?" Mel asks in an accusing tone once my bedroom door closes behind us.

"I told you. Nothing happened." I say tucking my hair behind my ear as I start to grab a few more things to add to the bag I didn't bother unpacking from last night.

"Then why didn't you correct Jake when he called Jess your boyfriend?" She grills me, putting her hands on her hips. "And what's with the handholding?"

"Who is Jake?" I ask, changing the subject.

"The cop. Officer Underwood." She explains, flustered.

I knew she had to know him.

"And how exactly do we know Jake?" I smile, finding it both a good distraction and great fun to tease my best friend.

I would much rather talk about that than Jess. Especially since she wants answers I don't have. But she is a persistent little bugger.

"Don't change the subject," she says pulling a few things out of my closet and dresser and adding them to the bag. "Jess, handholding?"

"I don't know, Mel. I started to correct him and Jess cut me off." I huff. "I don't know why he cut me off. But nothing has happened. I would tell you."

"The hand holding?" she pushes, reminding me that her

tenacity is unmatched. She isn't going to let it go, but I don't even have an answer for her.

"I think he was just trying to be comforting," I say, trying to convince the both of us.

She gives me a look of disbelief but doesn't push any further. "You'll tell me if that changes?"

"I will," I say, knowing that my promise to her is also an admittance to the possibility.

"Okay." She says, handing me my bag. "I am going to hold you to that."

~

We are back at Jess's in no time. He drove us back here in my Jeep because I didn't really feel up to driving. Like on the way to my apartment, we didn't say much. I don't think he's upset anymore though. It was more like he was giving me room to process, which I am grateful for.

When we get out of the Jeep we find the back kitchen door is cracked open. The light from the kitchen pours out of the door making me freeze in my tracks. Internal sirens go off in my head, no doubt intensified by the interview we just left.

"Come here," Jess says, wrapping his arm around me protectively.

I cling to his side as we cautiously make our way into the kitchen. I don't see anything out of order, other than the open door. Thankfully, Jess doesn't ask me to wait somewhere while he checks it out. I've seen enough horror movies to know that splitting up always results in trouble. We make our way around the rest of the house like this, with Jess's protective grip on me, until we are satisfied that we are the only two here.

"I must not have shut the door all the way when we left this morning." Jess reasons with himself out loud.

He releases me but I stay close while he carries my bag into his room and puts it down on the bed.

"Do you want to take a shower before bed?" Jess offers, pointing over my shoulder to the bathroom.

"That sounds like a good idea." I nod, exhausted from the day, or the week, maybe more.

Either way, a good hot shower is always what I need to feel better.

"Okay, I'll be out on the couch if you need me." Jess offers me a half smile and starts to step around me.

"Don't," I say, grabbing his wrist as he takes a step.

He stops in his tracks and looks from my hand on his wrist to my face.

"Don't what?" he asks, his eyes moving side to side as he tries to read mine.

"Don't sleep on the couch," I say, willing him to stay close to me.

I know it's safe here, but I don't want to be alone. Having him next to me makes me feel comforted. Even if things from this morning aren't resolved, I'll sleep better with him next to me.

"You're not sleeping on the couch, we've been over this." Jess protests, not understanding what I mean.

"I know." I take a deep breath trying to find my words, "Just stay with me. Please."

I pause long enough for him to see the sincerity in my eyes. Jess's expression softens, seeing what must look like desperation in my eyes. My shoulders relax noticeably when he nods in agreement. I give him a soft smile of appreciation before I let go and walk into the connecting bathroom.

I don't take a very long shower. I don't want to think about Leah anymore or worry about the argument with Jess this morning. I know if I stay in here long I won't be able to stop my mind from overthinking. I really just want to lay down in my sweats and sleep for a week.

Once I finish drying off, I realize that I don't have any clothes in here. I left my bag of clothes on the bed. I wrap the towel around myself and crack the door open to the room, where Jess is sitting on the bed. He looks up from the book he is reading when he hears the door squeak softly. I don't know why it surprises me to see him reading, instead of watching TV or scrolling on his phone, but it makes me smile.

"I uh.. I forgot clothes." I bashfully explain why I am still in a towel.

Jess looks me over in my towel and just stares. He doesn't say anything for a few seconds and I remember his comment about me in a towel before. He told me he couldn't speak in full sentences if I wasn't wearing clothes. It made me blush a little but I thought it was a joke. Yet, here I am in a towel and I don't know if he even heard me. *Could I really have that kind of effect on him?* My cheeks heat at the thought.

"Sorry," I say tucking myself further behind the door. "Could you grab some clothes out of my bag?"

Jess grabs my entire bag and brings it to me, without trying to look inside.

"I just needed clothes," I say, taking it from him.

"That's like asking me to dig through your portable underwear drawer," Jess says, his smile failing to hide his embarrassment. I can't help but laugh.

I'm not sure which one is more attractive, reading Jess or blushing Jess.

"Do my underwear make you nervous, Jess?" I tease him.

"More than you know." He admits through the door while I close it to get dressed.

Maybe I do affect him.

I am still smiling when I open the bag to discover that almost none of what I packed is in there. I saw Mel removing some things earlier. I assumed they were dirty from yesterday or she changed her mind about whatever she'd added. Instead, she has taken out all of my loose comfy underwear and pajamas and replaced them with lacy undergarments and nightgowns. I roll my eyes to myself at her obviousness. When it comes to meddling, she's as bad as Chad. I don't have any other options though so I put them on.

When I get to the bed Jess is lying back, on the side closest to me and the bedroom door with his book. He has changed into a pair of basketball shorts and removed his shirt. I guess that makes sense. He probably doesn't sleep in a shirt or actual pajamas. He is a bachelor after all, but a small part of me hopes it's because he's trying to look good for me. Even if he isn't, it's working. I pull at the hemline of my nightgown, suddenly worried that it's too short while Jess looks up at me.

"I see you picked a side of the bed." I point out to break the silence.

His throat bobs, taking in the nightgown that covers less than the towel and I swear he forces himself to look back at his book to avoid it.

"It's closest to the door." Jess clears his throat. "It's my spot by default."

Ever the gentleman. Of course, he chose his side based on my safety.

"Do you normally have a side? Or are you a middle sleeper?" I ask curiously.

His brow creases while he thinks about it before he says, "Middle, I guess."

That's what I was worried about. My issues with Leah are starting to affect Jess. Maybe it's not the biggest thing, but I don't like other people having to deal with my problems. It makes me feel guilty and embarrassed, even though it's not something I have control over.

"I'm sorry," I say fidgeting with the lace in my hem.

"For what?"

"That you got stuck looking out for me." I look up to see him looking at me with a smoldering intensity.

"I'm not stuck, Doll." He says with a soft sincerity, which contrasts the serious look on his face. "I'm right where I wanna be."

"I haven't ever seen you reading before," I say, wanting to talk about something less serious.

Jess looks dumbfounded at my change of topic, as I walk around to the other side of the bed.

"You didn't think I could read?" He smirks at me, playfully pretending to be offended.

"Of course, I know you CAN read." I joke back shoving him lightly as I sit next to him. "I just haven't ever seen you sit down and read a book."

"It's not exactly a social activity," Jess explains. "I don't recall you pulling out a novel when we are all hanging out either."

I think about it for a second and I suppose he is right.

Reading isn't something I usually do around people. I read a lot, but I always put my book down when I have someone around. I wonder how much Jess reads and briefly think about sitting next to him reading. The thought is so domestic, but like every other thought of Jess right now it brings me comfort.

"I guess you're right." I concede happily.

As soon as my head hits the pillow I hear a buzz from my phone. I turn over to see it on the nightstand on my side, where Jess must've put it. It's just a reminder to print something out for my students. I can do it in the morning at school.

I put the phone back down, but I stay on my side facing away from Jess. I just want to shut my brain off and go to sleep. Somehow I think it'll be easier facing away from his shirtless body inches away from me. I feel Jess's weight shift off the bed as he gets up to turn off the light. I guess bachelors don't exactly think to use lamps on the nightstands. I hear him leave the room for a minute before he comes back in and closes the door behind him. I can feel the warmth coming off of him as soon as he climbs under the comforter beside me.

"Good night, Doll." His deep, but somehow soft voice gives me goosebumps on my arm. I am grateful that he can't see them with the blanket pulled up over my shoulder.

"Night, Jess." I sigh a response.

We lay there in silence for a while. I am not sure if it's two minutes or twenty. Usually, I would read before bed, or watch a little TV. Just laying here, I have no way of tracking the time unless I check my phone, which I am avoiding doing since I am pretending to already be asleep. Instead, I try to clear my mind and force myself to sleep. Of course, trying to sleep harder means I am only going over the interview from today in my head a hundred times.

What's with the hand holding?

Mel's question comes to mind as I remember Jess's reassuring gesture. He was comforting me, I know that. Jess saw my reaction when Underwood was talking about Leah and just wanted to comfort me. That's what I told Mel, and it's what I keep trying to tell myself…except one thing. Jess didn't let me correct Underwood when he called Jess my boyfriend. By the sound of his breathing, I don't think he is asleep yet either.

"Why did you cut me off?" I say, barely above a whisper, once again losing the battle with my sleepy impulsive thoughts.

I feel Jess's weight shift towards me before he responds. "What are you talking about?"

I don't turn around, I'm afraid if I do I'll lose my nerve. I just stare ahead at the wall as I muster up the courage to finish the conversation I started.

"Underwood called you my boyfriend, and you didn't let me correct him," I say, unable to get my voice any louder.

I feel him instantly stiffen behind me at my question. I don't think he was expecting that. This wouldn't be the first time that someone mistook us for a couple. Usually, Jess or I would correct them and laugh it off, but this was different. I can feel the tension building in the silence as I wait for him to say something. I hold my breath, willing my heart rate to slow back down. It hasn't worked the other few times I tried it, so I don't know why I bother now.

"He wanted to know if you could stay with me," Jess says, avoiding the question, and his weight shifts again.

"I know but.." I start, but he interrupts me.

"I didn't want to have to explain it." His voice is soft, but I can tell it's closer over my shoulder now.

He breathes deeply waiting for me to respond. I don't say anything though. I just nod in agreement, not willing to be the one who admits first to what has been building between us. I feel Jess's arm on the top of my waist as he puts his hand on my stomach and pulls me to his chest. I stop breathing again, but it's no use. No amount of holding my breath could stop my heart from beating this hard and when I finally do breathe again I have to fight even harder to keep my breathing even. I wonder if Jess can hear how loud my heart is beating, or maybe his is beating just as hard and he can't hear mine over his own. I place my hand over his, silently reciprocating all of the emotions unspoken at this moment.

I'm in Jess's bed. Jess is holding me. Is this really happening? Is he making a move?

"Get some sleep, Doll," Jess says, interlocking his fingers with mine.

I can't think of a time I have ever felt so nervous, and somehow so comforted at the same time. It feels like all of the comfort of being home, combined with all of the thrill and fear of skydiving. This isn't the first time Jess has had me in his arms in the past few days. The other times were different though. Then he was comforting me, and we weren't in his bed. Not to mention how this nightgown that Mel packed isn't leaving much between us and I can feel the warm skin of his bare chest against the top of my back, where my nightgown doesn't cover.

I think to myself, *there is no way that I am going to get any sleep with Jess's arm around me.* I am wrong though, it's not long before the comfort and warmth have me lulled to sleep.

Chapter 20

Jess

I wake up with my arm still wrapped around Samantha, who is sound asleep. Her back is to my chest which leaves her butt pressed up against me and the fresh scent of fruit and sunshine fills my nose. I kept waking up last night, worried that I dreamt up having Samantha in my bed. Each time I woke up to find her still in my arms I was relieved. Now that it's starting to get light outside though, I am starting to get nervous. There has been a lot unsaid between us recently. After last night I'm afraid we've reached a point of now or never. When Samantha wakes up we are going to have to address whatever it is that's been between us.

I carefully lift my arm from around her, trying not to wake her up. Lifting the comforter so I can slide out, I can see where her nightgown has ridden up in her sleep. The bottom of her nightgown only hides the waistband of her lacy white panties. I bite my lip and take a mental picture in case I never get to see her like this again. After having her in my arms, I *really* want her back in my bed again. There's no room to be a chicken shit today.

I carefully sneak out of bed and quietly close the door behind me on my way to the kitchen. I decided to make her coffee again, even though it didn't go very well yesterday. The pot still has yesterday's unused coffee in it. I think about investing in a single-serving coffee maker while I wash out the coffee pot and refill it. It always seemed like a wasteful thing to have around before but if Samantha is going to be spending more time here, (*at least I hope she will be*) I think she would appreciate it. Maybe I am getting ahead of myself, but I really don't care. I'm all in at this point.

I grab my phone off the counter where I left it last night and open the Amazon app to order a new coffee maker for her. It doesn't take long to realize I have no idea what I am looking for. I scroll for a minute and settle on one that looks kind of like the one she has in her apartment, plus it has same-day shipping. I add it to my cart along with some coffee pods in a flavor I hope she will like. I almost check out my cart before I see the blue coffee mug she left on the counter yesterday next to me. It reminded her of Leah, so I pick it up and throw it into the garbage. I don't want any reminders of what Leah is putting Samantha through in my house. The only other coffee mugs I have are a couple of black ones that came to the shop as samples from an advertising company that says "Adams Auto" in white. I decide to add a mug to the cart that I think she would like and then check out.

Once that is done, I fish the Adam's auto mug out of the cabinet and grab the creamer from the fridge. *This time, I am gonna bring the coffee to her.* As soon as the coffee is ready I take the mug back to the room, planning to put it on the nightstand next to her and then hop in the shower. *Hopefully, I will be done in time to see her in that nightgown again before she wakes up.*

Unfortunately, when I open the door to the room the bed

is empty. I didn't expect her to be up this early. If she had come out of the room I would've seen her from the kitchen, so she must be in the bathroom.

"Doll?" I knock softly.

The door swings open right away to reveal Samantha standing in front of the mirror primping her hair. To my disappointment, the nightgown has been exchanged for a pair of pants, a button-up shirt with a colorful pattern, and a green cardigan. She couldn't be more covered up if she tried, but she still looks beautiful.

"You're up early," I say handing her the coffee and trying to pretend that I am not still imagining the sight of her in those little white panties.

"Yeah, school doesn't start 'til eight thirty but teachers have to be there by 8." She explains.

I completely forgot she had to work today. I knew it was a three day weekend, but in all the chaos I didn't keep track of each day. Which means she is going to be gone all day and I don't even know if she plans on coming back.

"Thank you." She smiles up at me through her eyelashes.

"For what?" I ask, trying to focus on her and not the panic setting in about her leaving without knowing where we stand.

"The coffee." She raises the mug to take a sip.

"You're welcome, Doll." I clear my throat trying to cover up my deep swallow in reaction to the hum of approval she makes when she takes her first sip and licks her lips.

She is avoiding addressing the elephant in the room just like I am, but the way she is looking at me has me hopeful. I back away to let her finish getting ready and go into the room to get dressed. Even though Carlos makes me being at the shop useless most of the time these days, I am gonna go in. I need something to do besides sit around here thinking about Samantha in my bed all day. I catch Samantha looking my way as I take off my basketball shorts and pull my jeans on, through the still-open bathroom door.

"Nice underwear." Samantha playfully catcalls at me walking into the room.

Is she flirting with me?

Oh, it is on.

I pick up my shirt from the bed and sling it over my shoulder as I walk over to her. She is standing in front of me holding the coffee mug with my last name on it in both hands when I bend over and whisper into her ear, "Not as nice as your white lacy ones."

Her eyes go wide as she looks up at me and gasps so quietly, I wouldn't have heard it if I wasn't this close to her. Her cheeks are undeniably flushed and this time there's no doubt, I'm the one who made her blush.

"Have a good day at work, Doll," I say putting on the best sideways smile I can manage, and walk out of the room back into the kitchen.

One of the perks of owning the shop is that I get to choose when I come and go. Which, means I don't plan on leaving until Samantha does, but after my dramatic exit I need to find a way to busy myself until she comes out. I thought about making breakfast, but years of knowing her have taught me that coffee is breakfast to her. I decide to busy myself making room for the new coffee maker and tidying the kitchen instead.

A few minutes later Samantha makes her way into the kitchen with her laptop bag on her shoulder. She smiles at me cautiously while she puts the mug in the sink and rinses it, but she's quiet. This is it, she is going to work and I need to know that I'll see her tonight. I take a deep breath as I ready myself to say just about anything to stop her from leaving. I can't decide what to say though.

"Well, I better get going." She says, pointing towards the back door.

Say, something idiot.

"Okay, have a great day," I say and I swear my voice almost cracks like a prepubescent boy scout.

Not that moron.

On her way to the door, she walks over to me and leans in to hug me. The scent of her fruity shampoo is combined with something else I can't place when she wraps both arms around my shoulders. I wrap both of my hands around her lower back and pull her closer to me, trying not to inhale too loudly as I drink in her heavenly scent. After what feels like a minute, but I am sure was probably only a few seconds she pulls her head back and looks up at me, but I keep my hands firmly placed on her back, refusing to be the first to let go.

"I'm gonna see you after work right?"

Thank fuck, I finally said something useful.

Samantha looks from my eyes to my mouth and then down to where she has slid her hand on the front of my chest. My heart has been racing and I think she is actually able to feel it through my shirt at this point.

"See me… here?" She asks, dragging those caramel-colored eyes back up to mine and biting her bottom lip.

I nod my head, unable to articulate words that convey how much I want her to come back. Hell, how much I wish she didn't have to leave at all. I remove one hand from her back and bring it up to brush a strand of hair behind her ear.

"Okay." She agrees, shyly smiling at the brush of my hand against her cheek.

Just as she starts to let go I tighten my grip around her waist and grab her chin with my free hand, lifting it so her eyes meet mine. I pause for just a brief moment, giving her the chance to push me away if she wants to, hovering my lips just a whisper away from touching hers. I can feel her breath slow and briefly wonder if she is trying to hold her breath.

When our lips finally touch I am not sure which one of us closed the gap, but I am incredibly grateful for it. Her lips are soft, warm, and full as she lifts up onto her tiptoes and grabs a fistful of my shirt pulling me to close any amount of space left between us. When her tongue grazes against mine a low growl escapes my throat. I turn and guide her towards the counter, never taking my mouth off of hers. Once I feel my arm between her back and the counter I bend down slightly and hoist Samantha onto the counter in one swift move. She wraps her legs around my waist while I plant kisses down her neck, denying myself a break to catch my breath. Samantha grabs me by the neck and leads me back to her mouth, where a slight moan escapes her as I kiss her deeply and push myself between her legs. I put every feeling I have ever held back from her into this kiss and she matches me every hot, panting step of the way.

This woman is going to be my undoing. I think, will myself to have a little self control. Now I really don't want her to go, but I know she has to. We are both breathing hard when I pull back and cup both of her cheeks in my hands. I take a moment to look at how beautiful her mouth looks, swollen from my kisses. If she didn't know how I felt before, she sure as hell does now.

"If you don't go now, I am going to make you *very* late," I tell her reluctantly, trying to ignore my dick aching against my zipper.

She smiles in agreement and holds onto my shoulders as I guide her down from the counter with my hands on her waist.

"Have a good day," Samantha says flirtatiously mimicking me as she picks her bag back up from where she must have dropped it.

I give her one more quick kiss before I force myself to step back so she can get to work.

"Just try and stop me, Doll." I don't even try to hide the enormous grin on my face.

Chapter 21

Samantha

What a morning.

I smiled like an idiot the entire way to school. I can not believe how incredible it felt when Jess kissed me. I mean, I have kissed men before and thought it was good, but there is something different about being kissed by Jess Adams. The way he took control of my mouth and hoisted me onto the counter effortlessly made me feel…I don't have a word for it but if you could combine fear, comfort, need, and passion and have it shoot out of a geyser at the speed of a rocket, you might be close. And that was just one kiss. I am going to have a hard time concentrating today at school after that.

I just get into my classroom and set my things down when I hear a message notification on my phone.

Jess: What time does school get out?
Samantha: 3:30 why?
Jess: Just checking how long it will be until I can kiss you again.

I think my face is going to break from smiling so hard. *Jess is actually flirting with me via text.* I have known him for years, and we have spent most of that time joking around playfully, but this is different. This is a bold, flirtatious side of Jess that I haven't seen before. I am tingly from the excitement I have to see this new side of him.

Samantha: That depends…Don't you have work today too?

Jess: I am at the shop now, but Carlos does a pretty good job of managing so I don't have to stay long hours like I used to.

Samantha: Children are starting to show up. See you this afternoon. Xo

Jess: Can't wait, Doll

I have to tell Mel.

Checking my calendar I see that today my students have music class for their "specials". I can tell her then since we will both be kid free and I can't wait until lunch, let alone the end of the day. Thankfully the time seems to go by very quickly this morning. We go over some trick spelling words and basic fundamentals.

One of the kids points out that I am "in an extra good mood" today. I tell him it's because I had a really good cup of coffee to start my morning with, which is technically true. I have to try hard not to think of Jess handing me the Adams Auto coffee mug, or him whispering into my ear with his shirt off.

Maybe going back over tonight isn't a good idea.

I don't know how much self-control I can maintain with this new side of Jess. I also have no idea what his expectations are.

I hurry off to find Mel as soon as my students are safely in the music classroom. She has just dropped her own class off at Art for their specials of the day. She is facing away from me, heading back towards the first grade hallway when I catch up to her. I am a little out of breath because I all but jogged trying to catch up to her. She didn't hear me call her name from farther away.

"Hey." I breathe heavily, grabbing her elbow to grab her attention. "Didn't you hear me calling you?"

Mel looks up from the phone in her hand as she closes the screen, then puts the phone in her back pocket.

"No, my bad I was zoned out," she explains looking at me quizzically. "Why are you out of breath?"

"I was trying to catch up to you," I explain. "I need to talk to you and it couldn't wait."

I know she is going to make it awkward when I tell her about Jess, but she did seem at least a little intrigued by the possibility. I need to talk to someone about it anyway, so I prepare myself for the *I told you so* and the way-too-personal questions and ready myself to spill the beans.

"Oh no. What happened?" Mel asks.

The worry in her tone is the only thing all day that makes me remember Leah. Maybe I should have included that it was about Jess. I feel bad for making her worry.

"Nothing bad," I reassure her, but I want to get out of the hallway before I give her all the details. "Let's go into your classroom. It's closer."

"Okay spill it," Mel demands the second the door closes behind us.

She always hated surprises as much as I did. Patience isn't

exactly one of Mel's strengths. But again, that comes with growing up anticipating turmoil at any turn. I take a deep breath and decide that ripping the band-aid is the only way to go here. I'm just going to tell her quickly so she can stop worrying, have her big reaction, and get it over with.

"Jess kissed me."

I instinctively cover my blushing cheeks while I wait for her to respond. I have told Mel about every boy I have ever had a crush on since the 7th grade. But somehow, even this feels different in the context of Jess. It feels more serious like it has more meaning than just telling her about some cute guy I met in passing.

It's *Jess.*

"Finally," Mel shouts, throwing her hands up victoriously over her head. "How was it? Did your toes curl? Did your leg pop like in Princess Diaries?"

Yup. That's pretty much the kind of reaction I was expecting.

"It's kind of hard for your leg to pop when you're being hoisted up onto the counter," I say hiding my face entirely behind my hands so I don't have to see her gawking reaction.

"Oh, that is hot!" Mel gushes. "I bet it was intense. Jess doesn't strike me as the gentle type."

"Mel!" I squeal cutting her off, "Stop or I won't tell you anything ever again."

My face must be redder than the fake apple sitting on Mel's desk at this point.

"What? We always talk about guys like this." Mel laughs, defending herself.

"I know." I hesitate while I try to figure out why this time is so much harder. "It's just…"

"It's Jess." Mel finishes my sentence, placing her hands over her heart. The only way she could look any sappier is if she had cartoon hearts coming out of her eyes.

"Yeah," I say, softly acknowledging the weight we both know hides between that simple phrase.

It's Jess.

"So, what now?" Mel asks the question I have been unable to answer to myself all day.

"He asked me to come back over after work," I tell her.

"Are you staying over?" She pries, wiggling her eyebrows suggestively.

"I don't know," I admit. "I mean everything is different now. I don't know what he is thinking or expecting. I don't know how to date someone I haven't just met. Hell, I don't even know if that's what he thinks this is, or if it's what I want. I mean there is an order to things. Boy meets girl, asks her out, they usually at least go on a few dates before he starts whispering about her panties in her ear and dry humping on the kitchen counter."

For once my best friend is actually stunned to silence when I finish rambling. She just stares at me with her mouth open, surprised by what I have just told her.

"Say something." I implore her.

"Your panties?" she whispers, trying to clarify the part of my rant that apparently got her attention the most.

"Yes," I say. "And it's your fault for your clothes switching ridiculousness."

A proud smile sweeps across Mel's face when she realizes what I mean.

"I was nervous last night after the interview with that cop." I start to explain, "When we got home the door was open and no one was there but it freaked me out so I asked Jess to stay with me instead of on the couch."

I take Mel's silence as my queue to continue the story. "That was before I went to take a shower so I didn't know that you switched out my clothes. I was expecting to crawl into bed in my sweats, not a skimpy nightgown which apparently rode up in my sleep giving Jess the full view of my very lacy underwear. A fact, that he decided to whisper into my ear, shirtless."

"Wait. You were shirtless or he was?" Mel jokes.

"Obviously he was. I was wearing this." I gesture towards my outfit. "Which is not nearly as sexy."

"So you *do* find him sexy?" Mel asks, pushing her limits.

"Of course I do," I admit, to both her and myself for the first time.

I think about the way Jess's chest hair tapers down to a smaller amount of hair leading into the top of his jeans, and about how strong his hands felt against my back. Not to mention the back-flips my stomach did when I was looking into his bright eyes seconds before he kissed me. He is not the type of guy that I have traditionally dated before. Most of them were more like Ross, prettier and less rugged. Even thinking of the two of them comparatively for a second makes me laugh audibly.

"Why is that funny?" Mel asks, raising an eyebrow at me.

"I was just thinking about it. I don't honestly know how I didn't see it before." I tell her. "I mean I can't even think straight, because that's how attracted I am to Jess right now. I never felt like that with Ross."

"Good. Ross was an asshat." Mel chimes in, which earns her a laugh.

"It's more than that. Jess is so much more… I don't know." I say rubbing my hands over my face again.

"Hunky," Mel says wiggling her eyebrows teasingly. "He's a *real* man."

"Oh my goodness," I say rolling my eyes at her, even though she just hit the nail on the head.

I look over at the clock on the wall and see that we only have five minutes left until we go pick up the kids from their special classes.

"Come on. We have young minds to nourish." I say, not disappointed that we are out of time.

"Fine," Mel says following me out of her classroom.

Stereotypical girl, swooning over the guy helping her feel safe.

In one quick thought, my inner cynic undermines my excitement. I try to ignore it, but I can't help but wonder if she, or rather, *I* am right. What happens when Leah grows bored of her games and I don't need Jess's protective side anymore? Do I even really need it now? I need to figure out if the pull I feel towards him is really what it feels like… or am I a real-life troupe of a girl who projects her yearning for security onto anyone who will have me?

For the first time, I don't find myself grateful to my inner cynic, and her cautionary warnings to keep my feelings in line. I kind of resent her, and that feeling of resentment reminds me of Carol. I suppose Freud would say there's a connection there. Between my reluctance to accept that my relationships have merit, and the fear of abandonment instilled in me by my mother's sporadic participation in my childhood.

My phone vibrates in my pocket, thankfully interrupting

my train of thought.

Jess: *I very much intend to kiss you again in 3 hours, be warned.*

Whatever reservations I was having have been shaken away, and a stupid schoolgirl grin takes over my face again.

~

"Miss Bunting, you seem like you're in an extra good mood today." One of the little boys in my class points out again when we get back to the classroom.

"I suppose I am, Max." I agree.

"Does that mean we can cancel the math quiz?" Max asks.

Naturally, all of the other kids perk up and start to get excited. The math quiz isn't actually today, it's tomorrow. I don't tell them that though.

"Sure, we'll do a few extra practice worksheets instead so everyone is prepared and we'll do the quiz tomorrow instead," I tell them.

"Yes!" Max and a few others start to clap in celebration.

"Best teacher ever!" Chloe yells and a few others nod their agreement.

And just like that, math turns into the best part of their day. The rest of the day passes very slowly. I have a text from Gramma, checking in on me. I feel bad that I haven't updated her since I showed up at her door unannounced. I am not sure I could even condense all that has happened into a text message. I decided to call her from the Jeep later and catch her up. She wouldn't expect me to respond during school anyway.

Chapter 22

Samantha

Jess is already home when I get back to his place. I open the door to the smell of food cooking, but I don't see him in the kitchen. I suddenly feel weird about just walking in. *Should I have knocked?* I was so excited on the way over here that I didn't stop to think about it. I've always knocked before, but between the sleepovers and the kiss this morning I don't know what the protocol is.

"Jess?" I call out.

It's bad enough that I let myself in. I don't want to go barging into his room unannounced as well. I consider going back outside and knocking, but that seems like it would be weird now that he likely knows I was already inside. Jess comes walking out of the room in the same Adams auto shirt he had draped across his shoulder this morning, which now reflects the day of work he put in at the shop. I take in the sight and think again about how attractive I now find this man's rugged attributes. To my relief, he smiles as soon as he sees me and doesn't question me for letting myself in.

"Hi." Is all he says as he walks toward me standing in the middle of the kitchen where I saw him last.

"Sorry. I wasn't sure if I should knock." I tell him,

nervously fiddling with the strap of my laptop bag that I have yet to set down.

In a few long strides, Jess closes the gap between us. Without saying another word he interlocks one of his hands in mine. Then he takes the bag off of my shoulder with his other hand and drops it next to us on the floor. I keep my eyes locked on him, curiously anticipating what new side of Jess to expect after this morning. He looks over me in a way I have never seen from him before like he's unabashedly taking in every detail as his eyes explore me. It's the first time that I have ever felt self-conscious in front of him. The way his eyes greedily move over me makes me wish I had stopped at the apartment to change. When his eyes finally land on mine after a few of the longest seconds of silence, he leans in and plants his lips on mine.

This kiss is different than the one we shared in this same kitchen this morning. This morning was hot, almost carnal. The way Jess is kissing me now is more gentle, slower, and yet, somehow more intimate. He runs one hand into my hair, deepening the hold his mouth has on mine, but taking his time. My body melts into his hands as I give in, letting him take control. He takes a steadying breath when he pulls away from my mouth, leaving me dazed and wanting more. I don't know what I was expecting when I got here, but this is better.

"You don't have to knock," Jess says brushing my cheek with his thumb.

My chest rises and falls as I try to steady my breathing and find my composure. *When did he start to have this much effect on me?*

"You hungry?" he asks, releasing me and stepping backward. "I threw some taco meat in this morning before I headed into the shop."

"Is that what I smell?" I ask, trying to play it cool. "You didn't have to make dinner."

I don't feel cool though. I feel anything but cool. My stupid face feels like it's probably red hot from the blood rushing to my cheeks. I don't know what to say, or how to act.

What do normal people do with their hands?

How can so much change in 24 hours? All of a sudden I am nervous in front of one of the people who has known me the longest. I don't even know if this feeling in my stomach will allow me to eat.

"I don't know if anyone told you… but today is Tuesday. Therefore I am pretty sure it's the law that we have tacos." Jess jokes, reaching into the cabinet to pull something out.

How is he so calm right now?

"I have heard of Tuesday." I play along, picking my bag back up from the middle of the floor. "I just didn't know about the law."

"It's a new law." He shrugs, placing two wine glasses on the counter in front of him.

Dinner and wine? Is this a date?

"I am just gonna put my bag up and get out of my work clothes," I tell him, making an excuse to go gather my thoughts.

When I get to his room I immediately pull out my phone and send Mel a message.

Samantha: SOS! Jess made tacos and there are wine glasses. What do I do?

Mel: Get off your phone… weirdo.
Samantha: I don't know if this is a date?
Mel: Then you're an oblivious weirdo.
Samantha: My toes for sure curled.
Mel: What?!?
Samantha: When he kissed me.
Mel: This morning?
Samantha: No. Just now.
Mel: He kissed you again? I haven't even been home long enough to take my bra off!
Samantha: He just walked up and kissed me as soon as I got here. And girl… it was toe curling.
Mel: WHY ARE YOU TEXTING ME THEN?!?
Samantha: I panicked and said I needed to change out of my work clothes. Idk what to put on. I don't have a lot here.
Mel: Walk out naked. He'll love that.
Samantha: Why are we friends again?
Mel: Point taken. Do the jeans that make your butt look amazing with that daisy covered flowy top. It's casual but flirty. And if you insist on underwear, make sure they're sexy.
Samantha: I don't plan on him seeing my underwear tonight.
Mel: Bet you didn't plan to make out with him twice today either…
Samantha: You can stop being helpful now.

I toss the phone down on the bed. The top that she suggested has little white daisies all over the sheer light green fabric which is see through on the arms and back, but just modest enough in the front. I ignored her suggestion not to wear underwear, but due to her repacking skills, the only ones I have are skimpy and made of lace. I run my fingers through my hair, pin the top half back then make my way back out to the kitchen. Mel and I might have different approaches when it comes to dating, but I am grateful for her outfit choice when I see the look on Jess's face.

"Here you go." Jess hands me one of the now half full wine glasses.

I notice his Adams apple move as he nervously swallows when our hands touch. Another first, I don't think I have ever seen him nervous before. At least, not in this context.

"Thank you." I smile shyly, taking the glass.

Maybe wine will help both of our nerves.

We each make a plate and sit at the small table against the wall. We only make small talk about how good the tacos are, both too nervous to say much more. Though Jess does joke that I shouldn't get used to him cooking unless I only want to eat tacos, as that's all he can make. The longer we sit here the more anxious I get until I can't take the quiet anymore.

"I don't know how to do this," I admit abruptly once my tacos and half of my wine glass are gone.

Jess is clearly taken by surprise at my candor, but after the initial shock he laughs a little and says, "That makes two of us, Doll."

"I don't know.." I disagree. "You seem to be doing alright."

"Nope." He shakes his head, trying (and failing) to keep from smiling at me across the table.

"Nope? That's what you have to say?" I laugh, both flattered and befuddled by his response.

Just then the doorbell rings and startles me a little. I didn't hear a vehicle pull up.

"It's just Amazon," Jess reassures me as he walks over to the front door that rarely gets used.

I am cleaning up our dishes when he brings the box over to the kitchen counter.

"Open it." He says scooting the box a little closer to me.

"Isn't that a felony? Like opening someone's mail?"

"Just open your damn box." He playfully nudges it, eyes locked on me.

"It's for me?"

"Technically, it's for you to use when you're here," Jess says.

I look from the box to him curiously. "You got me something?"

Just as I start to open it Jess places his hand on top of mine and stops me.

"Yes." He sighs nervously, "But before you open it, let me preface by saying that I ordered this *before*. So just… it wasn't like I was assuming anything. Okay?"

"Okay." I agree skeptically, moving his hands out of the way.

My mind races with the possibilities of what might be in the package. Whatever it was worried him that I would read into it, which makes sense since he's not in a habit of buying stuff for his friends.

Friends, is that what we are?

Jess is anxiously watching me, propped against the counter on his elbow. When I open the box I see one of those single cup coffee makers, like I have in my apartment.

"You got a new coffee maker?" I ask, my brow pulled

tight in confusion.

"Yeah well, I just thought you were spending a lot of time over here and you drink a lot of coffee. I just figured there's no need to make a whole pot every time since you're the only one who drinks coffee here and.. It was stupid." Jess rubs his beard, nervously waiting looking for me to say something.

"You got a new coffee maker for me? For your house… *Before.*" I repeat, more for myself.

"Yeah." Jess sighs nervously waiting for my reaction.

"And you got coffee to go in it?" I say looking back into the box and pulling out the rest of the contents. "And a coffee mug with flowers on it?"

My voice lifts in awe as I pull out the blue coffee mug with little white and yellow flowers on it and inspect it. It's beautiful, exactly something that I would've picked out for myself.

"It looked like you." He explains pointing from the floral mug to the flowers on my shirt.

"Thank you, Jess," I say holding the mug to my chest. "I love it."

I really do. Ross's gifts were usually just something he picked up on a trip at the airport. Never something he put in effort to choose specifically with me in mind. In the year we spent together I don't think he ever did something this thoughtful.

"You're welcome." He smiles and his shoulders relax noticeably.

"Can I ask you something?" I ask looking down at the mug in my hands.

Jess looks at me like he is trying to read my mind before he gives me the okay to ask what's on my mind, then says

"Yes."

"Is this.." I pause, looking for the right way to end my question without sounding presumptuous.

"A date?" Jess finishes my question for me.

"Yeah." I look up to find his eyes locked on mine.

"I think it might be." He confirms.

His eyebrows furrow like he is worried I might bolt out the door at the very idea. Instead, I put the mug on the counter and step closer to him until I am looking up at him through my eyelashes then I place my hand on his chest. I can think of a hundred different responses at this moment, trying to find the perfect thing to say, to let him know what I want. My pulse racing and his smoldering eyes on me pressure me to say whatever I come up with quickly. I feel my words get tangled up in the nerves and nearly get stuck in my throat, and the only thing I can do is manage a single word.

"Good."

"Good?" Jess repeats, his eyebrows shooting up and a crooked grin melting my heart as he brings his hands to my waist.

"Yeah," I say, pulling him down towards me with the collar of his shirt. "Good."

I lean up on my tiptoes and give him one long, slow kiss. Jess doesn't let go of me when I am flat on my feet again. He holds onto me and tucks my head under his chin. I can hear his heart racing like mine has been. I'm not sure why it's comforting to know that he seems to be just as nervous as I am, but it *really* is.

"Does this mean I have to sleep on the couch again?" Jess asks reluctantly.

"I don't know," I admit. "I've never slept *next* to a guy

before our first date. I'm not really sure how any of this works."

"Fair enough," Jess says stepping back. "What if I promise to be on my best behavior?"

The flirtatious look he gives me makes me bite my lip. *Maybe it's the wine.*

"I did sleep pretty well last night," I say taking a step backward toward his bedroom. "But I am expecting you to behave like a gentleman."

"Scouts honor," Jess says drawing an X over his heart.

"You weren't a boy scout," I call him out, laughing.

I turn on my heel and walk into the room without looking back. I am riffling through my bag to find something to sleep in when I feel Jess looking over my shoulder. I pull out another spaghetti strap night dress that Mel packed, this one is a deep purple, with lace around the low neckline and the bottom hem. *She really is an evil mastermind.* Even a real Boy Scout would have trouble resisting this thing.

Not that I am trying to test his resolve. I remind myself.

"You're wearing that to bed?" Jess gawks, looking at the nightgown from behind me.

"Is that a problem?" I challenge him, looking back over my shoulder and up to meet his gaze.

"Nope." He clears his throat and steps back, gesturing me towards the bathroom to get myself dressed.

When I come back out of the bathroom Jess has lost his shirt and exchanged his blue jeans for a pair of gray sweatpants, making me wonder if he's heard how gray sweatpants are basically a thirst trap for men and is trying to level the playing field. I lay in the bed on the same side as the night before, and Jess takes his place beside me. The tension in the air between us has amplified a hundred times since we were in this same place yesterday. Neither of us seems to want to break the silence first, or maybe neither of us knows how.

My phone, still on the bed from earlier, starts to ring. Leaning forward I see the name on the screen says "Briggs & Associates". It's the firm that Ross works at. I turn off the screen, deciding not to answer it.

"You not going to answer that?" Jess asks.

"No." I shake my head. "It's Ross. I don't have anything to say to him."

"You sure about that?" Jess asks, no doubt trying to gauge if I still have feelings for Ross.

"I haven't even thought of him," I admit. "Him cheating on me was a blessing in disguise. I know you're supposed to be crushed after a breakup like that, but I was just relieved."

"Ouch." Jess feigns sympathy. "I almost feel bad for the guy."

"No, you don't." I roll my eyes playfully.

"No, I don't." Jess agrees, giving me a devilish grin.

When I turn towards the nightstand to plug my phone in, Jess wraps his arm around my stomach. He playfully pulls me closer to him so we are in the same position he was holding me in last night.

"Jess," I say as a half hearted warning, feeling his arousal grow against me.

"I promised I wouldn't try anything." He says softly behind me. "I didn't say I could control wanting you."

I'm taken off guard by his brazen honesty. I wonder briefly about other sides of Jess that I have never seen, and the few new sides I've caught a glimpse of. *Flirty Jess. Cuddly Jess. Romantic Jess. Sexy Jess. Raging hard bulge Jess.* His lips touch my shoulder lightly sending a wave of nerves rolling down my body. His hand moves from my hip, down my thigh, causing me to shift my thighs as the tension between us grows. Jess moves a hand back up to my hip to still my movement as he tries to stifle a growl in his throat.

"Okay… Nope." Jess announces, suddenly rolling away from me and leaping out of the bed.

I turn over to see him pulling a navy Adams Auto t-shirt out of his dresser, which he tosses at me.

"What is this for?" I ask holding up the shirt as he continues to dig through another drawer.

"Put it on." He says, then tosses a pair of plaid pajama bottoms along with them. "These too."

"You can't be serious." I challenge him, cocking my head to the side. "It's not like what I was wearing has ever bothered you before."

Has it?

Jess takes a steadying breath and rubs his face. There's something incredibly hot about seeing the effect I can tell I am having on him now. *Horny Jess.* The thought makes me giggle out loud.

"It's not funny."He shakes his head, his expression torn. "I can't sleep next to you in that."

I sit up onto my knees on the bed and pull Jess's shirt on, over my nightgown. Once it's on I get off the bed so that I am standing in front of him. Pulling my arms inside the sleeves I shuffle the nightgown down over my hips and remove it. I bend over to pick up the nightgown and hold it out to Jess in the small space between us.

"Is that better?" I lock onto his intense eyes. Testing his self-control, even though I told myself I wouldn't.

It's definitely the wine.

If I'm being honest it's a test of my self-control too. Seeing how much he wants me makes it that much more obvious to me how attracted to him I am. Lucky for me, he is the first to give in. Jess's lips crash into mine as his strong hands pull me against him. My fingers find their way up to his hair while my other hand is pressed between us, still holding onto the nightgown. Our mouths intertwine between heavy breaths. When Jess's fingers trace my thigh at the hem of his shirt I drop the fabric and move my hand lower to his waistband. Before I can decide my next move Jess's hand closes on my wrist, and he pulls away with a heavy sigh.

"Pants." He says breathless.

I look down at the front of his pants reaching out for me and swallow in anticipation. I am already being stupefied by him and the strength that he has when he touches me. I don't know how much more of his impressive masculinity I can handle.

"Not those pants," Jess says following my eye line. "Pajamas. Put them on… for my sanity."

I don't understand. *Did I do something wrong?*

"You want me to put pants on?" I say mystified.

"Absolutely not." He shakes his head. "But I need you to."

The confusion and disappointment on my face must be easy to read because his expression softens as he gently cups my face before he continues.

"I need to make sure this is what you want." He says seriously.

His eyebrows furrow with a look of sadness, or maybe it's worry, I'm not sure. What is clear to me though that his words carry a lot more weight than asking if I want to sleep with him.

"Jess.." I start, but I am not sure what to say next.

I know this attraction between us has been building recently but I am not sure if I am ready to promise him what I think he is silently asking me for. My heart is still beating but instead of being fueled by the heat of the moment, it's now being driven by the fear of what happens next.

What if I don't want more with Jess? Or perhaps even more terrifying… what if I do?

"You don't have to say anything." He says before I can say anymore. "Let's get some sleep."

Jess leans down and kisses my forehead. I close my eyes, taking in the air slowly. I don't know what will happen if I admit to what I think I want. What scares me more is what happens if I don't say anything. What if I let this moment pass and he doesn't try again? The twisting fear in my gut seems to have decided for me.

"I do," I tell him, nodding my head.

Jess pulls back quickly to look down at me. His eyes narrow as they move over my face, no doubt looking for confirmation that he heard me correctly.

"I want this," I admit, then watch the worry in his eyes melt away.

"Thank God." He says grabbing me by the waist and hoisting me up so that my legs are now around his waist.

Jess keeps his eyes on mine as he walks us back to the bed where he lays me down. I am on my back as he presses his weight into me and parts my lips with his tongue. I let out a surprised moan when I feel him between my legs. His sweatpants are doing next to nothing to conceal his arousal, and under his shirt, I am still only wearing a pair of lacy panties consisting of little more than two small triangles. Our lips and tongues continue to intertwine as Jess's hand slides up the outside of my thigh, to my hip just under the bottom of the shirt. When his fingers find the small string holding the triangles together he lets out a throaty growl, like his hunger for me is amplified, and damned if it isn't the sexiest noise I have ever heard.

He moves from my mouth, planting kisses down my neck and collarbone as he slowly hooks one finger around the string and begins to move it towards the triangle piece that is in his way.

I should have listened to Mel and skipped the underwear.

Jess's hands feel strong, even though he is using them carefully. His calluses intensify the sensitivity of my nerves, leaving a trail of sensation in their wake. My hips instinctively pivot up towards him and he responds with a steady thrust that might have sent me right over the edge if there wasn't anything still separating us. He continues to follow the string forward with his fingers, then just as he reaches the side of the lace triangle there is a loud knock on the freaking door.

Jess's shoulders sag and he shakes his head slowly in disappointment. I don't let go of my grip on him. *Maybe if we don't say anything they'll go away.* He presses his forehead to mine, and I can only assume he is hoping the same thing.

"Go away!" Jess yells.

We steal another moment, still intertwined, neither of us wanting to walk away from what we started. Whoever it is doesn't listen though. They continue their loud assault on the door.

"Damn it," Jess grumbles.

He kisses me firmly once more before reluctantly standing

up.

"Who is it?" I ask, unsure if he was expecting anyone.

Though, on second thought it seems a silly question. I doubt we'd be where we are right now if he was expecting to be interrupted.

"I don't know." He shakes his head, as the knocking persists. "But if it's Chad I'm gonna kick his ass."

I grab the pajama bottoms off the bed and attempt to put them on in a hurry as Jess heads out of the room. After a few fumbling missteps I follow him out of the room, now swimming in his clothes. He gives me an appreciative smile when he sees me behind him. It feels so natural, him looking at me that way. It's mystifying the things I feel about him. It's like someone removed my blinders and now that I've allowed myself to look at him this way I don't know how to do anything else. There is one more knock, reminding me that whoever is on the other side of the door is going to have one look at me and know exactly what we were just doing. I could have just waited in the room I suppose, but for whatever reason I don't feel the need to hide it. Whatever this is, as new and undefined as it is, I don't care who knows.

Chapter 23

Jess

Samantha fumbles out of the room behind me as I go to answer the door. I look back at her wearing my t-shirt and pajama pants. She's practically drowning in them, but she still looks sexy as hell with her hair a mess from my hands being in it and my last name on her chest. I wanna kick the ass of whoever is banging on the door for interrupting us, but I still can't help but smile.

She's here, *and she wants me back.*

I turn back to the door when the knocking continues, then turn the handle and open it.

"What?" I snap, opening the door before I see fucking Ross, of all people, on the other side.

"I need to talk to Sammy." He says, looking past me at Samantha behind me. A sense of Deja Vu hits me in the stomach, reminding me that the last time this happened it didn't go well.

Shit.

What the hell is this guy's deal? Why does he keep showing up when it's the least convenient? I step aside and turn around to look at Samantha, frozen in place with a confused expression on her face. She isn't saying anything but judging by her ignoring his call earlier and her lack of response, I don't think she wants him here.

"Come on Sammy," Ross says, gesturing for her to come towards him.

She doesn't move though. She just looks at me and shakes her head a tiny bit.

"Looks like she doesn't wanna talk," I say to Ross, glad to be already closing the door.

"It's important." Ross protests, putting his foot in the door, which just pisses me off more.

"Didn't you get the hint when she didn't answer your call?" I say, now making more of an effort to put myself between him and Samantha.

"Sammy, please." He says, ignoring my comment and looking over my shoulder. "Just come out for a minute and let me talk to you. It's serious."

"I'm not going anywhere," Samantha says, appearing by my side. "What do you want?"

Ross's expression changes when he sees her this close. My guess is he didn't realize what she was wearing from further back. He doesn't look too happy about it either. His brow furrows as he looks her over then looks between the two of us, piecing together the reason for her baggy sleepover look. I watch as Samantha looks down at her outfit, realizing what Ross has just figured out, and brace myself for her to act embarrassed or try to explain it away. She doesn't though. Instead, she puts on a bold, almost competitive look and interlocks her hand in mine.

What she just admitted with that one subtle move spreads the biggest shit-eating grin across my face while Ross's mouth tightens as he clenches his jaw, trying not to react. I give

Samantha's hand an appreciative squeeze and think to suppress a smile for a split second. But then I remember that I don't like this asshat, so I don't care to spare his feelings.

"Seriously?" Ross says looking at our hands in disgust.

Yeah, seriously, Pretty Boy.

"You can say whatever you need to say to both of us," Samantha tells him.

"Fine." He concedes, "Can I at least come in?"

Hell no.

"Fine." Samantha sighs.

My eyebrows shoot up, surprised. "Fine?" I repeat.

She gives me an apologetic shrug.

I want to disagree, but I don't have much of an option here. Things are still new and I don't have a right to tell her who she can or can't talk to. No matter how much I hate the guy, I need to bite my tongue and just be grateful that this time she isn't running off with him to hear him out. She wants me here, and she made sure he and I both know that. I try to find comfort in that and suppress the urge to roll my eyes. I step aside, with Samantha's hand in mine, to make room to let Ross in. I need to keep my composure and not let this dickhead get under my skin.

"What's this about?" Samantha asks, sitting next to me on the couch as Ross takes a seat in the chair. She still hasn't let go of my hand until Ross opens his damn mouth.

"Leah," Ross says heavily.

"Okay, I'm not doing this," Samantha says standing. "I don't care that you slept with her. I don't care if you're with her. I'm fine. Thanks for whatever apology you were trying to do, but it's not needed."

I watch her reaction carefully, trying to assess if she means her words. I hope that she isn't just deflecting. I try to block out the twist in my stomach, warning me that she might just be trying to comfort herself with me. *She wouldn't grab my hand just to piss him off, would she?* I do my best to hide my self-doubt and pretend I am unbothered by this interaction. After all, none of what happened before he arrived was because she wanted to spite him.

"It's not that," Ross says. "It's about your dad."

"What about my dad?" Samantha snaps defensively.

Clearly, she wasn't expecting Karl and Leah to be brought up together, and neither was I.

"Leah called me up, and said she wanted to get together." Ross starts to explain. "I thought she wanted to hook up or something."

He stops to asses Samantha's reaction while he rubs his hands on his thighs nervously. She doesn't seem bothered at all by his confession, but then she may be hiding her reactions just like I am. After a few seconds of silence, Ross looks down and tightens his mouth, trying to hide his disappointment that she didn't seem to care. He wanted her to react. The selfish ass cheated on her and then came here expecting her to still be pining for him. It's so pathetic that I could almost feel bad for him, but I don't. He deserves to feel like crap.

"Anyway, we went out and she spent more time talking about you than me." Ross continues.

"Of course she did," I say, remembering the way Leah obsessed over Samantha at Benny's diner.

Samantha's expression changes from stoic to worried as she takes her seat back at my side and gives me a knowing look. I put my hand on top of hers, trying to reassure her. I want to hug her but I am trying to let her take the lead on how much affection she is comfortable with showing our current audience.

"What does that mean?" Ross asks furrowing his brow.

"Leah didn't ever want you, she wanted Samantha," I say, rubbing her hand with my thumb. Trying to soothe away the anxious feeling I'm sure she has now.

"Yeah. Okay." Ross laughs, rolling his eyes.

It's almost hard to believe the gall of this guy, except he wasn't super present when Samantha had to move out. And he hasn't been around since they broke up to know everything that's developed.

"Let me guess, Mel and Chad want in on the action too huh?" he says sarcastically. "Just because you've been pining for her all along doesn't mean that *everyone* is obsessed with her."

The way he points towards Samantha when he says that makes me clench my jaw. I don't care that he's taking a dig at me, I probably would too if I were him. But I don't like the way he is trying to make her sound unimportant either. She was always too good for him, whether I had a shot or not.

"Except Leah *is* obsessed with her." I rebuttal. I don't bother denying that I had feelings for her before they broke up. Long before that, even. It's time she knew anyway. "There's a restraining order being made up and everything."

I continue making circles on Samantha's hand with my thumb. As much as my irritation with Ross is growing, it's more important to me that she knows I am here for her. I'm not just trying to have a pissing contest with her ex.

"A restraining order?" Ross says taken aback. "You filed a restraining order on her? Because she slept with me?"

Egotistical Douche. What did she ever see in him?

"What? No." Samantha says, rightfully offended by his self-absorbed interpretation of events.

"She slept with you to break us up. Then she tried to sleep with Jess." She explains.

Ross rolls his eyes when she says that but leans back in the chair and lets her continue.

"She set up for you to bring Carol to the bar that night. She heard that I was going to be there with Jess."

Wow, okay she's telling him everything.

"When I left with you, she made it seem like we got back together and tried to sleep with Jess."

"Tried?" Ross's eyebrows lift suspiciously as he looks at me.

"Yeah, *tried,*" I repeat, then say a silent prayer that even drunk Jess was a better man than this guy.

"She told Jess the next week that it was a setup. She actually admitted it." Samantha laughs a little. But I know she doesn't actually find it funny.

"Uhuh.. Still not sure how her trying to sleep with all of your *boyfriends* is grounds for a restraining order." Ross gives me a look over, failing to hide his annoyance when he says that.

Samantha ignores his comment and lets go of my hand to walk into the kitchen and grab something off the counter. I'm surprised when she comes back to see that it's my phone. She has opened the group chat and pulled up the picture Mel sent when she found the threat on the door. She slides it across the coffee table to Ross, who hesitates for a moment, but then curiosity gets the better of him and he picks it up.

"This is why I got a restraining order," Samantha says matter-of-factly.

I have to suppress a smile when she sits back next to me and grabs my hand again.

She didn't disagree when he called me her boyfriend.

Maybe I am getting ahead of myself. But then, I've probably been wanting this for a lot longer than Samantha has. I make a mental note to let her lead the pace she's comfortable with between us and try to refocus on the serious topic at hand.

"Shit," Ross says after examining the picture for several seconds. "I didn't know, Sammy."

He looks at her with pleading eyes, but she doesn't seem affected.

"I'm sure you didn't." She shrugs.

"You said she was asking questions?" I ask, pulling the conversation back to where it started. "About Karl?"

"Yeah." Ross nods. His head continues up and down for several seconds, getting more subtle as it goes on.

"She was asking about how you paid for school if you didn't have a family." He says raising his eyes towards Samantha.

"I told her you got some money from when your Dad passed and she started asking more questions. I didn't feel comfortable answering them so I changed the topic."

"More questions like what?' Samantha asks.

"She wanted to know what would happen if someone showed up and claimed to be Karl's kid. Like if you had a long lost brother your dad never knew about, would you have to pay them back the money you'd already spent." He shakes his head. " I just told her I didn't want to keep talking about you. Then suddenly she had to go. It was weird."

Samantha doesn't say anything, she just looks like she's

taking it all in.

"Are you breaking client confidentiality or something by telling us this?" I ask because it seems like Leah was more asking him as a lawyer than a date.

He shakes his head just before answering. "No. I'm not her lawyer, she never paid me anything so I don't owe her confidentiality."

Something is bothering me though. If he didn't know about Leah's obsession with Samantha, why did he feel the need to tell her about this? And why come to my house to do it?

"So why come here?" I ask.

"I figured she'd want to know if." He says casually. There is a subtle smugness in his tone that tells me there was more to it though.

"She said I have a brother?" Samantha asks, her forehead scrunched up in turmoil.

"She said *hypothetically*." Ross corrects her. "Still, seemed like you should know."

"So what? She found a long lost brother Samantha didn't know about and is gonna try and use him to get to her? Can she do that?" I ask, trying to work my thoughts out, out loud.

"Nah, Sammy's dad was broke. He didn't leave her any inheritance. The money you got was life insurance right?" he says at first to me, then to her.

"Yeah, it was life insurance," Samantha confirms.

She is quieter now and looks worried so I wrap my arm around her shoulder and pull her in to comfort her. I'm crossing the boundary I set for myself a few minutes ago, but it's hard not to when it comes to her. She sighs heavily like it's exactly what she needs when her cheek presses against my chest. Ross bristles briefly when she leans into me. Then, I see him swallow his feelings, trying to cover his displeasure in Samantha finding comfort in my arms.

"Right." Ross clears the emotion from his throat. "So you were the beneficiary that he named. Which means it wouldn't go to anyone else, no matter what."

Samantha sighs, releasing a tiny bit of weight off her shoulders but doesn't relax entirely. For a brief moment, I appreciate the civility of the three of us, in this uncomfortable conversation. I can respect that Ross is sitting here, giving counsel to her just because it's the right thing to do. Even if it is hard to see her moving on. I wonder if we would have been friends if he never dated Samantha. Probably not.

"But, I might have a brother?" she reiterates, so softly that I don't think she's talking to Ross or me. It's more like she's trying to break the news to herself.

Ross must think the same thing because he doesn't respond. He just leans forward, putting his elbows on his knees.

"Did she say who it was?" Samantha asks.

"I'm not sure." He shakes his head. "It'd be pretty funny if it was Jess, though."

And just like that he's intolerable again.

"Nice try, Pretty Boy." I roll my eyes and give Samantha a reassuring squeeze. "Both of my parents are still together."

"Yeah?" he cocks his head to the side. "Ever had a paternity test?"

I clench my fist, trying not to show my annoyance. Samantha seems annoyed by his antics as well because she answers before I get the chance to.

"Jess's Dad gave him a blood transfusion when he crashed

his dirt bike after graduation." She says dismissing his little mind game. "If that's all, I think it's time that you go."

That's my girl.

Ross looks like he wants to say something else but he bites it back.

"Well, this has been fun." He says excusing himself.

Samantha doesn't get up to walk him out, and I'm not going to let go of her first. So I let Ross show himself out. None of us say goodbye. He just leaves and I stay there holding the girl who used to be his, trying to comfort her.

Chapter 24

Samantha

A brother.

I've never had a brother before. Or any siblings. It was always just me and Dad. Sometimes Carol for short stints. But I've never considered the possibility of a sibling I've never met. Part of me wonders if this is another one of Leah's weird games. Maybe she was planning to have some guy pretend to be my brother and try to con me. Maybe there isn't anyone at all and she was just counting on Ross warning me to psych me out. Or, maybe I have a brother and she somehow found out before I did. The possibilities are so dizzying that if I weren't still sitting down I might fall over.

"It's gonna be alright, Doll," Jess says pressing a kiss into the top of my head.

That does make me feel a little better, along with the way he is rubbing my arm. Tonight started off so great. Now thanks to Leah, yet again, it's a mess. At least there won't be a huge misunderstanding about Ross with Jess this time. I don't know how he was so civil with Ross, honestly. Ross was acting like a pompous jackass and not hiding his jealousy very well at all. *Like he has the right to act jealous.*

"Thank you," I say into Jess's chest, not lifting my head.

"For what?" he asks, resting his cheek against my hair.

"For being here."

"I'm not going anywhere." He gives me a subtle squeeze and I can feel his words melt away the tightness in my chest.

His voice is so comforting. It sounds like the way he looks. Strong, but not angry, rugged, but not worn out, like all the southern charm without the small town accent, but somehow it has that same effect. It's the kind of voice that when you hear it, you feel at home. I think that over for a moment. I'm not sure if I have always felt this comforted by his voice. Perhaps it's similar to the way I feel when I look at him now. I have always known he was attractive, but I never allowed myself to think about him that way for too long. There was no point in opening myself up to feelings that he wouldn't reciprocate, so I never even gave myself a chance. Maybe I always found him comforting, and it's just elevated now that I allow myself to feel it.

"You didn't correct him," Jess says, trailing his finger up and down my arm.

"About what?" I ask.

"He called me your boyfriend, and you didn't say anything about it." He says.

I don't have to look up at him, I can hear the smile he's trying to hold back in the change of his voice. He's calling me out for not correcting Ross about the same thing that I called him out for not correcting Underwood on. Only we both know that recent events and the fact that Ross is my ex make my lack of correction seem infinitely bigger in context.

Touche.

"I didn't?" I feign innocence.

"Hmm, let me think." Jess's tone is more playful, and the way he is rubbing my arm has changed from a comforting gesture to more of a caress.

"You corrected him about my Dad donating blood to me." He says.

"I did do that." I nod in agreement, still not lifting from his chest to make eye contact with him.

"You walked out here in *my* pajamas and grabbed my hand in front of him." He continues as if he's in the middle of a list.

"I guess I did that too." My face is molten lava, I cannot look him in the eye.

"You stayed."

My heart sinks a little when he says that. The last time Ross showed up, *also a Leah-related event,* I made him doubt what we both wanted. This time I want to be crystal clear, so I finally lift my head to find his bright blue eyes already waiting on mine.

"I did."

We say so much with our eyes in the next few seconds of silence. My eyes apologize for making him doubt. His eyes forgive and reassure me. And both of our eyes draw each other in until we're too close to see each other and I feel his breath against my lips. I close my eyes and tilt my head up, longing for him to kiss away the stress and return our night to how it was before Ross knocked on the door. But Jess isn't done with his list.

"And you didn't correct him when he called me your boyfriend." I open my eyes to see a wickedly flirtatious smile across his face, daring me to play along.

"I didn't want to have to explain it." I look up at him through my lashes, using his own words against him.

"Hmm." He barely laughs. "Very clever, Doll."

I feel his pet name for me all the way through my stomach and down into my legs.

Doll.

"Why do you call me that?" I ask him, running my finger over his chest the way he ran his over my arm.

His eyebrows shoot up and he pauses for the smallest of moments. Like a kid who got caught in a lie, he knows he can't get out of. He looks away for a minute like he's trying to decide if he should admit the true meaning behind this pet name he's given me. When he looks back at me and takes a steadying breath I know he must've decided to tell me.

"Do you remember the first time we met?" He asks, his lips tightening in worry while he waits for me to respond.

"Yeah, my Dad ordered a part from the shop, and your Dad had you deliver it, right?" I say thinking back.

"That's right." Jess nods. "When I pulled up the garage door was open, I assumed your dad was the one under the hood of that old Chevelle."

I smile at the memory of working on that car with my Dad. I still have it, but Benny keeps it undercover in a garage at his house. It's easier not to see it every day.

"But your dad must've been in the house or something." Jess goes on, tucking a hair behind my ear. "Because when I came around the side of the car I saw you under the hood."

"I remember, he was grabbing drinks for us." I nod.

"There you were, sweet talking the thermostat you were trying to get out, so you guys could put in the new one I was holding in my hand. Your hands were black, and the ends of your hair where they're lighter looked like honey in the sun, and you were wearing a light colored sun-dress with flowers on it."

"You said I was gonna get my dress dirty," I recall.

"And you told me it's rude to speak to someone using a socket wrench." He laughs. "I knew I had to know you then. I thought to myself I have never seen a girl who looks so beautiful, almost like a porcelain Doll. It was such a contrast to what you were doing at the time."

"You did not." I protest. "I was covered in grease."

"I did though." He smiles with one side of his face and raises a shoulder in a half shrug, almost as if he's relieved to get this off his chest.

"You scolded me for breaking your concentration, and then for offering to help." He laughs. "So I just put my hands in my pocket and said 'Have it your way, Doll.' And leaned up against the toolbox watching you work until your Dad came out and paid me."

I take it back, my cheeks were just flushed before. Now they're molten lava. I can't believe he remembers all of that.

"You thought I was pretty?" I ask shyly.

"Have you not seen yourself?" Jess asks like I am absurd for questioning it.

"But you always said I wasn't even like a girl to you," I say in disbelief.

"I lied." He admits casually as if he's telling me the time.

"What?" I am so shocked I yell it, louder than I mean to.

"I just figured you didn't like me so I was deflecting, that's what stupid teenage boys do." He explains looking somehow apologetic, embarrassed, and flirtatious all at once.

"And now?" I ask, moving from beside him onto his lap, with one leg on either side of him. I'm fairly confident after this evening I can predict his answer.

"And now," he repeats, moving his hands up the plaid on

my thighs until his strong hands have a firm hold on my hips. "I refuse to wait for another guy to come along and steal you away without you knowing what I want."

I try to catch my breath unsuccessfully as I lean forward until my chest presses against his. I can feel Jess's heart beating just like mine when I ask him the natural next thing that comes to mind.

"What do you want, Jess?" I whisper against his lips.

He pauses and moves one of his hands from my hip so that he's now cupping the back of my head with my hair intertwined between his fingers.

"I want you, Doll." He confesses bringing my mouth to his.

I don't know if it's Jess's confession, his strong hands on me, the way he is consuming me with his mouth, or a combination of it all, but I feel drunk even though I have more than sobered up from the glass of wine I had at dinner. My head is spinning and my stomach is doing gymnastics. With every swipe of our tongues together I am greedily craving more. Jess's hand on my hip moves up my back, reminding me that I am still in his clothes that are too big for me. Although if the hungry growl sound that comes out of his throat is any indication, his plan for this outfit to deter him was never going to work.

Jess stands up, with my legs still around his waist, and leads us back to his bedroom. He keeps one hand out behind my back in case we run into anything because neither one of us wants to take our mouth off the other. We are all hot breaths and hands and hunger until we reach the side of the bed.

Jess pulls back to look at me and smiles, like he is the

luckiest man alive which makes me feel just as lucky, to have him looking at me that way. He eases me onto my back slowly, soaking up this moment. His shirt that I am wearing is bunched up so my stomach is visible just above the waistline of the bottoms. All it takes is his fingers looping around the waistline of the pants to curl my toes before he slowly pulls them down my legs. He plants little kisses up my left leg on his way back up, keeping his eyes locked on me as I watch him. He stops when he reaches my panties and examines the lace, and the little strings on each side holding them together. He licks his lips looking up to me for permission to remove them. Without a word, I raise my hips off the mattress and his fingers are looping around the small strings this time, pulling them down at a tortuously slow pace.

Jess discards the panties on the floor and removes his own clothes at a much less patient pace. Then he is back on the bed, hovering between my legs. I gasp when I feel him press against me and he doesn't hide his proud smile as he confidently takes control over my mouth with his own again. He slides the hand that isn't supporting his weight up the last piece of clothing between us and that growling hunger sound escapes him again. My hips rise towards him in response. *That is my new favorite sound.* I have never heard anyone make such a sexy sound before, but then I have never felt as desired as I do in this moment either.

"You're on birth control?" Jess asks. It's his way of asking permission. He knows that I am, he and Chad have been privy to way too much girl talk between Mel and myself not to know.

"Yes." I breathe impatiently.

I wrap my legs around his waist, bringing him closer to

me. Jess puts one arm under me and with impressive strength lifts me off the mattress, giving me room to pull the shirt overhead and toss it on the floor next to the rest of our clothes. He lowers me back down, more urgently this time. We kiss like each other's lips are the water we've been thirsting for in the desert as if the world or our very existence in this moment depends on it. When I arch my hips up at him once more and feel him finally start to enter me I start to shake. A loud moan escapes my lips, which only urges him on.

Jess takes his time, giving attention to my mouth, neck, and breasts with his mouth in turn as our bodies move together. My fingers curl through his hair, grasping for purchase in reality as my face starts to tingle and my mind becomes dizzy.

"Jess" I whisper, but I can't hear myself over my heart beating in my ears.

I feel him start to shutter on top of me and it sends me over the edge, feeling his undeniable attraction, desiring me, filling me, claiming me. When he comes to a still I am trembling beneath him, neither of us is able to catch our breath.

Jess props his weight on his elbow as he reaches his free hands to wipe the hair out of my face gently. It's such a sweet, intimate gesture that when he says, "My Doll." Softly and presses a kiss into my forehead, I believe him. I believe what he said about why he calls me that. And I believe in every tingle in my body, that I am his.

Chapter 25

Jess

It's early in the morning when I reach out for Samantha with my eyes still closed, but she must be up getting ready for work already. It's been a few days since the night Ross came over. Samantha hasn't brought up the topic of Leah, or a possible new brother so I take it she either doesn't believe it or isn't ready to talk about it. I don't push her to talk, I know from being around after Karl's crash that she'll talk when she's ready. I've spent the last few days busying myself at work to quickly kill time so that I can be back here with her.

She talked about going back to her apartment yesterday since things have been quiet for a few days. I can't tell if she wants to go home or if she just feels like she's overstaying her welcome. I am already dreading the thought of her going home. Maybe it's because things moved so quickly. You don't usually have a week-long sleepover at the beginning of a relationship, *I hope that's what this is*. We sort of skipped over the *will they text me back* segment and fell head first into coming home to each other. Only she doesn't live here, and it's too soon for me to already miss her this much at just the thought of her going back to her apartment.

It's been the perfect week. The only thing that I could possibly complain about was the damn raccoon that knocked over the garbage. I found it that way when I got home yesterday. But then, that's what it's like to live out of town. Other than that I get to look forward every night to finding myself tangled up in Samantha. We eat, we laugh, we flirt. Flirty Samantha is incredibly sexy. She's always been witty, beautiful, and easy to be around. But there's something about being on the receiving end of her flirtatious smile that makes me feel like I am mid-air, the second after realizing your parachute opened successfully. Not that I have ever been crazy enough to jump out of a plane, but that's what I imagine it feels like.

A smile spreads across my face as I grab a pair of boxers from my top drawer and pull them on quickly. I knock on the bathroom door but she isn't in there. I decide to go pee and brush my teeth before going to find her in the living room or kitchen.

"Good morning." She says without looking back at me as she pours creamer into her coffee. She's been using the new coffee maker and the mug I got her with the white and yellow flowers every morning. I felt like a fool giving them to her, but now I'm glad I ordered them when I did.

"Good morning, Doll," I say, wrapping my hands around her waist from behind and pressing a kiss into her hair.

"Hmmm." Samantha hums, leaning back against me.

"I wish you didn't have to work today," I admit.

I move the loose curls of her hair to the other shoulder and trace her neck with small pecks.

"You know it's not really fair." She says smiling at me over her shoulder.

"What's not?" I ask, twirling her to face me.

Samantha giggles when I twirl her around and puts her

arms up over my shoulders, running her fingers through the hair on the back of my head.

How did I get so lucky?

"You already have a nickname for me," she fake pouts. "Now I am tasked with finding one that measures up."

I can't help myself, I laugh. It's outrageous and adorable and so *Samantha.*

"It can't be something lame and generic like *babe.*" She crinkles her nose a little like she smells something sour.

"Yours is personal and perfect." She says that part as if it's a complaint but I take it as the highest compliment. "I've been doing some thinking. And I have a few options I'm noodling with."

"Noodling you say?" I raise an eyebrow, feigning skepticism.

"Mhm. Noodling." She says confidently.

"How much coffee have you had this morning?" I tease.

"None yet, just made my first cup."

I love the thought that she is this chipper just because she's here with me.

"Okay give me your options," I say.

"I was thinking something embarrassing." She says teasing me back. "Like, cupcake."

I scrunch up my nose and shake my head in disapproval. "Veto."

"No? How about Schpoodle." She raises her eyebrows, pretending to actually be proud of that one.

"Veto." I kiss her on her cheek.

"Hmm, picky guy, huh? How about pumpkin?"

I am glad I can tell she is joking, there's no way Chad

would ever let me live down any of these options.

"Veto," I say again and boop her nose with my finger. "You see this is why you should have been work-shopping your nicknames, not noodling them."

She laughs at that and turns to pick up the coffee she was making from the counter behind her.

"Be careful what you wish for," Samantha warns me. "If you send me out of here without settling on something I am liable to let first graders choose a nickname for you."

I laugh quietly at that idea and then wonder if that means she is going to tell her class about us. *Has she told Mel?* I don't honestly know who she wants to tell, or when. We haven't exactly defined anything, outside of us both not correcting people who call me her boyfriend. I hope it feels as official to her as it does to me. *Maybe I'll bring it up tonight.*

When she turned around I expected to see her new mug in her hand. I like seeing her use a gift that I picked out for her, even if it's just a mug. Instead, in her hand is the plain blue mug, that I know I threw away.

The Leah mug.

"Where did you get that?" I say taking a step back and trying to file through my thoughts.

I *know* I threw it away. I even remember seeing it in the bag when I tied it up to take it out. So she couldn't have thought I threw it out by accident and taken it out. Samantha's eyebrows pull together as she notices my change in demeanor. I never told her I threw it out so she probably thinks I am just upset she isn't using the one I got her.

"It was in the cabinet." She says like it's a silly question. "I thought I left the flower one here yesterday, but I can't find it. I must've taken it to work with me out of habit and forgotten it."

Shit.

"I'm not worried about where the one I got you is." I start to explain. "That mug isn't supposed to be in there."

She looks at the cabinet I am pointing to and then back to me. I am doing a crap job explaining this, the confused look on her face confirms as much. I'm just having trouble articulating what my mind hasn't quite grasped yet or where to start to explain. I run my hands over my face trying to focus while she waits for me to say something that makes sense.

"I threw that away." *There. That makes sense, doesn't it?*

"The cup?" she questions me pointing to the mug.

"Yes." I nod.

"Why would you throw it away? It's not broken?" Samantha asks, but it's the wrong question.

Who put it back in the cabinet?

"You didn't know I threw it away?" I clarify.

I don't want to worry her unnecessarily. I want to make sure she didn't grab it out of the trash before I say what I am thinking next.

"No?" she's looking at me like I'm crazy.

"I threw it away because when I made you coffee it reminded you of Leah being here," I tell her.

As much as I don't want to bring that back up I need her to understand what I am trying to tell her.

"I threw it in the trash, ordered you a new mug, and I swear I remember seeing it when I tied up the bag and took it out to the big garbage can."

She looks down at the mug in her hand and then back up

to me, processing what I just told her. Her eyes go wide as the realization sinks in.

"Then who put it back in the cabinet?" she asks, finally on the same page.

I don't say anything. I just shake my head indicating that I don't have the answer, at least not one that I can say out loud. Samantha starts to shake her head along with mine. I take the mug from her hands and step to pour the coffee down the sink. I'm not sure the person who put it back in the cabinet was considerate enough to wash it first.

"I'll make you a new one," I tell her, tossing the mug back into the trash can.

Samantha stands frozen for a moment, while I grab one of the Adams Auto mugs from the cabinet and restart the coffee maker. She still has to leave for work in a few minutes and I know she will want the caffeine, especially now. While we wait for the coffee to start brewing I wrap my arms around her back and pull her into a hug. I can feel by the way she sighs and leans into me that she is thinking the same thing I am.

It had to be Leah.

I don't know why, or how, but nothing else makes sense.

"How do you think she got inside?" Samantha asks, without taking her head out from under my chin.

"I don't know," I say, squeezing her tighter. "Do you want to call the cops?"

"And tell them what?" Samantha sounds defeated. "Here's a mug, and no proof of anything at all."

She's right. It sounds ridiculous. I'm not even sure I believe it.

"Why don't we stay at your place tonight?" I offer. "I can

have Chad help me install some of those camera doorbells on the front and back door, but for tonight we can just crash there."

"Okay." Samantha nods pulling back to look up at me. "I am running out of things to wear here anyway."

"Alright, you want me to meet you there after work?"

"Yeah, that sounds good." She says. The sides of her mouth turn up but the smile she is faking can't hide the frown in her eyes.

I hate that Leah is doing this to her. Making her worry and wonder about something new every few days.

"I don't get it." I shake my head. "What's the point of breaking in here to just replace a mug?"

Samantha thinks for a second while she pours creamer into the new cup. Then she grabs the handle and looks as if she's had a disappointing realization before she can bring the mug to her lips. Only after she takes a small sip of coffee, and a deep breath does she say, "To let me know she can."

"Not for long," I reassure her.

I don't know how Leah got in here, but damned if I won't change all of the locks, secure all the windows, and have cameras up faster than she can plan her next stunt.

Chapter 26

Samantha

"Are you sure he didn't have two blue mugs?" Mel asks.

I guess it's a valid question. And just like every other thing Leah has done, it's so subtle that anyone else would be skeptical about it having any real meaning. Small enough to wonder why she bothered to do it. The photo she knifed into the door wasn't subtle at all, so the confusion continues. The only thing I can think of was that she was trying to send the message that she could get into Jess's house, or that she has been watching us.

"I'm sure," I tell her. "He only had two of these, the one blue one he threw away and then the pretty one he bought me."

I point to the Adams Auto mug on my desk I brought in this morning. I didn't have time to drink it before I had to leave for school. When I got here this morning I checked for my flower mug, but I didn't find it. I asked Mel to come to my room to eat lunch with me since we didn't have time to get together before now because we had a meeting while the kids were at their special classes.

"It just seems like a weird thing to do." Mel shrugs. "I mean, not that anything she does isn't weird. I just don't get the point of digging in his garbage to put a mug in a cabinet. It's such a small thing that could've gone unnoticed."

"Maybe that's the point." I think out loud. "I wonder how many things she's done that I never noticed, or second-guessed and just brushed off."

"That's a scary thought." Mel cringes, stirring her lunch with her fork.

It is a scary thought. One I try and fail to avoid. I don't want to waste more of my free time thinking about Leah, but it's hard to keep the thoughts from creeping in.

Did a rodent really bite the wire when my car broke down?

Was there even a raccoon when Jess found the garbage spread around?

How many things have I swept under the rug, that could've been her?

"Change of subject," I say and straighten my posture, as if that will straighten out my mood as well.

"Okay," Mel perks up. "How is it?"

She wiggles her eyebrows suggestively and sits forward, waiting for my answer. My cheeks start to feel flushed and I put my hands over them, trying to suppress the bashful smile I am fighting. She always knows how to bring me out of a mood.

"Miss Eddy, I do believe we are in a school," I say in my best southern bell accent.

That makes both of us laugh.

"I don't know how to explain it, Mel," I say dreamily. "It seems weird to talk about it because he's *Jess*. He's the same as he's always been in some ways but in others.."

I trail off, amazed that he can even incite my heart to flutter without being present.

"Oh, you got it bad." Mel teases me.

"I think I do," I admit, now fully hiding my face in my hands.

I know I do. But I don't need to admit to Mel that I can't seem to slow my feelings down to a normal, healthy pace when it comes to Jess.

"He does the book growl," I tell her.

"He doesn't." She squeals, bouncing in her seat.

"He does," I smirk, hesitant to look at her reaction. "And let me tell you, it's one thing to read about and an entirely different thing to be on the receiving end of in real life." Just thinking about it makes me squirm a little in my seat.

"I take it Ross never did the book growl?" she laughs.

"Ross never did *a lot* of things."

"That's it, I am officially jealous." Mel proclaims dramatically. "I need a man."

This is nice. I was nervous about talking to Mel about Jess. It's different than talking about guys together that the other doesn't know, or at least doesn't know well. She isn't treating it any different than if I was dating some rando she's never met, though. That makes me feel better about talking to her about him. It's a good thing too because if things continue like this, I don't want things to be awkward when the four of us hang out.

"What about that cop?" I suggest. "You think he does the book growl?"

"Jake?" Mel's mood shifts instantly when she says his name. "Not a chance."

"Bummer." I shrug, "Bet he would've used the handcuffs."

This time I am the one with the suggestive eyebrows and

Mel is the one left rolling her eyes.

~

Jess is leaning against the side of his truck waiting for me when I pull into the parking lot behind Benny's. Good gracious, he's gorgeous. I mean, technically he is a mess. He's rugged and greasy and it looks like he's probably been harder at work than any of his employees today. But still, there's something incredibly sexy about seeing him here, waiting for me and covered in grease.

He scoops me up into his arms and twirls me around the moment I step out of my Jeep.

"Well, hello to you too." I giggle.

"Hi, Doll," Jess says.

I give him a quick kiss, smiling as he puts me down.

"Seems like you're in a pretty good mood this afternoon," Jess says, grabbing my work bag from the passenger seat.

I catch myself biting my bottom lip as I watch him reach across the driver's seat and pick it up with ease. It's silly, really, but I would have to walk around to get it out because I am not tall enough to get it from this side. I chalk it up to a combination of the thoughtful gesture and the way his arms look in his work shirt. Not to mention that he is right, I am in a very good mood after talking to Mel today.

"I talked to Mel at lunch," I tell him.

Jess stops for a beat, surprised by my explanation for my good mood. My stomach sinks at his pause and I wonder if I should have talked to him before opening up to our friends. Another thing that's different than dating someone from outside of our friend circle. Technically Mel is his friend too, and I didn't check to see if he wanted to tell her or Chad. *Is this weird for him?*

"I'm sorry, I didn't think…" I start to apologize but Jess cuts me off.

"Don't be sorry." He smiles, pulling me against him at the bottom of the stairs that lead up to my apartment.

"I've been wanting to talk to Chad too, I just didn't wanna rush you."

"You're not upset?" My shoulders drop, relieved by his response.

"Am I upset that you talked to your best friend about *us?*"

The way he says *us* feels like his voice just lit a furnace in my chest.

"No, Doll. I am very much *not* upset." He reassures me as he runs his fingers through the base of my hair and pulls my mouth to his.

Even though my eyes are closed I can feel his smile as his mouth takes control of mine. I reach my hands under his shirt and feel his strong back muscles. My hum of approval only seems to egg him on. Jess's mouth doesn't leave mine as we climb the stairs. I'm not sure how we made it to the top. I really should be more careful considering the last time I went up these stairs in a hurry I rolled my ankle. But of all the thoughts racing through my mind right now, that doesn't seem to be a priority.

When we reach the top of the stairs I fumble breathlessly trying to get the key into the door. It shouldn't be that hard. I only have two keys on here, one for my Jeep and one for this apartment. Jess's mouth on my neck is making it harder to use my fine motor skills though. When the door finally swings inward Jess drops my bag on the floor, still kissing me, and kicks the door closed behind him. *Holy crap, he's hot.* I am so swept up in feeling his strong hands in my hair and under my shirt that I drop the keys on the floor, missing the counter as we make our way back towards my bedroom.

In a few confident moves, Jess successfully removed every school-appropriate item I was wearing. He's down to his boxers when he reaches around my back to undo my bra. His mouth moves from mine, down my collarbones, planting hungry kisses on the way down. When he brings my nipple into his mouth he lets out that hungry growl that sends an instant wave of tingles all over my body. He continues his journey down my stomach and stops on his knees, eye level with the waistband of my very see through, skimpy excuse for underwear. Jess looks up at me with a wicked grin as he rubs a finger across the front of the sheer fabric.

"Are these for me, *Doll*?" he asks as my hips push me closer, craving more of his touch.

"Mhm." My response catches in my throat.

How can he form complete sentences right now?

My head rolls back as he kisses my inner thigh, and then slowly works the sheer fabric down. Jess stands, dragging his hands over my body on his way up. I waste no time helping him out of his boxers. He uses one hand to caress my breast, rolling my nipple between two of his fingers as his tongue brushes against mine. I melt into his other hand as he reaches between my thighs and begins making circles with his fingers right where I am craving his touch. I moan into his mouth as he moves the first hand from my breast to my back, pulling my weight into him as my knees start to weaken. My head is already spinning from his vigorous touch.

"That's my girl," Jess says in a low voice, leading me to the bed.

I spin him around before he can continue his teasing assault and push him on his back. I can't wait anymore. I want him *now*. I start to crawl slowly up him on the bed, trying to hide how badly I want to feel him inside of me again. But I need to at least pretend that I have some self-control left. Jess's mouth hangs open as he watches me stop halfway up his body. I look up at him through my eyelashes as I take him into my mouth and greedily start to move my mouth up and down.

"Fuck, Doll." Jess groans.

Yes, please.

My hum of approval only coaxes him on more, sending his hands into my hair and his hips flexing up to my mouth. My plan is failing because this is only making me crave him more.

"Get up here." He pleads.

I do as he says, trying not to show my desperation. I bite my lip and position myself above him, bracing for the way I know he is about to fill me.

"Damn, you're beautiful, Doll," Jess says, pressing his mouth against mine.

I moan into his mouth as I ease myself down onto him. His hands find my hips, following as I rock on top of him. His mouth takes turns with each of my breasts, amplifying the intensity of everything I am already feeling. His hips flex up into mine over and over, matching the rhythm I set. His strong fingers start to dig into my hips and I start to shutter with only the strength of his hands keeping me upright. The edges of my vision go dark and everything from my face to my toes is covered in tingles. I let out moan after moan, forgetting that we were above a restaurant and people might be able to hear us.

When I collapse against his chest Jess wraps his arms around me, securing me while he presses a kiss to my forehead. We are both panting, and our hearts seem to be in competing drum lines with my chest resting on his. We should probably get up and clean up. I definitely need some water, but we both just lie there in silence while our breaths and pulses slow over the next few minutes.

"You are dangerous, you know that?" Jess says, breaking the silence.

I smile bashfully at the confidence his words make me feel.

"I think I forgot we weren't at your place," I admit, not as embarrassed as I should be about my lack of volume control.

"All the more reason to pack heavily." He smiles proudly, then presses his lips to mine.

I let him up to go grab us water as I go turn on the shower in the bathroom. *Pack heavily.* His words echo in my thoughts while I wait for the water to warm up. I can't help but light up.

Chapter 27

Samantha

There is a case of water on the edge of the counter, so Jess doesn't have to go into the kitchen to grab them. Thankfully he returns before the water is warmed up for me to get in the shower because I am dying of thirst. Once I finish most of the bottle, I hop into the shower. I am letting the water wash over me when I hear Jess slide the curtain ring aside to join me.

I don't open my eyes, I just continue running my hands through my hair in the water as I feel his mouth on me once more. He starts at my breast, while his fingers find that perfect spot they were massaging in the bedroom. This time it's intensified because everything is still sensitive from what we just did not five minutes ago. He continues his way down planting kisses as he did before, this time replacing his fingers with his tongue. I rake my fingers through his hair and begin to moan again, trying to be more quiet this time.

It doesn't take long before his mouth has me needing to support myself by leaning against the wall behind me. When I do, Jess pulls one of my legs over his shoulder, gaining his hands better access. He starts to work his fingers in tandem with the rhythm of his tongue, and when my new favorite noise that he makes reaches my ears I scream out his name.

Just when Jess has me right where he wants me, someone begins banging on the apartment door. I hear that someone is yelling something while they knock but my head is too dizzy from Jess's performance to make out the voice. Much to my disappointment, Jess stops and laughs at the timing of our visitor.

"I hate surprises." I huff.

"I'll get it." He rakes his hands through his wet hair, then gives me a quick kiss before stepping back out of the shower.

I wash my hair and body quickly. Luckily I just shaved yesterday at Jess's so I don't need to do much else. I can hear Jess and another muffled male voice out in the living room so I dry myself quickly, throw a quick sun dress on, and wrap my hair in a towel. I try to hurry to get out there and see who it is.

Ross's visit comes back to mind, making me pause before I open my bedroom door. He said Leah mentioned a possible brother. I have tried not to give it much thought, but right now my stomach feels like the elevator floor just fell out. If Leah knows I have a brother out there somewhere does that mean he knows about me? Is he who's out there talking to Jess? Or was it all just another mind game?

After what feels like a long time of just standing there frozen I finally swallow my nerves and open the bedroom door. I'm sure it was probably only a few seconds, but these things have a way of dragging out time. I'm relieved when I reach the opening of the hallway to see the back of Benny's head. He is turned the other way, talking to Jess.

"Seems we have a noise complaint, Doll," Jess smirks at me over Benny's shoulder.

This. Isn't. Happening.

My hands fly up to my face, attempting to hide my

embarrassment. I seem to be doing a lot of that today.

"I just wanted to make sure it wasn't anything serious," Benny says. He looks just as embarrassed by the situation as I am. The poor man can't even look at me. Benny practically helped Dad raise me. He's more of a parental figure to me than Carol ever was. I might prefer to have a brand new brother barging in the door to this.

"We're sorry about that, Benny," Jess says, patting Benny on the arm. "Won't happen again. Will it, Doll?"

Jess winks at me when he says the last part. Evidently, he finds my shame amusing. And okay, maybe it will be a *little* funny to look back on in a hundred years… but right now I am mortified. Benny shakes his head and lets out a small chuckle making his way back to the door. Before he opens it he turns around and looks right at me with an unexpected look of pride. "It's about time, Sam."

I don't get the chance to respond because Benny makes his exit. I pick up the squirrel throw pillow from over the arm of the sofa and chuck it at Jess's head. Naturally, he grabs it mid-air, which should annoy me but it's just another unexpected turn on.

Pillow catching, really? That's what does it for me.

I try unsuccessfully to ignore Jess's sexy sideways smirk.

"Will it, Doll?" I say mocking him. "Are you trying to watch me actually die of embarrassment?"

Jess tosses the pillow back onto the sofa and saunters over to me. He still has that stupid panty-melting grin on his face when he wraps his arms around my lower back.

"Are you ashamed of me, Doll?" he softly asks, with his lips hovering just over mine.

"No," I answer, annoyed that my pulse is already reacting

to him. "I was embarrassed that Benny had to come up here because he heard us."

"Technically he came up because he was worried you were being attacked." Jess teases, putting a little more space between us. "So I think he only heard one of 'us'."

"That's not helping," I say, playfully shoving his chest, which of course doesn't budge because suddenly he's Hercules. And here I am, the damsel going weak in the knees while he effortlessly sweeps me off my feet.

Get ahold of yourself, this isn't a rom-com. My inner cynic rears her ugly head.

Maybe she's right. I'm not supposed to be reacting this way to a man, even if it is Jess. Deflecting a pillow, reaching a bag, or not budging when he gets shoved aren't reasons for me to stand around here swooning. Even if he did just leave me weak in the knees…twice. If there's anything I should be embarrassed of at this moment, it's the fact that I am acting like a twelve-year-old fan girl at a Justin Bieber concert.

"Are you hungry?" I ask, walking towards the kitchen.

I need to put space between us so that I can think straight. I probably don't have anything worth a darn to eat in here, since I have been staying at Jess's, but I pretend to go look anyway. I pull a carton of Chinese take-out, out of the fridge that must be a week and a half old and hold it up.

"Probably going to want fresh take out I'm guessing?" I jest.

Jess's nose crinkles as he shakes his head at the old takeout container in my hand.

He's even sexy when he's disgusted. I can't catch a break.

I step on the pedal to open the trash can. Then I jump back and drop the carton of noodles on the floor when I see what's on top of the other trash.

"You okay?" Jess asks jumping up to come help me clean up the mess.

I just stand there in the noodles, shaking my head, at least I think I am shaking my head. I haven't been home in days. Not even to get clothes. There's only one explanation for this. Even though it's possibly the most subtle threat in the history of stalkers, that's exactly what this feels like. Officer Underwood was right, Leah is threatening me.

Jess studies my shocked expression for a moment before following my line of sight to the trashcan. He does his best to step around the noodles and then steps on the pedal for himself. When the lid flips open once again Jess looks from the can, to me and back again. He is just as surprised as I am to see my new flower mug, sitting amongst the rest of the trash. There is a small piece of paper inside of it that says "*much better*." That I only catch a glance of before Jess slides it back into the cup and steps back.

"Don't touch it." He says firmly. "I'm calling Underwood."

I watch the lid slowly close as he releases the pedal and I can't see the mug anymore. But I know it's still there. He saw it too.

"I need to clean this up," I tell him, shaking in a much less enjoyable way than I was earlier.

"I got it," Jess assures me. "I'll sweep it up and put it in a Publix bag so it doesn't get onto any evidence."

I hate that. *Evidence.* Just like that, my beautiful gift has been turned into a menacing message. Not only is she watching me, she's taunting me. She's showing that she knew I'd come here next. I may never know how many things I have second-guessed in the last few weeks that she played a hand in, but I know one thing.

Leah is a step ahead in a game I didn't even realize I was playing.

Chapter 28

Jess

After I got off the phone with Officer Underwood, I sent a group message out to let Chad and Mel know what was going on. Mel responded that she'd be over right away but I haven't heard back from Chad yet. He's been a little harder to pin down sometimes.

Samantha hasn't said much of anything since she opened the trashcan and saw the mug I got for her inside. I cleaned up the old takeout noodles on the floor while she went to the living room. She's been sitting in her Dad's old chair, staring out the window. I tie up the plastic grocery bag that I put the garbage in and hang it on the doorknob so I don't forget it later. I don't want to leave her alone to go down to the dumpster.

As I loop the handle of the bag around the doorknob I hear heavy footsteps coming up the stairs outside of Samantha's apartment door. I look through the peephole and see Mel coming up the last few stairs. It's not her footsteps I heard though, she's too light to make that much noise. As Mel reaches the top step and moves to the side, I see Officer Underwood following not far behind. Mel has a sour look on her face and she looks like she can't get up the stairs fast enough. Neither of them are talking to each other. I step back from the peephole and wait for Mel to knock before I open it. I don't want it to look like I was just sitting here waiting for them. I don't know what it is about this cop, but he seems to bother Mel. She is still grimacing when I open the door.

"Mr. Adams." Underwood uses my name as a greeting.

"Just Jess." I correct him.

It's an uncomfortable feeling, having someone so close in age call you something so formal. Mel doesn't bother to address either of us. She just barrels past us straight to Samantha in the living room.

"Why does Mel hate you?" I ask in a hushed voice, so she doesn't hear.

I know it's not really my place, but Mel hasn't been chatty about it which is unusual for her. I wanna make sure he's someone Samantha can trust. He looks surprised by my question, his head tilting to the side and eyes darting over to check if Mel is listening. I can't tell if he thought I already knew, or if he's just shocked at my directness. He fidgets with his radio while he contemplates his response.

"It's complicated," Underwood says, mirroring my low tone. "I knew her brother a long time ago. I just think she doesn't like having me around as a reminder."

"Mel has a brother?" I ask.

This is the first time I have ever heard it. I know Mel and Samantha bonded over both living with just their Dads before Mel's dad got remarried. I remember hearing that she didn't exactly get along with her stepmother. But I don't remember ever hearing much about her birth mother or any siblings. I'm sure Samantha knows more. I haven't known Mel as long, and to be honest I have never been as close to her as I have been to Chad and Samantha.

"Listen, I didn't come here to get into Melissa's business," Underwood says with a hand on the back of his neck. "Can we just get to what you called me over for?"

I nod my head towards the kitchen. He doesn't want to give away more than Mel wants to share, which I decide is respectable. Not to mention he is right. I am letting myself get sidetracked from the reason I called him here. Most likely because I don't even know how to go about filing a police report for this situation.

"Well first, if you ever wanna get off of her bad side you should probably not call her that anymore," I warn him as we round the counter and cross the tiled floor.

Mel never likes to be called *Melissa*, another thing I am realizing I never really asked about. I just assumed she liked Mel better.

"Thanks for the tip," Underwood says.

The sides of his mouth try to turn up in a smile but it doesn't come across as believable. Samantha stays with Mel in the living room while he follows me into the kitchen. I didn't give him much explanation on the phone. I just told him that I needed him to come to Samantha's apartment. When I open the trash can and point to the mug sitting on top Underwood gives me a puzzling look. Which is understandable, I probably look like a lunatic.

Please come to my girlfriend's house and look at her garbage.

Not that we've made our relationship official yet, but it certainly feels official. Hell, if we were going by my clock she would already have her stuff moved into my house and we'd have one less thing to worry about. I know it's too soon for that though, I need to give her time for her feelings to catch up to mine.

After one more curious glance between me and the garbage can, Underwood raises his eyebrow and snaps me out of my thoughts.

"What am I looking at here?"

"The mug," I say.

He takes a skeptical step forward to take a closer look.

"I gave Samantha this mug at my house. She hasn't been back here since I gave it to her, and somehow it ended up here." I start to explain.

"So you threw it away?" Underwood's question prompts my heavy sigh of frustration as I rub my face, trying to figure out the clearest way to explain this to him.

"I didn't throw *this* mug away. It was like that when we got here." I say with my foot still holding the pedal to keep the lid open.

"What do you mean by *this mug?*" Underwood straightens up.

"I threw away a blue mug at my house. Just plain blue, no flowers. It reminded Samantha of one of Leah's manipulative stunts, which I guess is another long story, so I threw it away. Then I replaced it with this flower one." I point to the flower mug again.

This time his eyes follow my finger, but I don't think he's following my explanation so I continue.

"A few days ago I threw away the plain blue mug. I tied up the bag and took it out to the can myself. I never told Samantha I threw it out. Then I ordered this flower mug for her. This morning, I walk out to the kitchen and Samantha is using the blue mug I tossed in the garbage. She said she couldn't find this one. Then we get here and she goes to throw some old takeout away and it's in the trashcan."

Mel and Samantha walked over to the counter while I was explaining. They take a seat at the bar stools on the other side of the counter. I let go of the foot pedal and let the lid start to close slowly, leaving the mug in place still. Samantha leans forward on her elbows, waiting for the officer to say something. I hate seeing her look tormented like this. I just want to get the cameras I ordered today put up and get her back to my place. Underwood gives it a moment of thought, looking between all of us, and then he walks closer to the counter.

"You haven't been here since this mug was given to you?" he directs his question to Samantha.

"No." Is all she says shaking her head.

"Where did you get the mug that was thrown away at Mr. Adams?" he asks reaching for his notepad.

I think it's the same notepad he had before. He rifles through it for a minute like he's trying to find the same notes he took the last time we saw him.

"In Jess's kitchen cabinet," Samantha says.

"You didn't know he threw it away?"

"No." Samantha shakes her head again.

Underwood's mouth scrunches together while he carefully decides his next question.

"You sure you didn't just throw this one away because you didn't like it? Maybe you just didn't wanna hurt his feelings?"

"Are you serious?" Mel snaps at him. "She is being *stalked,* you jackass."

We all gape at Mel in disbelief.

"Mel, you can't call him a jackass." Samantha intervenes. "He's in uniform."

Samantha's tone and the look they share make me think maybe she does know more than I do about why Mel hates the guy.

"It's fine, she's just defending a friend," Underwood says.

I think my shoulder and Samantha's both relax at the same time, relieved that he isn't too upset by Mel's insult. We need him on our side.

"No I didn't throw it out, I loved it," Samantha tells him. "I was looking for it at school, I thought maybe I took it there and forgot it."

The cop uses the back of his pen to slide the paper inside of the mug up, enough for him to see the handwritten note inside of it. Then he scribbles something else down in his notebook and takes a few photos while we all wait with bated breath.

"So what now?" I ask.

Underwood sighs when everyone's eyes turn to him for an answer.

"Unfortunately there's not a lot to go on here. There was no sign of a break-in, nothing to prove anyone else was here. It doesn't sound like there was much to go on at Jess's house either."

A heavy sadness presses on my chest when Samantha's eyes fall in disappointment. What are we supposed to do? Obviously, Leah doesn't care about the restraining order. Does he expect us to just allow Leah to get away with her psychological warfare as long as no one sees her do it?

"So you're going to sit back and do nothing?" Mel's accusing tone asks what the rest of us are thinking.

"I know it's frustrating." He ignores Mel and directs his answer to Samantha instead. "But building a case like this will take time. It's good to have a paper trail, even if it's just bizarre notes like these."

He holds his little notepad up when he says that, before closing it and putting it back in his pocket.

"You're useless." Mel groans, not accepting his answer.

Not that I disagree, but I'm beginning to think we shouldn't invite her next time. *Oh God, please don't let there be a next time.* I start to make my way around the counter to Samantha, wanting to be closer, to comfort her. Underwood follows my lead, this time not ignoring Mel's rude comments.

"Melissa, I'm doing what I can. I can assure you.." But he doesn't get to finish because Mel cuts him off.

"Don't call me that." Mel jumps up off the stool pointing her finger at him. "And don't make excuses. You don't get to just sit by and watch while terrible things happen."

Samantha and I watch in shock as Mel's finger digs into the front of Underwood's uniform shirt and he starts to slowly back up towards the door. The shift in his expression makes me think there's something deeper in her comment. Like she struck a chord.

Why is he letting her get away with this?

"That's not what I'm doing." Underwood defends himself.

It's no use though, Mel reaches around his waist and my eyes go wide as her hand passes the handgun holstered on his hip. The cop doesn't flinch though. I say a silent prayer that he doesn't reach for his gun at her sudden movement, then another when I see what she was reaching for.

"Make yourself the tiniest bit useful and at least take this on your way out." Mel's words are sharp as she shoves the bag of old takeout I hung on the door into his chest.

Underwood grabs the bottom of the bag as Mel pulls her hand away, barely catching it from dropping. With a frustrated huff, he looks over Mel's shoulder and tries to regain his professional composure, as if Mel didn't just have him looking like a scolded puppy.

"I'll do what I can, keep your eyes open and call me with any updates." He tells Samantha.

"Will do. Thank you." She says, but the look of shock at Mel is overtaken with disappointment. She looks hopeless.

"Mr. Adams, Miss Eddy." Underwood nods his goodbye,

careful to not call Mel by her full first name this time. For some unexplainable reason instead of tazing Mel for reaching near his gun, the officer starts to leave with the bag of garbage she assaulted him with.

"Just Jess and Mel, it's not that hard Jake," Mel grumbles walking away as the cop makes his exit.

I don't feel like we got anywhere, but I am still grateful for him to be gone. Whatever secret issues Mel has with him are not something I want added to Samantha's plate right now.

Chapter 29

Samantha

It's been a little over a week since I've been back to my apartment. I've been sitting on Jess's bed looking down at the paper in my hand, like I have every day, though I haven't brought myself around to using it. It's Carol's phone number that she left on my counter. I took it out of the junk drawer the last day I was there. I have been holding onto it, along with this awful feeling that things are going to get worse where Leah is concerned.

Besides not receiving any real help from the police, I can't seem to shake the conversation with Ross out of my mind either. Leah told him I might have a brother out there somewhere. I have been talking myself in and out of calling Carol to ask her about it all week. There's no use asking Gramma. I am sure that if she knew about it, I would too. And I don't want to upset her unnecessarily if it isn't true.

It couldn't be true, right?

The Dad I had would have gone to the ends of the earth for me. He used to tell me stories about his younger wilder days. How he'd partied, the times he'd skipped school and ended up in Dukes of Hazard type cop chases and narrowly gotten away. He'd even spent some time in prison before meeting Carol. Dad would never say a bad word about Carol, he'd wanted me to make up my mind about her on my own. It was clear to me once I was old enough that my dad grew up for me, in a way that Carol never cared to. When I was born he sobered up and worked so hard to take care of me that his boss had to hire two people to replace him when he died. My dad spent every evening watching shows with me and doing homework, and every weekend with me exploring or working on things. He was always looking for the little life lessons he could teach me while we drove down the road or worked on things together. I can't imagine that he wouldn't fight for another kid as much as he did for me.

I put the phone number down, deciding for the umpteenth time that calling Carol is never a good idea, and that it's more than likely another of Leah's schemes to mess with my mind. Then I go to get into the shower. Jess is still at work. He and Chad installed the camera doorbells last weekend which gave him enough peace of mind to not rush back here just because I get off work earlier than he usually does.

Jess said he was glad that Chad managed to show up since he's been harder to make plans with lately. Almost every time we ask him to do something he claims he has to work or has some other reason he can't come. I'm starting to worry that he is coming around less because of all the recent drama. I don't want to come between him and Jess if that's the case.

Who wouldn't want to avoid all the drama following me?

I hope that Jess doesn't think the same thing. Staying here with him has been amazing, but I know we got thrown together faster because of Leah's drama and I hope he doesn't come to resent that. I know if Jess was home, I wouldn't be thinking about any of this. He's given me no reason to think he isn't ecstatic to have me here. If anything it's the opposite.

Nothing else noteworthy has happened, but that hasn't stopped me from waiting for the other shoe to drop. It's just been several days of the same cycle on repeat. Work keeps my mind busy, then I get back to Jess's and it's quiet while I wait for him to get home. That's when I do my best over-thinking. When I can't shake the feeling that regardless of the cameras and restraining order, Leah is somehow still watching and plotting. Either way, as long as I think about it, this is the time of day when Leah is winning. *She said she wanted to see you break.* Jess's words feel heavy when they come to mind in these quiet times. Like the gravity of her threats could pull me down until I fold into myself.

Then Jess comes home (well, his home), and everything that isn't him fades away. I don't know how he does it, but I hardly think of anything else when I'm with him. Sometimes he tries to subtly check on me, like he doesn't want to upset me, but he just wants to know that I am okay. Which I am, as long as he's here. Sometimes he's playful, just like he always has been with me. Sometimes he's comforting. And other times I am swept up in his flirtatious smile and the way that his body seems to know exactly what mine craves.

I can't think of any way to describe the feelings that I have developed for Jess, other than *all consuming.* I feel at home with him near me. I feel at home being in his house, which my inner cynic frequently reminds me is not my own. Don't get me wrong, I love Benny for letting me move into the apartment. It's just that no matter how much I tried to make it my own, it never felt like a home. Not the way that Jess's house does, maybe that's just because he's here. I rinse the shampoo from my hair and let the water roll over me while I think about that.

I wonder why I never felt this way with Ross. He was the most serious, long term boyfriend I ever had. I thought that I loved him, and I maybe even would have said yes if he'd asked me to marry him. But looking back I can't think of a moment when I craved Ross this way. He was just there, or he wasn't and I was fine with it. I think Gramma was right, I wasn't as in love with him as I thought. Maybe that's what this ache that I have that only Jess seems to soothe is. That thought scares me as much as being alone these days.

It's too soon to feel this way.

I find myself thinking that things have been propelled forward because of this drama with Leah, worrying that maybe the cute little dance we do around officially calling this a relationship is his way of sparing my feelings.

Why would he want to be stuck with you? My bitchy inner voice reminds me that along with me, comes baggage that he probably doesn't want to commit to. In fact, I've never seen him commit to anyone for more than a short time.

I open my eyes when a loud *slam* scares me, causing me to scream. I grab my towel and turn off the water quickly, then open the shower curtain slightly. All I can hear is my heart racing as I try to slow my breathing down. I wait a few seconds. Then, when I don't hear anything it's all I can do to stick my head out of the shower curtain. My feet are planted in place, unwilling to budge.

"Jess? Are you home?" I call softly, despite the fact that my throat feels like it's closing up.

When there is no reply I force myself to step out of the shower, preparing for the cold tile underfoot. I learned my first time showering here that one of the many women's touches Jess's house lacks is bath mats. I regret keeping my eyes up as I step out when my foot starts to slip. Luckily I catch myself, only losing a few of the shower curtain hooks in the process. Once my feet are firmly planted on the tile I reach down to find the conditioner bottle that I must have knocked over. Some of it spilled out and must've caused me to slip. Holding the towel around my chest, I rush back into the bedroom, my heart racing to catch up with my panicked breaths.

All that happened was I dropped a bottle of conditioner on the floor, I know that. But with all of this looking over my shoulder it sent my adrenaline through the roof. I am on edge looking around every corner for Leah's next move and I am starting to feel paranoid.

She wanted to see you break. And it's working.

I quickly dress myself in a pair of black leggings and a loose T-shirt that has cartoon cats on it. Then I throw my hair into a messy bun and without thinking about it I grab Carol's number off the bed and start dialing. I pace the floor anxiously and the adrenaline turns into nausea as the line rings.

Asking Carol if my dad secretly had another kid out there isn't going to solve my Leah problems, but I have to do something. Before I can change my mind again and hang up, I hear Carol answer the call.

"Hello?"

"Hi, it's me," I mumble, instantly regretting this.

I have to tell my own mother who is calling, and I am barely able to spit that out. How the hell am I supposed to ask her what I need to know?

"Sammy?" Carol asks on the other end. "Hey baby girl, how you doing?"

If she were anyone else's mom I'd think they were close by how chipper she sounds to hear from me. But it's always been like this. When she reappears, she acts as if she was never gone. Like she and I are close, which used to work when I was younger, but now makes me feel uncomfortable and annoyed. But I need answers, and she's my only lead. So there's no turning back now.

"Are you in town?" I ask, not wanting to waste time on fake pleasantries.

"Yeah, I am staying with a friend. Why?" Carol says.

"I need to talk to you, where can we meet?" I try to hide the emotions behind my voice, not wanting to scare her away.

Carol was never good with confrontation. If she thinks I am upset with her she might bolt. Even after coming to terms with who she is, I think sometimes I still coddle her, afraid to be the trigger that sends her into her next manic episode turned bender.

"You wanna meet now?" she sounds surprised, but hopeful so I know I've played it calm enough despite my nerves feeling fried.

"Yeah," I hold the phone with my cheek and shoulder and start pulling my shoes on. "Are you near downtown? I can meet you on the dock by the lake in like 20 minutes."

"Yeah. I'll be there, Baby Girl."

"Okay, see you then," I tell her, ignoring the knot in my stomach when she calls me that. I hang up before she says anything else and grab my keys and purse then head for the back door.

~

Before I know it I am on the downtown dock of one of the biggest lakes in town. This one connects to another lake that we pass to get to town from Jess's, Lake Minneola. Then they connect through a few local towns with canals that I know like the back of my hand. I grew up on these lakes, me and Dad and Benny. Carol was never there for the boat rides, or to see me learn to wakeboard, or fly off a tube behind the boat with Mel teasing that she hung on longer. Over the years the memories eventually included Chad, who worked at a marina in high school so he was always on the water, and Jess because they were inseparable. Nowadays we are too busy to spend much time on the water. I miss it.

"Hey, baby girl." Carol's telltale greeting pulls me out of my thoughts, with a twist in my gut.

"Hi." That is all I manage because neither Mom nor Carol feels appropriate to say to her face.

We walk around the dock and beneath the trees around the lakeside for a while. I let her ask questions about teaching and other things that any other mom would probably know, just because I am avoiding getting to the point, and maybe because every once in a while I still slip up and trust her a little too much with myself. I know that I can't put off what I came here for forever though. So after a couple walking their poodle mix dog passes us, I steady myself for the coming conversation.

"You and Dad never had any other kids right?" my question makes Carol stop on a dime.

"Why would you ask me that?" her face twists and it's clear that for once, she's the one acting suspicious of me.

"Someone was asking Ross what would happen if my Dad had a kid we didn't know about out there." I shrug, pretending for us both that I don't hold much weight to it. "Like if I'd have to pay them back for the life insurance money or something."

"Would you?" Carol's eyebrows shoot up and knit together in a way that shockingly feels like concern. I'm surprised by the flitter of warmth I feel at her concern until I realize it means there could be something to be concerned about.

"No, Ross basically said he could have 100 kids, but the life insurance had my name on it." *Cool, calm, don't spook her yet.*

"Thank God." Carol's words surprise us both.

I watch her tense when she's realized her slip up.

"What does that mean?" I stop her with my hand on her arm.

"Sammy, I didn't mean anyth-..." She tries but it's too late to take it back. And she knows it.

"Bullshit." I snap. "What. Does. That. Mean?"

She shakes her head a little, and I can't tell if it's in warning that I don't want to know or to herself not wanting to say it. Either way, I pin her with a glare that says *I am not letting you bolt without answers.*

"Karl, your dad I mean, he had an affair when you were little."

My heart sinks (no, maybe it was my stomach) and then time slows as she continues. It's as if the faster I want her to spit it out, the longer I have to wait to hear her words and understand them.

"I forgave him at first, but it kept happening. I started drinking on nights when he was with her, which turned out more often just to tolerate him when he was home. Then the other woman got pregnant and I couldn't take it anymore."

I don't believe it. I was expecting her to debunk the whole thing, or maybe say he had an older kid that he never knew about from his wild teen years. I never thought I'd hear that I have a younger sibling out there. And is she blaming him for her addictions?

"He told me that he was done, he wasn't going to see her anymore and he was choosing us, his first family." Carol continues, her voice wavering the more she speaks. "I didn't believe him. I wanted to, but I didn't. So I left."

She pauses, waiting for me to say anything, to pity her maybe.. but I don't.

I can't.

"That's why it's always been so hard for me." She goes on. "Every time I saw you both it just reminded me of his betrayal, and I wanted to forget."

"Are you seriously making this about you right now?" my words fly like daggers and it's one of the few times I speak my mind and don't feel guilt as she actually recoils.

"Sammy, you need to understand-.."

"No." I cut her off again. "You don't get to come here after all these years and dump all of the blame on someone who died because he can't defend himself. You can't blame him for leaving and not caring to take me with you. For not choosing to be sober for *me*."

The tears start to fall as I feel the weight of my chest pulling down like gravity itself. I loved my dad, and I know I was better off with him. Still, there's always been a part of me that wondered why she never bothered to take me with her. Even if he had cheated, why hadn't she wanted *me*?

"You can't blame him for twenty five years of never being

there. And you sure as shit aren't going to blame him for stealing my money, my TV and God knows what else just so you can keep getting high."

"That's not what I was trying to do Samantha. I know you've always loved him more. I wasn't trying to get you on my side." She tries to play the martyr. One of her favorite manipulations, but that doesn't work on me anymore.

"Who was she?" I demand.

Her shoulders sink when she realizes that I am not going to try to comfort her. I just want answers. Then Carol can go back to whatever hole she crawled out of, for all I care.

"Maeve." She says reluctantly. "Maeve Woods."

No.

The world spins. My skin feels like it's on fire as I start to run away from my mother, to the edge of the water where I fall to my knees and I think I am going to vomit but it could just be my heart trying to climb out of my throat and throw itself into the water. My phone rings in my pocket but I can't move to answer it. I fall forward on my hands, the gravity of Carol's words seemingly trying to drag me to hell. Carol (to her credit) tucks my hair behind my ear and rubs my back, despite me having just ripped into her. Thankfully, she doesn't say anything else until I stand and try to steady myself.

"I'm sorry, Sammy."

"I have to go," I say, then get into my Jeep without another word.

It's only a few minutes from the lake to Benny's, which means I am about halfway there when my phone rings again. Jess's name pops up on the stereo and I know he will be worrying because I wasn't there when he got home. It was probably him calling a minute ago also, so I answer it.

"Hey," I say trying to hide all the emotions that I just had tsunami through me.

"Hey Doll, you okay?" he asks, and I can tell he's trying to keep worry from his tone. "I thought you'd beat me home."

Home.

The word hits me in the stomach and I am glad I have parked because my eyes are starting to blur with tears again. I wipe them away to see droplets start to hit my windshield as if to say that the sky understood what I was feeling and wept with me. Though logically I know that makes no sense, I find a little comfort in the storm I know is coming.

Why the hell would he want you? My inner cynic tears into me with the same ferocity I used on Carol.

Broken.

Baggaged.

Unwanted.

"Yeah, I uh… I'm just getting to my apartment." My lip quivers and I hope he can't tell over the phone. "I just thought it was probably time to go back, you know. I can't invade your space with my issues forever."

"What? Invade my space? Doll, that doesn't make any sense, I want you here."

"I'm sorry Jess, Benny is flagging me down. I'll talk to you later, okay?" I lie, and then hang up quickly before he can hear the sobs that threaten to overflow. Then, the rain picks up just like my tears do.

Why couldn't it have been anyone else?

Even my inner cynic doesn't bother answering.

Chapter 30

Jess

Florida is going through its preheating season, meaning we are starting to see more rain, and pretty soon we will have nightly thunderstorms. Right now it's drizzling, which is more than a sprinkle but less than a downpour. We had a couple in the shop earlier who hadn't heard the term drizzling before, a clear indication that this is their first summer here and they'll be miserable once the real heat hits. Technically it is still spring, but unlike northern states, we really just have the two seasons and mostly just start calling it summer once it's too hot for pants again.

That's what I tried to think about on the drive to Samantha's, to distract myself from worrying. It doesn't work though. I don't know what's going on with Samantha, but I could hear in her voice that she wasn't okay. No way am I buying that she decided it was time to go back to her apartment and just took off, leaving all of her stuff behind. Something happened, I just don't know what. That's why I took off the second she hung up on me, pretending Benny needed her for something.

Coming down Brookhill Road, at the stop sign the white painted line in the road looks brightly repainted. It's been worn out for so long that I never even noticed there wasn't one until I come to a stop at the bottom of the hill. When I start to accelerate my car begins to slide, unable to get good traction on the slippery painted surface. All it takes is for me to ease off the gas a fraction until I feel the tires grip and then I am turned onto Lakeshore Drive, thinking briefly about how many accidents that might cause for people who aren't from here, who aren't used to driving in our rains, especially when it takes fifteen seconds to go from a drizzle to torrential.

The closer I get to Samantha's apartment, the heavier the rain seems to come down. Lightning starts to strike off in the distance ahead of me, contrasting the picture in my rear view of a sunny, light blue sky with only a few wispy white clouds. *Typical Florida, bipolar weather.* The amount of time from the lighting strikes to the thunderclaps gets closer together before I arrive, so I know we are at the center of the storm. I plan to make a quick dash to the door, but when I pull into the parking lot, Samantha's headlights are on and she's still in her Jeep.

Between the rain pouring over both of our cars, I don't think she noticed me pull up. It's hard to make out anything more than her silhouette, but even that's enough. I'm pretty sure she is crying, or at least has been, since her hand wipes at her cheek. Not wanting to startle her by walking over and opening her door, I decide to take out my phone and call her. The line rings and I watch as her head turns to the touch screen on her dashboard. She hesitates, long enough for me to worry that she might not answer, but after the fourth ring, she picks up.

"Hey," her voice sounds chipper, but I know it's forced as I watch her straighten her shoulders and wipe the tears away faster.

"What's the matter, Doll?" I ask her.

"What do you mean?"

I don't know why she's trying to hide whatever is going on. Part of me wonders if she is trying to push me away for some reason. A louder part of me is screaming that even if she was, she doesn't want to or she wouldn't be crying.

I hate seeing her cry.

"Look to your left, Doll," I tell her, then watch the outline of her shoulder sink when she sees my car.

"You wanna go upstairs and talk about it? Or do you wanna talk like this?" I ask.

I can barely hear her sigh over the rain pouring on the windshield, followed by a quiet moment before she finally responds. "Like this."

"Okay." I nod a little, though I'm not sure if she can make it out. "Why didn't you come home?"

I see her stiffen a little, and remind myself to be patient in the long pauses. I know better than to push, she'll say what she wants to when she's ready.

"I did go back to *your house*." She answers. I note the infliction of her words, and disappointment coils in my gut at the implication.

Samantha is subtly reminding me that I am lightyears past her when it comes to how we both feel about each other. Hell, I nearly told her that I loved her after our first night together. I've wanted to tell her every single day since, only being held back by the same self-doubt that has kept me from showing her my feelings for all these years.

"I'm sorry." My voice is laced with hurt and caution. "I didn't mean it like that. I don't want to push you too fast."

Lightning strikes somewhere over by the lake and we sit in

silence as the thunder rumbles overhead.

"It's not you, Jess." Her silhouette turns towards me. "I just.."

The silence kills me and even though I told myself not to, I push. "You what? What happened between this morning and now?"

"Leah."

Thunder cracks again, giving us a few more seconds of pause as it tapers off.

"I don't understand," I say when the thunder is quiet enough.

"Jess, I can't do this. It's not fair." She starts to cry again and the urge to hold her nearly pulls me out into the storm, but I know she needs to get out whatever she's about to say. I can hear it in her voice. So I wait, knuckles gripped tight to my steering wheel and shifter, even though I've been parked for a while now.

"I can't pull you into this shit. I can't ask you to be my bodyguard and have you install cameras, meeting with the police, and reworking your schedule for me. I can't have people showing up at your door and breaking into your house to mess with me. I can't finally let myself see what it would be like if I let myself imagine a world where *we* get a chance when it's not real. It's all wrong. Everything is tainted. Around every corner is some new fucking surprise. You've never been bothered to keep *any* girl around for *any* length of time, much less with a shitload of baggage tagging along with her. I can't expect you to want to be my boyfriend, with all of the baggage that comes with me, which just means now nothing will ever be the same."

I let her finish her rant, noting that none of what she said was about *not* wanting to be with me. "For the love of God, Doll, please tell me what happened."

Anticipation itches at me while she takes a steadying breath.

"I talked to Carol. I don't have a brother." The rain lightens up a little more so I can see her more clearly. Her eyes meet mine through the droplets on both our windows, the look on her face almost apologetic for what she is about to confess. "I have a *sister*."

Fuck.

Realization hits me like a bolt of lightning to the chest. The shock is so jarring that I can't imagine what Samantha must be feeling right now.

"Leah?" the question barely comes out, and Samantha's only response is a single, slow, conforming nod.

Leah is Samantha's sister.

The weather starts to pick up again, the rain suddenly pouring harder than it has all day. It doesn't stop me though, from needing to be close to her, to hold her, to comfort her. It takes only a few seconds for me to kill the engine and fly around the hood of my car, ripping her door open to hold her. She practically leaps into my arms from her seat, arms wrapped around my neck as the rain soaks us both in no time. I reach across her turn off her engine, and shut the door, saying a silent prayer that she is letting me comfort her.

"I'm not going anywhere," I shout over the rain and the thunder that's now moved off into the distance somewhere. She looks up at me from where her face is buried in my chest, squinting against the rain while I cup her face in my hands. "I wake up with you in my arms and I can't believe I get to hold you. I go to work and I can't wait to get off to come see you.

Hell, I haven't kept any of those girls around for longer than a few months because no matter who you were dating or how hard I denied it, it was always gonna be you, and I think they knew that."

Samantha looks down sheepishly like she can't quite believe what I'm saying. Or maybe she isn't sure how to accept what I'm saying, with all the hurt she'd felt today.

"I mean it, Doll." I continued loudly over the rain drumming against both our vehicles. "I don't give a shit about Leah, or Carol, or Ross, or any of it. They can all come give me hell for all I care, but I am not walking away from you."

"It's not worth it, Jess." Her words are laced with defeat, but she holds onto me like she can't bear to let go.

"The fuck it isn't. I love you, Samantha. I have loved you probably longer than I ever knew and I am not letting you go unless you look me in the eye and tell me that you don't want this. Not because of Leah, or any other bullshit reasons, either."

Her jaw falls open and the rain running down her face rolls onto her top lip and into her mouth. "Say it again."

She licks her lips and tightens her grip as I move one hand into the back of her wet hair and another to her back, pulling her flush to my chest.

"I love you, Doll. And I am not going anywhere."

Her arms shoot up around my neck and I use the momentum to hoist her up around my waist as our lips collide. The warmth of her mouth is amplified, reminding me that we are both soaked to the bone. I walk us to the back door that leads to her apartment steps and only stop kissing her just long enough to ensure we make it inside.

The door closes behind us, as I press Samantha against the

wall, her legs still around my waist. In the stairwell light, I can see her every curve, as her rain drenched clothes cling to her body. Her breasts heave up and down with heavy breaths and her nipples peek through the lace of her bra and the fabric from the combination of the AC and the rain. The site elicits a guttural hum of approval as I plant kisses down her neck and collarbone, trying to warm her with my mouth and tongue.

Her legs tighten against me, hips flexing forward for friction that I am eager to provide. I thrust into her, letting her feel how much the site of her like this drives me wild. The breathy moan I get in response is enough to send a shudder through me.

I need to get us upstairs quickly before I lose control and take her right here on these stairs. The thought has my cock flexing against her warmth again and it takes all of my self-control to pull back and lower her down. I absolutely plan to take her over these stairs, and anywhere else I can manage, but not right now. Right now I want to take her upstairs and show her just how much I mean my words.

After a breathy pout, she takes my hand and follows me up the stairs. Once we are inside I lead her into the bathroom where I grab two towels. I wrap the first one around her and use the other one to wipe my face and hair before pulling my shirt off over my head. Samantha follows suit, peeling off her shirt and leggings, as I dispose of the rest of my clothes. She is standing before me in her red lacy bra and a black sheer thong that I know isn't only wet from the rain. She slides them down, then reaches behind her back and the bra drops to the floor, revealing her nipples, practically reaching for my mouth to warm them.

"You are fucking gorgeous, Doll."

Her eyes hungrily sweep over me until they lock onto the site of my cock, pulsing with the need for her and she licks her lips in anticipation. In one quick move, my hands are in her hair, tongue caressing hers, panting our way to her bed. I lower her onto the bed, standing between her thighs, and revel in the way her body responds as I trail my hand up her right thigh and take her nipple into my mouth.

"Do you see what you do to me, Doll?" I say, as her hand reaches down to stroke my cock.

She quivers with anticipation and her hips roll in a silent plea, showing how much she needs me. I circle my fingers over her sensitive clit while she pumps me, rocking her hips in time with her strokes. I swear I could come right here and now, if she keeps going, so I drop to my knees making her release me. I slowly trail my fingers down as I kiss her inner thighs on each side of her lips, then drive two fingers into her core. I work my fingers in and out as I tease her with my mouth, planting warm kisses that send her fingers into my hair.

My fingers work faster as she rocks against them and her moans beg me for more. Teasing little bites, with just enough pressure on each side of her lips, in turn with my fingers fucking her then finally letting her clit feel the warmth of my tongue driving into her, turn her moans into the most sensual scream I have ever heard as she comes apart for me.

"Jess." She whimpers, as I stand, taking the glorious site of her completely wrecked before me.

"Do you want more?" I pump my cock in my fist, as she watches licking then biting her lower lip.

"Yes." She nods, scooting back to make room for me.

"Then say it." I drawl, climbing between her legs on the

mattress.

Samantha reaches her hand between us and uses my dick to stimulate her clit, pumping me while I kiss her deeply, letting her taste herself on my tongue.

"Tell me, Samantha," I say pulling back enough to make her squirm with need.

"I love you too, Jess." She whispers into my lips as I shift forward, desperate to be inside of her. "I love you so much."

"Fuck, I love you Doll." I let her guide me as I push into her, but she doesn't let go.

Her hand holds a firm grip on my dick, pumping me as I thrust into her greedily.

"Who's pretty little cunt is this?" I say into her ear and barely hold back my load as I feel her tremble at my words.

"Yours, Jess." She moves her hand to grab my ass while the other one tears into my back and I sink into her as deep as she can take me. "I'm yours. Only yours."

I rock into her over and over, quickening the pace and she matches me with each thrust. Between panting breaths and moans, she screams my name and I know the thunder outside is the only reason no one has heard us downstairs, but I don't care. She is mine, truly mine and I hold out as long as I can, reveling in the feel of her until she comes apart screaming my name and pulsating, milking the cum from me, neither of us willing to relent until the last drop is deep inside of her.

Chapter 31

Samantha

My core aches as I slide out from under his arm, which is enough to make me blush at the memories of earlier tonight… or was it last night? I grab a robe off the corner chair, that I usually dump laundry on. It is dark out and Jess is fast asleep, wearing nothing but the rumpled comforter below his waist where his chest hair trails down his stomach.

The street lamp on the corner shines in through the blinds, casting enough light that I can see his rumpled hair and rugged muscles, even in the dark. I steal a moment to appreciate how beautiful he is. Everything about him oozes masculinity and strength, there's something to his gruffness that I hadn't known I was missing. Suddenly I don't know that I could ever look at a *"pretty boy"* like Ross, and feel attraction anymore. The floor creaks, despite my light steps, but his light snore tells me that I didn't wake him.

Okay, seriously, even his snore is cute?

Out in the kitchen, I help myself to a glass of water which I drink at the counter while I attempt sorting out my wild thoughts.

There's the thought that steals my breath and leaves me feeling like the luckiest girl in the world- *Jess loves me.* Which I assume means we're past the whole *is he my boyfriend or not* stage. I'm no expert, but I think being in love skips the line on that one.

In love. Lord help me.

I really am irrevocably in love with Jess. In that sickening way that makes you ache when you're not with someone. The kind of love that makes you feel blessed beyond measure. Then, just when the weight of how lucky you are to feel that kind of love settles in, your stomach flips with a sense of dread that you finally have something strong enough to break you if you lose it. Which brings me to my next thought- *I tried to push him away.* In my self-pity last night, I was so wrapped up in anger and shock from my meeting with Carol, that I just wanted to crawl inside of myself like a turtle in a shell and implode. Maybe I would have if it weren't for Jess refusing to let me go through this alone.

Maybe, if it weren't for Jess, the shock wave of emotions could have broken me from the inside out. Carol blaming my Dad for an entire lifetime of not being there for me, at least not in a way that I'd ever wanted her to be. Finding out that I have a younger sister that I never knew about. Being overwhelmed by the need to talk to my Dad, and ask him a thousand questions that I would never be able to ask. Realizing that Leah is my sister, and wondering how long she's known. Wondering if our secret familial bond is what drives her to do the things she does. Maybe it was the reason she wanted to live with me to begin with. Dreading having to tell Gramma about it all. All of these things plague my thoughts on repeat until the first bit of sunlight starts to creep in from the blinds.

Resigning myself to the fact that I won't be able to sleep, now that the sun is creeping up, I opt to make myself a cup of coffee, setting the water glass in the sink. After confirming that my creamer hadn't expired yet, and filling my reusable coffee pod, I open the cabinet to grab a coffee cup, staring blankly at the options before me. A Key West mug from a girls' trip with Mel, a Glenbrook Elementary mug I'd gotten from the school when I started, and a few silly mugs with animals wearing glasses or hats. All things that are a part of my life, or at least made me smile at some point, none of them appeal to me though.

Before I can think about what I am doing, I walk over to the garbage can, step on the pedal to lift the lid, and then take out the flower mug that we never bothered to remove. I loved this mug, and despite my new (to me) sister's games, this gift from Jess is the mug I want. I crumple up the note Leah left inside it and toss it in the can as the lid slowly closes.

Like fuck am I going to let her break me.

The thought runs through me in a wave of self-empowerment, as I turn on the sink and wash the mug. Once the coffee is done, I add enough creamer to make it the perfect Beyonce color and take it to the chair by the window.

I sit there for a while, watching cars go by out the window and nursing my coffee. The same thoughts continue to cycle through my mind. Jess, Carol, Dad, Leah, Jess, rinse repeat until my coffee is half gone. I find my phone in my still-damp pants, left on the floor from last night's rush to get into the door. I have a missed call and a message from Carol that I don't bother opening. Whatever it says is surely more about comforting herself right now. The battery is low, so I need to go put it on charge but I have one thing I want to do first.

I'm not usually the most present on social media. Mel does enough of that for both of us, always the first to take the pictures and share them with everyone. I don't much care one way or another, I like seeing the memories when they come up, but as long as she tags me I'll get those either way. What I need to do though, Mel can't share for me this time.

After fussing with my hair for a few seconds, using the camera as a mirror I decide that good enough will have to do. This isn't about looking good, it's a message for one person I know who hasn't stopped following me. I raise the flower coffee mug into the frame and take a few photos, testing out the angles before settling on the one I like best. Before I can overthink it, I upload it to my Facebook, knowing it'll automatically go to Instagram as well.

The caption reads: *To Family.*

Chapter 32

Samantha

Once Jess woke up we spent the rest of the morning at my apartment. His clothes from last night were still damp when we found them trailing from the front door to my bedroom. Naturally, they needed to be washed since he didn't have any other clothes at my apartment. Of course, his lack of things to wear while we waited led to us falling back into bed to pass the time. Oh, and on the couch… and the counter… let's just say if I thought I was sore this morning, I'm sure I'll feel positively bruised tomorrow.

And it was so worth it.

When we finally did get around to getting some clothes on, Jess insisted on packing up a few more of my clothes and random things to take back to his house. I didn't mention the fact that he yet again called it *home*, almost as if he'd forgotten that I don't technically live there. I didn't call him on it though, partly because I was swept up in the bliss of the morning. What distracted me was that in the same breath, he said the reason we needed to go *"home"*, was to get ready.

Jess Adams, Mr. Grumpypuss himself, who never kept a girl around long enough for us to learn their names, wanted to take me on a proper date. I couldn't disagree with him that it was long overdue, especially after the things we'd said to each other last night. Neither of us brought it up or said the weighted four-letter word again this morning, but the feeling was still there. I knew neither of us regretted it. We'd both meant it when we said we loved each other, it was just a matter of time before one of us said it again and the anticipation of hearing those words in that gravelly voice again was just delicious.

Once we got back to Jess's, I called Mel and updated her. She was reasonably equal parts shocked and her usual protective, fiery self about the revelation that Leah was most likely my sister. She also thought that must be why Leah had been trying to imitate me for so long. The thought that she knew the whole time we lived together gives me the creeps and makes me infinitely less comfortable trying to guess where the line that Leah won't cross could be.

I also used my typical pacing when I am on the phone as an excuse to wander out of earshot and fill her in on things with me and Jess. While I spared her the intimate details of our… *entanglements* (much to her disappointment), Mel's enthusiastic "It's about damn time!" came through the phone so loud I had to pull it away from my ear when I told her about his confession of loving me. Mel claims, much like Gramma, that everyone, except Jess and I, seems to have been aware of his feelings for a long time.

I couldn't bring myself to call Gramma yet, I still only had the word of Carol to go on after all. I didn't need to stir up feelings for her without evidence. She's been through enough, losing my dad, and then years later losing my Grandfather. I was almost sure she'd have died of heartache when Grampa died if her younger years hadn't conditioned her into the survivor she is. I resigned myself to only tell her when I had concrete proof, anything less than concrete would be cruel to bring up to her now. I wouldn't drag Dad's memory through the mud based on half-baked allegations the way Carol had.

Short of confronting Leah, I wasn't sure how to prove or disprove it anyway. Maeve Woods, Leah's mother had died when she was young. I'd never heard what happened to her, I only knew that Leah didn't like to talk about her and that Maeve's sister Maude had raised Leah.

Gramma had given me one of those saliva DNA kits as a gift for Christmas. She was very interested in the genealogy and wanted to see if it would match up with the stories handed down, about where her side of the family came from. I never did the test and sent it in though. While yes, It would have told me about my dad's side of the family, a part of me knew there was probably some distant cousin or aunt who'd done it on Carol's side as well. Something about linking myself in a worldwide confirmation to Carol made my stomach turn, so I put it in a drawer to be forgotten.

I had heard stories of kids who found their birth parents through those tests, or siblings who were split up by the foster system reunited. There's no way of knowing if Leah, or anyone close enough to her for me to recognize had taken the test. Still, I've been weighing the pros and cons of doing the test and sending it in. It wouldn't give me answers for months, and would symbolically link me to one (if not two) of my least favorite people. I needed answers though, and perhaps the cons were worth not having to face Leah myself to ask her for a DNA test. Not only would that show her that she had been getting under my skin, but I wasn't even sure if she'd agree or if it'd set off another of her schemes.

I told myself that I had the day, while Jess mowed the yard

and did a few other outside chores to think about it. I took that time to unpack the random things he'd packed from around my apartment. Some clothes, toiletries, and accessories, which I'd put away in his room and bathroom. A soft throw blanket that he decided his couch was lacking, as well as my Squirrel throw pillow, which I put on his bed. The flower mug, which had been my addition while he packed, I put back into the kitchen cupboard.

Home.

Technically, it isn't. But his words echo soothingly in my mind and this time not even my inner cynic has anything clever to say about it. Jess has more than shown that he wants me here. There is no denying it.

After unpacking I took a shower before Jess had the chance to hop in and distract me from getting ready for our date. I have already blow-dried my hair and am working on styling it and doing my makeup by the time he comes in from his yard work to take a shower of his own. I only have to get dressed, and then it will be the end of the time I'd allotted for myself to dwell on what to do about Leah. I decided that I would do the DNA thing, even if it gives me no answers. It had been a gift and I could at least do it for Gramma, to see what she wanted on her side of things.

I shut the thoughts of anything other than our date out of my mind as I pull the zipper up the side of my dress, just before Jess steps out of the bathroom. His towel hangs loosely around his waist, dragging my eyes down the contours of his stomach to…

"My eyes are up here, Doll."

My cheeks flush red as my eyes shoot up to his face to see the most panty-melting flirtatious smile I'd ever been privy to.

I roll my bottom lip through my teeth, cursing myself for already having done my hair and getting dressed. The things his smile made me want to do would wreck all the work I'd put in.

"Now if you'll excuse me, I am indecent." He drawls.

Amusement flickers in his eyes at my surprise that he would ask me to leave for him to get dressed. *Like we hadn't spent half a dozen instances tangled together, naked in the last twenty-four hours.*

"Are you kicking me out of your room?" I protested, half heartedly.

"What I am doing, is barely resisting the urge to keep you in *this* room." His voice shifts from playful and cocky, to a more restrained low rasp that brushes goosebumps up my arms.

"Oh come on," I protest, lowering my voice to a flirtatious tone to challenge his own. "A gentleman, like yourself can surely show some…" I briefly pause while I trail my finger down his chest, dangerously slow towards where he still holds his towel. "Restraint."

His low growl rumbles out and I can practically feel it in between my legs. Jess catches my wrist in his free hand and effortlessly spins me against the dresser. The towel drops and I feel just how little *restraint* he has, pushing against my ass as he pinned me in place. All I can do is watch as the mirror reflects my face, flushed with surprise and arousal. Jess's jaw clenches as one of his hands finds my side, just under my breast that he grazes with his thumb. The other hand slides its way up my thigh, under my dress until his fingers hook the thin material of my underwear.

"I need these off for what I have planned." His words

shoot down to my aching core and have me shifting against his erection.

Forget the hair and the dress. We can stay here, right?

Jess sinks down behind me and lowers my panties so slowly that the thundering of my heart amplifies, as well as my desire. I lean forward against the dresser, already wet with anticipation. His hungry eyes meet mine in the mirror as he raises the bottom of my skirt, exposing me further. I squirm with need and bend further forward, showing him just how ready I am for him to take me like this. Jess's hand moves achingly slow, gliding down my ass, to where I'm desperate for his touch the most. Then suddenly his hand is gone, and just when I think he'll push into me and put me out of my misery, he spanks my bare exposed pussy and my knees buckle at the surprisingly erotic sensation.

"Do you like that?" His voice is low and gravely in my ear.

Jess helps steady me with one hand and gently soothes away the sting with the other.

I can only muster a hum of approval and nod as I push back into his hand, begging for more.

"That's my girl." Jess smiles and kisses my bare shoulder next to the strap of my dress, then much to my distress, he turns away and busies himself getting dressed.

Chapter 33

Samantha

My many, not at all subtle, attempts to lure Jess into staying in for the night were unsuccessful. After getting himself dressed, he slipped my thong that he had removed into his front pocket. Then led me out the door to his car. I have to admit, I was a little disappointed to be taking the Mustang. I was sort of hoping after what happened while we were getting ready that the closeness the bench seat offers would work to my advantage in the truck. Especially since it's hard to keep your mind off such things when you're wearing a skirt with nothing underneath it.

Jess took me to a small mom-and-pop Indian restaurant on the other side of Glenbrook. He sat beside me in the booth instead of across from me, which I loved. It reminded me of how my grandparents always did the same thing. We laughed and flirted, and he held my hand afterward as we walked around for a little while.

At one point I pointed out a generic SUV and told Jess I might consider trading my Jeep in for something like that. He didn't try and talk me out of it. I'm sure it isn't hard to see why the vehicle I used to love has turned into something I dread using daily now. He did, however, suggest that the SUV was too boring for someone as "spunky as me." Instead, he asked why I don't drive the old Chevelle that's still sitting in Benny's garage. I explained to him that the car was a manual, and though I loved working on it with my dad, I'd never actually been tall enough to get that damn clutch engaged all the way to the floor. It stays at Benny's because I can't use it, but I can't bear to part with it either.

That's how we got here. Parked in a brand new, paved neighborhood that they've only started to build in. These neighborhoods are a car guy's (or gal's) wet dream. Freshly paved, no one around so you don't have to worry about traffic or noise complaints. Especially after sunset with the roads lit by the new street lamps. It's the perfect place, according to Jess, for me to learn to drive stick. Unlike my Dad's old Chevelle or Jess's old truck, the new creature comforts in his car mean that I can adjust the seats and pedals more.

For the first time in my life, I easily hold the clutch to the floor and engage it while the engine roars to life. Jess grins at me from the passenger seat, and I have the sensation of a bundle of vines twisting in my abdomen. I've never been into cars to impress guys, but damn if I don't want to get this right. I try to let off the clutch and start to hit the gas at the same time which doesn't work. I feel the car start to stall, so I quickly punch the clutch back down and let off the gas.

"I thought I needed to give it gas," I explain, embarrassed.

"You wanna let the clutch out slow, til you feel it bite first. Since it's new, the computers make it harder to stall so don't worry so much about that. Just try and get her rolling, Doll."

With one hand on the gearshift, I start to let the clutch out again, this time looking for the bite Jess mentioned. About halfway up I feel it. It feels like that split second before your car takes off when you punch it, like feeling potential energy before it's unleashed. When I am sure I'm in the sweet spot I'm looking for, I press the gas. A smile breaks out across my face when the car not only doesn't stall but starts to move.

Jess doesn't say anything, which I take to be him letting me concentrate. Now that the car is moving, it's smooth sailing. I easily shift through the gears, knowing from years of experience as a passenger, when to shift based on the revs of the engine. When I can't take his silence anymore, I spare a glance over at Jess. And if I do say so myself, he looks downright twitterpated.

"Great job, Doll." His praise rolls over me and I fight the urge to squeeze my thighs together.

I do a few laps around the new roads, stopping at the stop signs and then working my way up through the gears with a little more tenacity each time. Jess makes a few other critiques and compliments, and by the time I park the car I have gotten it up to 87 mph. Which granted, is only about half of Sally's potential, but for my first time, and the tiny roads here, I am pretty damn proud. Judging by the look on his face, I'd say Jess is pretty proud too.

"Out of the car," Jess says, reaching over and pulling up hard on the E-brake.

Before I can respond he is halfway around the front of the car. By the time I manage to stand, adjust my skirt, and close the door his arms are on my waist.

"Do you have any idea how fucking sexy that was?" He asks, then possesses my mouth with his before I can respond.

Jess leads me to the front of the car while he kisses me and his hands explore my curves. Between what happened before our date, and the way he's taking control over me, I can already feel how wet I am for him where my thighs meet. Jess leans me so I am just resting my ass against the still-warm hood of the car, as his fingers make their way up my skirt. I have a new reason to be thankful for the secluded venue since I can't help but moan at his teasing touch.

"You like that?" his gravely rumbles through me and I arch forward, wanting more friction.

"Jess. Please." I whimper, untying the top of my peasant top dress and letting my bare tits fall out.

I'm immediately rewarded with his warm mouth, pulling on my nipple while his hand works my clit faster. I reach down to undo his pants and free his dick. As soon as I wrap my hand around him and start to pump it I feel my climax building faster. There's something so sexy about feeling his dick while he controls me like this.

The tension builds but Jess keeps me right on the edge, until I'm a sated mess of moans, dripping down the hot hood of his car. I pull him closer, desperate for release.

"Jess, please."

"Please, what?" he says, gripping his cock and replacing the circles he was making on my clit with the tip of his dick.

"Please fuck me." I start to shake and my legs are feeling weak from pleasure.

"Stand up." He orders me, spinning me around.

Jess rolls my nipples through his fingers as he kisses my neck. Then finally, he bends me over the hood of his Mustang. I'm the perfect height to bend at the waist and be supported which is good because I know my legs aren't going to last long. The heat from the hood radiates through my nipples. Jess smoothly pulls my skirt up, his rough hands caressing my bare ass before he finally brings the tip of his cock back to my clit.

"You're so fucking sexy, Doll." Jess praises, burying himself inside of me.

I cry out from pleasure as he starts to pump himself out and back in so that I can feel every inch moving deep inside me. His hands find my hips and the possessive way his fingers dig into my hips is all the warning I get before his strides come harder. My vision starts to fade to black around the edges. An intense sensation spreads from where this man is relentlessly fucking me until every inch of me is tingling. I think he's saying something, but the only thing I can hear is my heart beating and the screams of pleasure rippling through me. The only thing holding me on the car is Jess's firm grip when I feel his cock start to jerk inside of me with his release.

There's something so hot and possessive about feeling him come inside of me.

"I love you so fucking much, Samantha." Jess pants over my shoulder, still supporting me as I come down from my orgasm.

"I love you too, Jess." I kiss him over my shoulder.

He goes to get some napkins from the car for us to clean up with, and then we spend a few more minutes just kissing, with me wrapped up in his arms. Before I can pull away to get back into the car Jess pulls my panties out of his front pocket and places the fabric in my hand.

"Told you I needed those off." He smirks and gives me a playful peck on the cheek before returning to his side of the car.

Chapter 34

Jess

"You guys are too cute. I think I am gonna throw up." Mel says, across the table from us. Samantha was just telling her about my latest packing antics at her apartment.

We met Mel and Chad at Bob Evans this morning, instead of going to the diner we usually go to. We all decided it was best to avoid it, considering Leah's aunt works there. Samantha and I are sitting on the same side of the booth. She's been nestled into me, stealing bacon off my plate while Mel and Chad give us shit. I couldn't care less about their playful jabs though. Even the comments about how it's weird to see me smile so much (Mel), or how I've gone soft (Chad) can't phase me.

Samantha loves me. The thought makes me grin outwardly.

She hasn't stayed at her apartment since the night I first told her I loved her. We have been by a few times to grab more clothes and odds and ends she needs. Every time we go, I have been adding a few extra things into her bag. She usually gives me the side eye or a playful smile but never outwardly protests. She's also stopped flinching when I call my place home, which I take as a good sign. I can't wait for her to officially move in. This time I added all of her lingerie drawer, as well as some of the books from the unread section of her bookcase.

"It's not cute, Mel." Samantha faux-pouts. "He's stealing everything I own."

"I'm soft-launching her moving in," I say with a wink, pushing my plate closer so she can steal the home fries.

"Oh come on," Mel says, noting Samantha's bashful response. "You're literally already living there."

"Temporarily." Samantha half-heartedly corrects her friend. "Don't you think it's too soon?"

"Is this how it's gonna be with you two?" I cut in. "Just gonna have the behind the scenes talks about the boyfriend right in front of me?"

"Yes," Mel says to me, before cutting her attention back to Samantha. "It's not too early if it feels right."

"Yeah, *Doll*, does it feel right?" Chad cuts in, clearly enjoying this.

"That's your one free pass, dude. Don't call her that again." I point at him, earning a hands up in surrender response from Chad.

"Ignore the boys." Mel waves her hands as if directing the attention back to herself. "Say you wake up tomorrow and it's time to move back to your apartment. You're now limited to one sleepover a week."

My smile broadens as Samantha's shoulders slump at the thought. She doesn't want to live in that apartment anymore, and Mel, for once, is being gloriously helpful. Samantha worries her lip between her teeth, and I can see the wheels turning in her head. She wants this, but she's scared. Given her history I get it, she likes to have her independence to fall back on.

"What if we keep paying Benny for the apartment until you're comfortable enough to let it go?" I offer.

"I think I need to pee." Samantha dodges.

If it weren't for the *that's girl code for come talk to me where Jess can't hear you* eyes she gives Mel, I wouldn't have even thought she'd heard me. Nevertheless, Chad and I dutifully stand to let the girls out of our respective booths.

"Nervous?" Chad asks once they're out of earshot.

"Nah, she wants it. She's just nervous." I tell him. "Plus, I think Mel will actually help."

"You two look good together bud. Glad you finally manned up." Chad teases.

"Yeah, yeah. What's been going on with you?" I change the subject. "You've been a little MIA lately."

Chad reaches up and rubs the back of his neck nervously. It takes a beat but he eventually nods, as if deciding to talk to me about whatever it is.

"Yeah, I know. Mom's been sick. I have been going over to check on her a lot."

"Shit man. Why didn't you say something?"

"I don't know. I mean we all got our own shit going on. And I was hoping it'd get better but I'm actually gonna just move her in with me."

"It's that bad?"

A shrug of the shoulders is his only response. One thing I've learned about Chad is that even though the bastard loves to meddle in our lives, he can be extremely private about any areas where he might need help. I've tried explaining the irony to him, but it always falls on deaf ears.

"I can come help. When are you moving her stuff?"

"Today. I'm heading over from here." He says glancing to see if the girls are coming back. Which I take as a hint that he doesn't want to share this with anyone else yet.

"Alright, I'll tell Samantha I gotta help you with something. I won't go into details though."

"No that's alright, you can tell her. I just don't really wanna deal with all the questions just yet." Aka don't pry or Chad will shut down instead of leaning on us.

"You got it, bud."

He leans out a little farther into the aisle looking behind me then says, "Um, I think the girls went back to the wrong booth."

Chad picks up his phone when a notification chimes while I turn to follow his line of sight. Sure enough, I see a small hand and wrist hanging into the aisle with a tattoo that says *Bigger than the Universe.*

"Samantha!" I call, my voice laced with amusement.

Honey blonde curls lean out of the booth. But when I expect to be met with sweet brown eyes and a laugh, staring back at me are a pair of noxious yellowish-green eyes.

When he sees my face shift to convey a mixture of confusion and disgust, Chad turns back around to see Leah getting out of the booth and walking straight to our table.

"What the fuck?" Chad's words mirror my thoughts as he puts the phone back down on the table.

I look from Leah's face to her wrist, triple-checking what I am seeing. Sure enough, it's there. *Bigger than the Universe.* The tattoo that Samantha got in memory of her dad, is now proudly displayed across Leah's wrist. A protective rage boils in my chest as she leans forward and places her hands on our table, positioning her wrist towards me purposefully.

"You've got some fuckin' nerve," I say before she gets out whatever she's about to say.

"Oh? Why is that?" her counterfeit innocent tone is a stark contrast to her nefarious body language.

I clutch my fists under the table, trying not to make a scene. Even though every part of me is internally screaming to get this psychopath far away from Samantha.

"Don't act stupid." I grit out, barely able to keep my voice low enough. "I should call the cops and tell them you're breaking your restraining order."

I didn't even notice Samantha and Mel walk back up behind Leah. Thankfully they see her first and stop a few yards back. Samantha catches my eye. I try my best to say *do not come closer* with my eyes, without drawing Leah's attention to her. I'm not sure if it works, or if she just decides to turn around. Either way, I am grateful when both her and Mel retreat.

"What are you going to tell them?" Leah challenges me, none the wiser that Samantha and Mel are now on their way out the door. "That I am in a public place? I don't see anyone here that the restraining order requires me to stay away from. Do you?"

"Yeah, we're just supposed to believe you being here is a coincidence right?" I scoff. "Following Samantha around, going through her apartment and my house. And that."

I point at her wrist still leaning against the table, then lose control of keeping my voice low. "That's just fucking sick."

She straightens up at that. As if trying to convince herself and anyone else watching that my words didn't hit her somewhere personal.

Good. Fuck her.

"You don't know what you're talking about."

"I know you better stay away from her," I say standing, forcing her to stumble back to make room for me and Chad to pass.

I don't want to give her the opportunity to be the first one to walk away. I need to get out to the parking lot to check on Samantha.

Chapter 35

Samantha

Jess and Chad filled us in on the insanity of Leah getting my tattoo copied to her wrist, which I am not ready to process right now. Then Jess told Chad that he probably should stay with me instead of going to help him like he'd offered. After getting more of an explanation, I insisted that he still go. It took me saying I was okay fifteen times, and Mel offering to stay with me for Jess to accept that he could still go help Chad.

The guys have been gone for a few hours now. I am not sure how much longer it'll take them, since it's been raining off and on all afternoon. I wonder if it'd be better for Chad if it did take longer. We've all noticed Chad pulling away. The last thing I want is to be the reason Jess isn't there for him when he does open up. Which is rare.

Mel and I have been working on getting our class shirts made anyway. Glenbrook Elementary has a long-standing tradition of teachers and their classes wearing matching tie-dye shirts during the most competitive day of the year, Field Day. Seeing as how Jess's house has become the new go-to for us to gather (because two of the four of us are already typically here) we set up our tie-dye station in Jess's kitchen last night.

Mel made her class colors the traditional colorful swirl but with black added to make it "look less corny". I went for a patriotic variation with blues on the top and a red and white bottom. We waited the traditional day to let the dye really set. Now we are just finishing up some pizza and almost ready to start unwrapping the shirts to rinse and wash them.

"Nice throw pillow."Mel snarks, pointing to the stolen squirrel on the sofa.

"I can't help the fact that the man is a kleptomaniac," I say, playing at being on the defense.

There may be a few extra things of mine around recently. Every time we go to my apartment Jess adds something else to bring here. Most of the clothes that I wear (plus my entire lingerie collection) have made their way over here. Several of my books have made their way onto the shelf under the living room TV. Even the lamp from my bedside table has made its way to Jess's room where it now sits on "my side" of the bed.

"Yes, I'm sure you're putting up such a battle." Mel teases, rolling her eyes. "We all know you're moving in. The real question is how long are you gonna make the man suffer before you admit it?"

"He is not suffering, don't be dramatic." I laugh, untying a shirt to rinse.

"Right. Because grumpy-puss himself, who hates joy, is now hosting regularly and decorating with throw pillows and faerie smut for the fun of it. That checks out. I'm sure whenever you get around to it, he won't be eagerly awaiting your move-in notice."

I fight back a smile and throw my head back in a groan. "What if it doesn't work?"

I keep myself busy with the shirts, avoiding looking at Mel's face.

"What if he doesn't want me to live with him anymore when it's not so new and fun anymore?"

"I don't think that's going to happen," Mel says with a confident nonchalance. "But, for the sake of your commitment issues, I'll play along. *If* it doesn't work out, you can move in with me."

She gives me a look to emphasize the weight of that offer. Mel has turned down being roommates with me on multiple occasions. Each time citing her chaotic childhood home as the reason she wanted to live alone. She's even ended relationships over refusing to live with anyone. Not only is her promise offering me a safety net, but it's also showing me how much even Mel thinks I should go for it. How much she believes it will work.

If I am being honest with myself, I want to move in with Jess. I've just been nervous to admit the desire, even to myself. My little apartment over Benny's doesn't feel like home to me. Even though I lived there and tried to personalize it for longer than I have been at Jess's house. There's just been something about Jess's that felt like home since the first night I stayed here. The more time we spend together, the more I realize that that feeling doesn't stay within these walls. It follows us wherever we go together. Because what makes it feel like home, is Jess and the idea I used to have that love wasn't as grand as I know it is now seems like a lifetime ago.

Mel's smug knowing smile gives away that all these thoughts must be written on my face like a flashing billboard. Telling her that my mind finally caught up to my heart's decision.

"Do I live here now?" I ask, my face mirroring a daydreaming teen with her first crush.

"Might wanna tell Grumpy-puss to make it official, but yeah, I think you do." She raises her eyebrows in that playful way she always does, and we both double over laughing.

My phone dings with a notification, so I put down the shirt I have half unwrapped. I have little stains on my fingers because I will forever be too stubborn to wear gloves. I decide to wash my hands before checking the message, which of course is fruitless.

When I double-tap on the screen, bringing it to life, I see a text from Chad that makes my heart drop.

Chad: *Jess got hurt. Meet me at the hospital.*

I immediately try to call Chad, waving Mel away frantically when she tries to ask what's wrong. He doesn't answer though and she reads the next message that comes through over my shoulder.

Chad: *on phone with 911.*

Chad: *Ambulance almost here.*

Chad: *Meet at hospital*

A hundred feelings battle all at once inside of me. Worry, twisting my stomach. Fear, tightening my chest and making it hard to breathe. Panic, trying to cloud my mind and spin me out. It's the tears that start to fall down my cheeks that bring them into balance and remind me that I need to remain level-headed right now.

"I need to get to the hospital." I look around in circles, aimlessly for a few seconds.

"Don't worry about all this. I'll finish cleaning it up and meet you up there." Mel says, misunderstanding my frozen panic for concern about leaving our project mess behind.

Truth be told I had forgotten about the shirts completely. Nevertheless, I thank her for her offer before grabbing my purse and slipping on the first shoes I can to get out the door.

Chapter 36

Samantha

This is Jess, with Adam's Auto. Please leave a detailed....
Voice-mail.

Because he's in an ambulance, on the way to the hospital. Of course, he isn't answering his phone. Some part of me hoped that he would. Maybe he'd pick up and tell me he broke his pinky toe when Chad let something slip from his grip. Or he'd thrown out his back trying to carry too much of Ms. Wilkins' bowling ball collection at once. Even though I don't know if she has such a collection.

This is Jess, with Adam's Auto. Please leave a detailed....
Dammit.

Chad hasn't answered either.

So I am driving down Brookhill Road, to get to the local hospital from Jess's place.

Our place? Not the time.

I shove the thought aside and force myself not to cry as I turn down the next street. My windshield is already covered, wipers frantically trying to wipe the rain away. After losing my dad so suddenly, it's hard to stop my mind from going to the worst scenario. With each *swish-thud,* my heart pounds a little faster. A little harder. If I didn't need to see where the hell

I was going I'd turn it off, if only to have one less thing amplifying the sense of urgency already overwhelming me.

Swish-thud.

Why won't anyone pick up the phone?

Swish-thud.

Please, God, let him be okay.

Swish-thud.

Will I make it there in time?

Swish-thud.

The tears well up and I want to let them run over. I want to fall apart and pull over and let the crying consume me. But I need to get to Jess. I need to prove to myself that he is okay.

I realize I must have slowed down, between the tears and the rain, when headlights appear in my rear-view. I try, again, to pull myself together and focus on driving.

I am driving through the last bit of turns on the road when my phone finally rings over the speaker of my Jeep. My chest does a flip when I see Jess's name on the screen. I urgently tap my finger on the touch screen to answer, as the rain comes harder.

"Jess?" I answer loudly, trying to make sure he can hear me over the pounding of the water against my roof and windshield. "Are you okay? What happened?"

"My phone died. Sorry."

Thank you, Jesus. He doesn't sound hurt.

"I thought you were home?" Jess says, and I can't be sure over the rain but it almost sounds like I hear a door shut somewhere behind him.

"Chad texted me that you were on the way to the

hospital," I explain, coming to the end of the road.

The rain isn't as loud now that I am stopped at the stop sign, so I figure I'll steal a few more seconds trying to hear him better before I turn left onto Lakeshore Drive.

"I'm almost there. Just give me about five minutes." I continue.

"Fuck." Jess's curse makes me flinch.

"Samantha, you need to turn around."

"What? No." I protest. "I am almost there."

I'm about to take my turn, seeing headlights coming up behind me before the urgency in his next words stops me.

"Chad didn't text you, Samantha. He hasn't been able to find his phone since breakfast."

"What do you m-" my words are cut off when the round headlights coming up behind me don't slow down, but barrel straight into the back of my Jeep.

"Samantha?" Jess's voice is laced with the same panic I was feeling over him just minutes ago.

My Jeep lunges forward into the intersection, and my head hits the steering wheel.

No. The airbag went off and hit me.

Maybe both?

I try to press the brake harder. It's no use though. Between the rain, going downhill, and the vehicle behind me still pushing, my Jeep continues to slide forward.

My ears have started ringing and everything seems foggy. It feels like things are tilting from side to side, but I know I need to focus.

"Brookhill and Lakeshore," I shout to Jess.

"What happened?" he asks urgently, but I don't have

time to explain.

The vehicle behind me isn't letting up, and it's all happened too fast to try and turn now. I'm running out of pavement and I know as soon as I hit the slick grass on the other side, I am going into the lake.

I look up in my rearview, remembering the round headlights the second before they hit. I can't see the lights now, but I can make out the outline of the rectangular roof line.

"Leah," I say, trying to keep my answers short as I yank up the emergency brake. "The lake."

It's too late though, the engine pressed against my spare tire is still revving aggressively. Forcing me forward no matter how much I fight it.

"I love you, Jess."

"Doll, no–" Jess's desperate, fear-laced voice is drowned out as Leah floors it, and I lose the last bit of traction I was holding on with.

~

My legs are cold. Wet. My vision is cloudy when I open my eyes. I only think to hold my breath for a second before realizing I feel blood dripping down my forehead, so my head can't be underwater. Pain radiates through my body when I reach up to feel my face. The adrenaline is wearing off and I am starting to feel all of the pain.

I blink rapidly trying to clear my vision and focus on what to do next.

"Jess?" I try.

Nothing.

The Jeep is waist-deep in water. The power has probably fried and I have no idea where my phone is, but I am pretty sure it doesn't work anymore.

I move stiffly, trying to remember what to do in these situations. I try the door, but I'm too weak to push against the water on the outside of the door, holding it closed. The power windows don't work when I try them, so that's also a bust. I vaguely remember reading once that vehicles are designed to float in the back and wonder if I can get out the back door.

I twist to try and climb over the seat but the seatbelt holds me in place. I push the red button trying to unbuckle, but it doesn't immediately release like I expect. After a few tries, I finally jiggle the seatbelt free. The water level is up to the bottom of my breasts by the time I can finally crawl over the seat. The back isn't sinking as fast but I don't bother trying the back doors, knowing I won't be able to push against the water on the outside.

When I get back into the cargo area I frantically look for a latch. A button. A glow-in-the-dark pull chord like they put in trunks, anything. But I can't find a way to open the back door from inside.

Fuck. Fuck. Fuck.

The front of the Jeep is now completely underwater, but I think it's slowing down. I reach down in the water and feel around on the floor of the cargo area looking for a tab to pull up the floor cover. Once I find it, I pull it back and get to work on my next search. Right by the back door, in the floor should be a latch to open a compartment. My hands are shaking, and I am trying to remind myself not to hyperventilate and use up all the oxygen. After a few seconds, I finally find the release and toss the lid behind me.

Thank you, Jesus.

I pull out the scissor jack that came with the Jeep. It'll have to do. I rear it back and strike the back windshield as hard as I can. Pain ricochets up my arm and shoulder as it bounces off the glass without leaving a mark.

The water level has reached the bottom of the rear window. Despite the pain, I keep hitting the window. I lose count of how many times I hit it before it finally cracks. Once it does I get another rush of adrenaline and hit it harder and faster until it finally breaks enough for me to push a hole through the crumbles of the safety glass.

I use the back of the seats as a foothold and pull myself up through the window. I can feel little cuts on my palms from the crumbles of the glass when I finally grab hold of the rear spare tire and crawl my way through the broken window. I'm sure I'll have more cuts and scrapes from the feel of my stomach and legs, but I am able to pull myself out.

The spare tire on the back of my Jeep is resting on Leah's hood under the water. It looks like it stopped me from going all the way under the water, but not by much. Her Jeep isn't as far into the water as mine, so the water isn't as deep. The hood of Leah's Jeep isn't that deep underwater when I climb off my spare tire down onto it and remember that she's a danger.

I crouch to look into the windshield. I don't know if I am relieved to see the driver's seat empty or not. Her driver's side window is down and since it isn't underwater like my jeep, which was pushed past the drop-off, I guess she must've climbed out the window.

I climb my way onto her roof, trying to stay out of the water as much as possible. Then, I hear the wail of a siren in the distance. Looking up the hill towards town, I can see the faint glow of red and blue lights in the distance.

Help is coming.

I fall to my knees right on the fucking blue Jeep that started this all.

Help is coming.

I don't have to keep fighting so hard. I can just lay down here and…

Chapter 37

Jess

As soon as I lost the call with Samantha I called 911. I told them the few things she was able to tell me before the phone cut off. The operator kept me on the line until the first officer arrived on the scene and told them they found someone on the roof of a Jeep in the lake. I was already in the car by then.

The operator said they'd be taking the girl to the hospital so that's where I am now. Rushing through the automatic doors to the emergency room fast enough for the security guard to stop me. I do my best to steel my nerves. Though I am sure this guy sees a lot of frantic worried people, I don't want to scare him from letting me in. I go back through the metal detector slower this time, with my phone and keys now in the bowl on the table next to the guard.

"Check again. Jess Adams. He should be here." I hear as I clear the security area and approach the front desk.

"Mel?"

How did she beat me here? How did she already know Samantha was hurt? Why is she asking for me?

Mel's face mirrors my confusion as she turns to see me standing behind me. She takes me in, then to my surprise, plows me into a huge hug.

"You're okay." She sighs, relief clear in her tone.

I remember Samantha saying that she got a text from Chad that I was hurt and realize that must be why she was here.

"When's the last time you talked to Samantha?" I ask her urgently.

"Right before she left your house," Mel tells me. "She got Chad's text and we were working on rinsing the tie-dye shirts. I told her to get up here to check on you and I would follow once I finished up."

My head starts nodding on its own. As if trying to put into order the events of the night. I push past Mel to the nurse at the desk, trying my best not to show how frantic and disheveled I really feel. She's not likely to help me any faster if I freak her out by panicking.

"Where is she?" Mel asks, turning to follow me.

I don't answer her. I don't have the answers.

"Excuse me." I try to suppress the nerves in my voice.

I put my shaking hands in my pockets, unable to get them to still.

"I'm looking for Samantha Bunting. Can you tell me if she's arrived?"

"She didn't find you?" Mel asks, putting herself beside me against the counter.

"She was in an accident, Mel." I manage, trying not to say anything else until we talk to the police.

I did tell the 911 operator to let the first responders know this is related to an ongoing case that Officer Jake Underwood has been working with us on. She said she'd pass along the info. I'll worry about calling him after I find Samantha. After I see that she's okay.

"I don't understand," Mel says before the nurse cuts in.

"I'm sorry sir, we don't have any patients here by that name."

"She was in a crash," I explain to the nurse and Mel at the same time. "In the lake, can you check if the ambulance is on the way?"

Mel's confusion is replaced with a worried one, like my own. The nurse promises to go see what she can find out, then disappears behind a door.

I explain the little I know to Mel while we wait in the hard waiting room chairs. Chad's missing phone, and the few things Samantha was able to tell me before the phone cut off. She has the same fear that I did when the 911 operator said they found a woman on the roof of the Jeep, and no one else around.

Where is Leah?

Was it her or Samantha on the hood?

Did one of them not make it out of the lake?

"Leah Woods." A familiar voice snags both of our attention at the same time. We turn to see Maude Woods, talking to the other reception nurse.

"Someone called me and said they'd be bringing her here."

"Maude." I jump up, not really sure what I am going to say to her. But I need to hear any info she might have that we don't.

While the nurse helping Maude types into her computer, and thankfully before I say anything else, the first nurse reappears.

"So, it looks like we have a bit of a situation." She says grabbing the attention of all of us, the second nurse included. "It seems there were two nearly identical vehicles involved in the accident."

My jaw clenches and Mel tenses next to me. Maude looks between the two of us and the nurse, understanding dawning on her.

"Rescuers contacted you," she gestures to Maude, "because you are the emergency contact for the driver of the rear vehicle. It was the only one they could read the license plate on."

"Where are the girls?" Maude interjects, wringing her hands. She looks equal parts worried and remorseful.

I briefly wonder how much she knew about Leah's obsession with Samantha. What it must've been like raising someone with this kind of evil in her heart. What kind of weight this might put on her? But I shake it off and focus on the nurse.

"Well, that's the thing. First responders only found the driver of one of the vehicles."

Mel's fingers dig into my arm as my heart thunders in my chest.

"Who?" I barely choke out the words against the lump of fear in my throat.

"We don't know. They couldn't pull identification out of the submerged vehicles. The best we can do is have one of you identify the girl they brought in."

"Fuck." I rub my hands over my face. Then through my hair as Mel and Maude freak out in their own ways to either side of me.

"Since I assume only one of you three is next of kin or even a relative of one of them," The nurse looks at us to confirm, which we do by looking to Maude, "We'd like to ask Maude to come back with us to identify our Jane Doe."

"Wait." Mel stops the nurse. "If she can't tell you who she is herself…"

"She's unconscious." The nurse interjects, knowing where Mel's mind is going. "But she *is* stable."

The three of us share a simultaneous sigh of relief, even though we aren't all hoping for the same outcome. Maude may not have anything against Samantha, but I know she is hoping that it's Leah back there. Stable, and being taken care of.

"We all know both of the girls," I tell the nurse, then turn to Leah's aunt. "Maude, will you tell us if it's Samantha? Please."

My voice cracks, tears blurring my vision. I hold my breath as she takes a second to look sorrowfully between Mel and me. Then the damn breaks and I fall to my knees right on the waiting room floor when she offers me a small nod.

I stay on my knees, as Mel kneels beside me with a hand on my shoulder. And I pray.

I pray for Samantha. I pray that it's her they've found. I pray for the doctors who are taking care of her. I pray for her to heal. Then, I pray for Leah. I pray that she's alive, out there somewhere. I pray that the cops find her and that she has to suffer for what she's done to the woman I love. I pray she gets locked away and we don't see her for a very long time. If ever again.

When I finally compose myself, Maude comes back through the door. The nurse follows behind her, and the torture starts all over again as Mel and I wait to hear what she has to say.

"I'm so sorry."Maude blubbers. "I should've never let them live together."

Maude's apology leaves us without a clear answer, so Mel and I both look to the nurse behind her expectantly.

"We have Samantha here."

"Thank God." Mel and I say in tandem, as Maude is overcome with tears of her own.

In another world, I'd comfort Maude. I'd do my best to reassure her as she worries for the girl she raised. I can't bring myself to hope for anything good for Leah though, so I say nothing and wait for the nurse to continue.

"It seems like she's trying to wake up. If I could have you two wait here, I'd like to give her a few minutes to talk to the doctor before I ask if she wants visitors. We'll need her permission for either of you to go back since you're not immediate family."

"Of course," Mel says, leading me back to our seats. "Should we call her Gramma?"

"Yeah, let's just get in there and see her first. I wanna have all the facts we can before we call." I say.

"Good idea." She nods. "What about Chad?"

"I think Leah took his phone off the table this morning at breakfast. He didn't have it all day while I was with him."

"How do we get ahold of him then?"

"I'll have someone run by and talk to him. I just wanna see her first."

"Yeah." Mel's nod slows as she cocks her head inspecting me. "You really love her, don't you?"

"I really fucking love her." I sigh. Then we sit in silence, waiting for the nurse to return.

Chapter 38

Samantha

"Miss Bunting?"

My name is accompanied by three taps against the open hospital room door, which I can't see from behind the drawn curtain.

Jess leans back in his chair, checking who it is before waving my visitor inside. He hasn't left that spot since the nurse let him and Mel in hours ago. He called Gramma for me and promised to drive me over to visit with her once I am released. He's been doting on me, making sure I am comfortable ever since.

Mel left just a bit ago when the doctor said I was cleared to eat. She said she wasn't going to subject me to hospital food after what I'd just gone through, which made me wince in pain from a small laugh.

The doctor says I sustained a concussion, and a few of my ribs are bruised, probably because I need to sit too close to the airbags to drive. My shoulder was nearly dislocated from the socket by the seatbelt when I lunged forward, so it hurts to raise my left arm. Other than that, and the obvious bruises and scrapes, and there's just the cut on my forehead, leading into my hairline.

The doctor reluctantly allowed me to opt out of the

painkillers they wanted to prescribe originally. I explained to him that I didn't want to be tempted, and my mother's history. He assured me that just asking was probably a pretty good sign that I wouldn't have to worry about ending up addicted. Still, I was grateful when he agreed to give me a cocktail of the maximum doses of Tylenol and ibuprofen instead. *And even more grateful when they mostly worked.*

"Underwood." Jess stands to greet the officer with a handshake.

I muster a small smile to greet Officer Underwood, in exchange for the pity smile on his face.

"I'm sorry to see you again under these circumstances," Underwood says.

I don't know what to say really, so I wait for him to get to what he's here for.

"Did they find Leah?" Jess asks.

I try not to flinch, hearing her name. But, I know both men noticed it anyway.

"We did." He nods. "That's what took me so long to come."

I close my eyes and sink back into the bed. Feeling a wave of relief and hope wash over me.

Maybe this is finally over.

"By the time I was updated, you'd already been brought by ambulance to the hospital. As soon as I got the call confirming that you were the one in the hospital, I knew she had to still be out there somewhere."

"She couldn't have gotten far by foot, right?" Jess asks.

"Right. So we went to her aunt's house about two and a half miles away by foot, if you cut through some neighborhoods and woods. Maude was just getting home when we arrived. She was very agreeable, upset of course. But she let us in and when we didn't find any sign of Leah there, she promised to call if she showed up."

"I think I saw her," I say.

I have talked to Jess and Maude, and the doctors of course. But this is the first time since Underwood arrived that I actually say anything out loud. There's something about him being here that intensifies how serious this all is. How close I was to not making it out of the water.

"Maude, I mean. I think she was in this room when I woke up."

"That's right." Jess wraps his hand around mine, reassuring me. "Since Mel and I weren't family, and you didn't have ID on you, they had Maude come and identify whether it was you or Leah they pulled off the Jeep in the lake."

Even though he's talking to me, I know he means it as an explanation for Underwood as well. I feel myself sink at the idea that they couldn't tell us apart. That I could've died and been buried under a tombstone reading *"Leah Woods"*.

Are we really so easy to mix up?

My inner cynic recoils at the thought, and I am right there with her.

"It was just the hospital covering their ass, Doll," Jess says, seemingly able to read my insecure thoughts. "Hair dye and a tattoo don't make her look like you."

"Did you talk to Maude?" Underwood asks, steering us back on topic.

"I was too out of it." I shake my head. "I think I heard her say that she was sorry about something before she walked out. I can't be sure though. I was in and out of it."

"Understandable." Underwood nods again, jotting things down in his little pocket notebook. "Maude actually turned out to be a tremendous help to us. We didn't expect to hear from her after we left. You rarely ever get the family turning in their loved ones. So, you can imagine my surprise when she texted me about an hour after we left."

"She turned Leah in?" Jess cuts in.

"Sure did," Underwood confirms. "I left her my cell number, in case she heard anything. I couldn't believe it when she texted me that Leah showed up looking for dry clothes and a place to lay low. Said she didn't want to spook her by calling it in."

"Maude seemed pretty upset when she was here," Jess says. "Like, she was worried of course. But, I don't know. She also seemed like she felt guilty for what Leah did."

"So where is she now?" I ask, fiddling with the sheet the nurse draped over my lap.

"She's officially been placed under arrest. She's being processed, and with your help, we are prepared to press charges."

"She's in police custody?" I ask, needing to hear it again.

"Brought her in myself," Underwood says. "After all you've been through, I wanted to be able to look you in the eye with something real."

I squeeze Jess's hand and the threat of tears wells up.

It's really over.

Jess gets up and scoots himself onto the bed beside me, gently letting me lean into him while I cry out my relief.

"If you'd like, I can give you a few minutes. But I do need to get an account of what you can remember from the accident. While it's still fresh." Underwood says gingerly.

I shake my head, wiping my eyes. "I can do it," I tell him.

"You sure?" Jess asks, then kisses me on the forehead when I nod my response.

Whatever it takes to end this.

Before I can start, a rush of takeout bags and bright red hair blows into the room.

"I'm sorry I took so long, but the frappe machine was down at McDonalds, so I went to Starbucks instead. Don't worry I brought decaf. I also got you some good snacks and…" Mel trails off when she notices Underwood.

"Miss Eddy." Underwood dips his head in a greeting.

"Mel. It's still just Mel, Jake." She sighs.

At least he didn't call her Melissa.

After all these years, I still don't understand why she hates being called her real name. I don't particularly know why she doesn't like him calling her Miss Eddy either, since that's what she goes by at school.

"He arrested Leah," I tell her before she can say more.

I don't really know what her deal is with him, but I don't want to hear them bicker right now. I just want to tell him what happened and put this whole thing behind me. Mel, to her credit, seems to soften at my announcement and offers him an olive branch.

"Good job, Donut. It's about time."

Well, sort of an olive branch.

Chapter 39

Samantha

"Come in." Gramma's familiar greeting through the storm door welcomes us.

Jess lets me go first up the stairs, doing a poor job of pretending he isn't still hovering. Despite my insisting I am okay, he's been dutifully taking care of me since the accident. The nurses even let him stay with me overnight in the hospital. After spending two nights in the hospital, I couldn't wait to finally go home last night. By home, I mean Jess's house.

When one of the registration staff came by to make sure the hospital has my most recent insurance info and such on file, she read me an old address. The look on Jess's face when I gave her his address instead of the apartment above Benny's was priceless. I wouldn't have been surprised if he pushed her out of the way and kissed me right then. He managed a remarkable amount of self-restraint. Though he was absolutely beaming when he told her the zip code since I didn't know it.

I also added him to my emergency contact list. Not that I am hoping for more emergencies. But it'll at least let him come see me if that's ever the case.

Inside Gramma's, I take my shoes off and lean into

Gramma's greeting as she presses her cheek to mine saying "Mwuah."

She repeats the process with Jess before ushering us into the kitchen table. Something warms in my chest, seeing the two of them interact like that. So familiar. I don't think Gramma has ever been like that with one of my boyfriends. But then, I suppose they've all been trying to be well-mannered and impress her, which is not the way to win her over.

If you wanna get on Gramma's bad side, just call her ma'am.

I smile at the two of them, sitting in the comfortable cloth chair beside her. Jesse takes the seat to the other side of me, and Gramma tracks his hand on mine. Even though I have told her about us on our many phone calls, it feels like an admission holding hands in front of her. One I am happy to make, but I still feel a flutter of nerves. Like the first time I asked Dad if a boy could take me to a movie.

"Maude Woods called me." Gramma says, surprising us both from across the table.

Jess and I look at each other, silently making sure we both heard her right. I'm used to Gramma jumping right into whatever she wants to talk about without preamble. I just didn't think she knew Maude. In fact, I was planning on giving her a very long detailed story about what happened with the crash, and what Carol had told me about Leah being Dad's secret love child.

"How do you know Maude?" I ask, leaning forward.

I suppose it's better to find out how much she knows and go from there.

"I've known Maude for a long while." She says, then takes a deep breath and fiddles with the fabric place setting on the table.

I wait, rather impatiently for her to continue, as Jess traces comforting circles on my wrist.

"When you were a baby, your dad came to me. He made his fair share of mistakes, as you know, and he was really trying to straighten things out. Well, it turns out he and your mom were fighting a lot and during one of their breakups he ended up getting together with Maude's sister Maeve."

Is this really happening?

Did Gramma know about Leah?

"After your Dad and Carol made up, Maeve came back around and told him she was pregnant. Once the baby was born, Grampa and I helped pay for a paternity test. We met Maude when she brought Maeve and the baby to the appointment. It turns out your Dad was not the father of Maeve's baby, but by then the damage was done with Carol."

"You knew about Leah?" I ask. Wondering how she could let me live with her.

"I never knew the baby's name." She explains. "I didn't know that Maeve's child was Leah until Maude called me yesterday. She said that right after your Dad died, she and Leah ran into Carol at a bar. Carol was drunk or high, maybe both. She went off on Leah, telling her it was her fault that she lost Karl, all those years ago. Of course, he'd told Carol that he wasn't the father of Maeve's baby. But, you know Carol."

"She wouldn't believe him, because then she'd have no reason to get high." I say.

She gives me a look that I've learned over the years means that she won't say a bad word against my mother, but she's glad I can see it for myself.

"Maude says she told Leah about the blood tests, and she

thought Leah understood that your dad wasn't her father. She'd told Leah that it would be cruel to bring up after the accident, and Leah agreed not to say anything. Maude claims it wasn't until Leah bought the Jeep and you moved out that she began to think that Leah still believed Karl was her father."

"So she thought for the past several years that my Dad was hers. The whole time we lived together. She thought we were sisters." I think out loud, still too shocked by what Gramma is revealing she knows to feel relief that the paternity test was negative.

"That's the way it seems." She says sorrowfully. "Maude said she found some strange emails from Leah these past years in her junk folder after the arrest. Ones that made it seem like Leah never believed that you two weren't sisters. She said it sounded like Leah was trying to convince you to see it for yourself… until you moved out."

"She's not though. Right?" Jess says to me, then to Gramma. "Leah's not your sister. She's locked away for the foreseeable future and you get to walk away knowing that you're not tied to her."

"That's right." Gramma says, offering him a small smile of appreciation.

My shoulder relax as I reconcile everything I just learned. Here I was trying to protect Gramma from this, and she knew all along. I knew something didn't sit right about Carol's story that Dad would turn his back on another daughter if he had one. Some part of me feels like his memory has been redeemed, healed of the blemishes and shadows this confusion cast. I never called Carol to tell her about the accident. She would probably find a way to make it about herself. Seeing as she planted the seed in Leah's mind to begin with, I think it's for the best. Some daughters were just not meant to have mothers.

"Well, anyway." Gramma taps on the table, then busies herself getting up.

That's our cue that she's done with the topic. She's moving on, and I think I am ready to move on from it too. Jess is right. Despite Leah's best efforts, I am still here. And I don't have to worry about her anymore.

"Jess, if you don't mind the light above my sink in the bathroom needs a new light. There's some new ones in the laundry room."

Jess smiles at Gramma, standing and pushing his chair in, then says, "You got it."

Jess is definitely not out of earshot by the time Gramma says, "I like this one, he's handy."

I know he hears her because he shoots me a wink over his shoulder on his way toward the laundry room.

We spend the next few hours at Gramma's. We play games. She comes up with at least five chores for Jess, which he does happily. Even though I am feeling much better, they both insist I do nothing. Then, she orders us lunch from Ubereats, which I'm sure is half to show off to Jess that she's a tech savvy Grandmother. The other half is probably because she thinks cooking for any less than a full holiday feast is a waste of dishes.

Chapter 40

Samantha

Jess wasted no time gathering the rest of the stuff from my apartment.

Most of the furniture was already there when I moved in. Jess "soft launching" my move in (his words) made things easier too. All we had to do was collect the minimal furniture I brought into the apartment and a few boxes. He made sure to make room by the window in his- I mean *our* living room, for my Dad's Chair. He also rearranged a side table to one side of it and put my bookshelf in the corner behind it.

Benny didn't seem at all surprised when I told him that I'd be moving out. He did, however, mortify me by joking that he no longer needs to consider soundproofing the space between the diner and the apartment.

I've been home from the hospital for a few weeks now. The cut on my forehead and bruises have all healed nicely. My shoulder still feels a little stiff, but I feel mostly good besides that. Mentally I am feeling better too, not having to look over my shoulder anymore.

Chad and I both needed to get new phones. Officer Underwood said they did recover Chad's from Leah's Jeep. It was fully submerged underwater, but just the fact that she had it was enough to likely prove that she intended to lure me to the lake. Therefore, she could be charged with attempted homicide. Thankfully that, compiled with Underwood's meticulous notes from the other incidences, should earn her about a fifteen-year sentence.

I haven't gotten a new car. I'm still waiting on things with insurance. I've browsed a little, but nothing really calls to me. Jess and Mel have been giving me rides to and from school for work in the meantime. I know I can't ask them to do that forever, but for now, I am grateful they don't mind.

I told Mel in no uncertain terms that I didn't need a housewarming party, since Jess had already been living in the house most of his life. I also told her that I didn't need a party to celebrate Leah's arrest, or as she put it "kicking death in the teeth." Naturally, that means that we are having a small get-together. Of course, I expected that from Mel, but I was surprised when Jess and Chad were both on the pro-party side of the conversation.

Jess had justified having people over, stating that he needed to expand his cooking skills beyond his amazing tacos. Apparently, that means that he has to pull out his dad's old smoker and be up at the crack of dawn filling it with seasoned meats. Meat-smoking Jess is just another new side of him that is inexplicably attractive. He was out back tending to the smoker when people started to show up.

Mel, thankfully got here a little early and has been helping me make sides. Cooking has never been my superpower, but I think we pulled off an edible mac and cheese and various other sides.

How hard can baked beans be, right?

Chad hasn't opened up much more about what's going on with his mom. He does seem better now that she has moved in with him though. Like he's stretching himself less thin by not having to take care of both of their places and drive to check on her so often. Jess said he couldn't tell what kind of sickness Ms Wilkins had when he saw her. Maybe that's a good thing, I'm not sure.

After Mel and Chad, Benny and his son Matt are the next to arrive. Mel wasn't happy when Underwood showed up moments later. She reluctantly agreed to play nice, since he was such a big part in resolving things with Leah. Which, in Mel's terms means passive-aggressively calling him "Donut" anytime they needed to talk. I don't think she's going to be happy to know he and Jess have been hitting it off.

"How you doing, Doll?" Jess asks, pressing a kiss into the side of my head as I put out the paper plates.

He just brought the last of the meats inside, and they smell heavenly.

I turn around and put both arms over his shoulders so his hands reach my hips before I answer. "I'm perfect." With a smile.

Something about having all of my favorite people together, the smell of good food, and the man I love pressed up against me feels that way.

Perfect.

Perhaps it shouldn't. Maybe I am supposed to be scarred or depressed after what I went through. Maybe I'm supposed to fester on it for longer than I have. Maybe it's the years of learning not to hold on to things because of Carol, I'm not sure. What I do know is that Leah is where she cannot hurt me anymore.

I am still standing.

I know I am supposed to hate Leah after what she did, but

I don't. In some ways I pity her. I do know what it's like for her to not have her mother around, but I can't pretend being stuck with Carol compares to your mom dying at a young age. I'm glad I had my dad for as long as I did, and if he had been Leah's father like she believed, she would've lost him without ever getting to really have him the way I did. I know that doesn't justify what she did. She is certifiably crazy. But she's also alone, and despite all she put me through there is a small, possibly equally crazy part of myself that's thankful to her.

If it hadn't been for her delusions and deranged responses, I might not be here right now. In a house that finally feels like home. Finally able to say without a doubt that I know what love is. For the first time in my life, I feel like someone is worth loving with my whole heart, something I have never wanted to risk before.

"Get a room you two." Chad pulls me out of my thoughts, shooing us with a paper plate.

"We have a whole house." Jess counters, offering me a melt-worthy wink as he pulls away.

We all take turns piling our plates with barbecue and sides. No one bothers finding a seat. We just all stand around the counters, picking at our food while we chat. We feel like a family, which in some ways I suppose we are.

"So, Underwood you drive that Tundra out there?" Jess asks, pointing out the back window.

"You can call me Jake." Underwood laughs, nodding to confirm. "Yeah, that's mine."

"Mind if we go check it out? Samantha's been looking at getting something new."

"Be my guest." Jake tosses his plate of rib bones in the

garbage before heading towards the door.

I don't really know that I would consider driving a truck. I don't have a strong need to pull or haul things, but I still take Jess's hand when he offers it and let him lead me outside.

While Jake shows us around his truck, everyone else makes their way outside as well. Chad busies himself making a fire and Mel and Matt help pull out lawn chairs, placing them around the fire pit in a circle.

"Thank you for letting us take a look at it," I say to be kind, even though it's not my kind of vehicle.

"Anytime," Jake says.

He is so well-mannered, that it's hard not to wonder what made Mel hate him so much.

"If you're not gonna be helpful at least get outta the way, Donut," Mel says, as if she could hear me thinking kind things about the poor guy.

"Here, let me help." He reaches for the chair she's carrying only for her to use it to push him out of the way.

Before I get the chance to pull her aside and finally ask her what the deal is I hear another car coming down the gravel drive. The familiar rumble of an old V-8 pulls my attention to the driveway. Two white stripes grace the top of the hood on the beautiful midnight blue Chevelle I haven't laid eyes on in over five years. When it comes to a stop in front of me I am surprised to see Benny driving it.

When did he even disappear?

"What is this?" I ask as Benny closes the door and hands me the key chain.

Benny only smiles and tilts his head towards Jess with a knowing look, which I follow.

"You need a car." Jess shrugs, his smile contradicting the

casual tone.

"But, I can't drive this." I start to protest, while Jess opens the door and ushers me inside the car.

"You *couldn't*." Jess corrects me. "If I recall, you learned to drive a stick recently."

I don't hide my blushing smile at the rest of the memories of that night. The look in Jess's eye tells me he is remembering it too.

"Also, the boys and I made some adjustments to the pedals and seat. I think you'll find no problem adjusting them to your liking now."

I slide further into the seat and Jess's hand grasps the bar below the seat between my legs, bringing me closer to the wheel. Looking down I see where he replaced the pedals with new ones, which my feet easily reach. When I press the clutch all the way to the floor with ease and start the engine my eyes fill with tears.

Dad would love this.

"Mel and I are still happy to drive you around until you get more comfortable with the stick," Jess says. "And I will gladly still help you car shop if you don't want to daily-drive this. I just couldn't stand the idea of it sitting away forever when I could easily solve the only reason you never drive it."

I can't believe this man is giving me the first surprise in months that doesn't have me running for the hills and he seems almost apologetic.

"I love it, Jess," I tell him, wiping the tears away. "It's perfect, thank you."

After a few rusty laps around the back roads, (*because the older stick shift really takes more skill to drive than Jess's modern Mustang*) we spend the rest of the night around the fire with our friends.

My chosen family.

Slowly, they trickle off, each making their excuses to leave until it's just Jess and I left. *At home.*

The next morning, after spending the night wrapped up in Jess's arms, I slip out of bed and throw my hair up into a bun, careful not to wake him. Before I leave the room I steal one more look at him sleeping with the sheets hung low on his waist.

I can't believe I am in love, and living with Jess Adams after all these years.

Then, I make my morning coffee in my flower mug and drink it on the hood of my old car in my cartoon cat pajamas.

EPILOGUE:

Jess

"That was insane," I say as we pull into the driveway.

"I told you." Samantha laughs.

I take a second to appreciate her playful smile. I was right, Leah never had a chance at dulling her shine. Samantha has always, and will always be unspeakably bright and filled with joy.

You could've warned me about the bull horns. I would have worn ear protection."

My ears have been ringing since we left the school. Today was field day at the school Samantha and Mel work at and they roped me into coming to volunteer. I mostly held the clipboard for Samantha's class, watching in horror as the children competed against other classes while the teachers cheered as if they were watching gladiators. It was intense, to say the least.

"Field day is no joke at Glenbrook Elementary, Puddin'. Next time, come prepared." She says teasingly.

I smile at the ridiculous name that she allowed her first-grade class to assign me.

"Do I get any vote on this nickname?" I say, only playing at putting up a fight.

She finally made good on her promise to let her class pick out a nickname for me. Her criteria for them was that it needed to be something sweet, but also slightly embarrassing. Then, because she is always looking for teachable moments, she had the children nominate names and hold a class election to decide the winner. I should just be thankful that the kids voted against Poptart, Cake-pop, and Snugglemuffin.

"No chance. You used up all of your veto power." She winks closing the door and walking around to the back hatch of her new Bronco.

Samantha has been driving her dad's old Chevelle here and there, but I always knew she wouldn't want to daily drive it. The Chevelle is the kind of car you take out for a weekend car show, maybe drive it in the Saturday night parade in Old Town. Not so practical for a daily commute.

I knew from the look on her face the first time she saw the green Bronco on the lot that she was instantly sold. Samantha now parks her Bronco (Satirically named Tamlin, due to the emerald green paint job and bronze rims which she assures me give *high fae energy*, whatever that means) next to Sally under the carport. The Chevelle never went back to Benny's, it now lives in the garage with my old truck.

Since she moved in, everything just feels so right. When one of the kids in a red white and blue tie-dyed shirt today asked me if he was going to have to start calling Ms. Bunting "Mrs. Puddin'" soon, I grinned like a fool. Of course, I explained to the little guy that she would be Mrs. Adams if we ever did get married. He said that would be better for her, so her name was in the front of the alphabet, which made me laugh so hard that I distracted the other team during the cup and bottle competition. Luckily Samantha was too busy celebrating to ask what the little guy and I were laughing about. I want to give her some time to settle in after the crazy year she's had, but when the time is right... Samantha Adams does have a nice *ring* to it. In the meantime, I have Chad on his way with a surprise that I think she might like.

Who am I kidding? She's gonna love it.

I help her carry the cooler and other things inside and set them in the kitchen. Once we are done, I pull her into my chest and wrap my arms around her back as she reaches over my shoulders to link her hands behind my head.

"Seriously, I had fun today," I tell her. "Thank you for inviting me, even if all I did was hold the clipboard."

"The clipboard is very important." She says in a sweet tone, raking her fingers through the bottom of my hair. "Don't sell yourself short."

"You know, I'm surprised you still have a voice after such aggressive cheering all day." I give her side a playful squeeze, earning a squeal in response.

"I know." She giggles. "I feel like I need some tea and a huge spoon of honey, and I wasn't screaming nearly as much as Mel."

"Don't remind me. Mel was terrifying." I chuckle. "Someone needs to tell her it's a school event, not a gladiator fight to the death."

Seriously, I knew Mel watched football aggressively but she was way louder today. When it got down to the big tug-of-war event at the end I think she could've burst eardrums. What's crazy is that she wasn't even the most enthusiastic teacher there.

"Cut us some slack. It's our first year." Samantha playfully shoves my chest, then furrows her brow when I don't budge.

Before I can respond Chad honks twice, announcing his arrival.

A few months ago I was watching Samantha flinch

every time we heard a car pull up. She was so on edge, constantly waiting for the other shoe to drop, or the next unexpected terrible thing to happen. I can't help but feel a warm pride in my chest when she doesn't even flinch at the arrival of an unexpected guest. I lean forward to place a kiss on her forehead and tell her to stay put before going outside to meet my friend.

Chad has the biggest shit-eating grin spread across his face when he sees me come outside. Hell, I'm just grateful he was able to keep his mouth shut and not give it away after I told him a few weeks ago. I know he's just happy for me though, even if he hasn't stopped giving me shit about knowing all along that I had feelings for Samantha.

Part of me thought about asking Mel to help out with this, but I decided to save her help for when I finally pop the question. You know, when the time is right. In the meantime, Chad has earned some points for his discretion in "*Operation Snoop Dogg*" (Yes, I let Chad name it.)

"You ready for this?" Chad asks, pausing at his passenger door, waiting for me to give the go-ahead.

"Absolutely." I nod, then look back over my shoulder to make sure Samantha isn't peeking out the window. "She's gonna love him."

"Well if she doesn't, he can come home with me," Chad jokes, opening the door.

Samantha

I am sitting in my dad's chair in the living room, reading one of my "shadow daddy romances" as Jess likes to call them, when the back door opens. I can hear Jess and

Chad laughing on their way in, and also something that almost sounds like the pitter-patter of little… Ooof!

A yellow blur of fur with a waggly tail barrels at me at full speed, jumping into my lap. Puppy breath covers my face as I try to pull my book away, so it doesn't get crumpled. Once I manage to get my hands free I wrangle the little intruder back to get a good look at her. Oh, erm, I mean *him*.

"Well hello, little guy." I smile at him, ignoring Jess and Chad staring at me from the other side of the sofa. "Where did you come from?"

When the pooch only continues to lick at my face in response, I finally turn to the men.

"Chad, you got a puppy?" I ask, rubbing the soft little ears between my fingers.

Chad shakes his head, with that all-too-familiar smirk on his face. I follow Chad's gaze to Jess, who has his hand rubbing the back of his neck nervously.

Will him being nervous every stop being incredibly cute? Probably not.

"Actually, Doll, he's for you," Jess says, voice hesitant. As if he is having second thoughts on how I will react to the puppy.

"You got me a puppy?" I say in awe, squeezing the poor pup to my chest. Though his tail wiggles indicate that he doesn't mind.

Jess's shoulders relax, then he makes his way over to kneel by the chair. I reluctantly allow Jess to pet my new best friend (sorry Mel) and the little traitor practically jumps into his arms.

"What's his name?" I ask, not bothering to hide how much I am enjoying looking at my incredibly strong, sexy boyfriend holding a baby Labrador puppy.

"You get to name him, Doll." Jess smiles, carefully depositing the fur ball back onto my lap.

"I've been calling him Snoop Dogg." Chad chimes in proudly, earning a synchronized eye-roll from us both.

"Veto," Jess says, causing us all to laugh.

"Well, Puddin'," I say "Looks like I'll have to do some noodling."

Sent from: Leahwoods@gmail.com
To: Maudewoodstock@aol.com

You wouldn't lie to me right?

Yet, in a certain light I can see it, when she turns her head just right. And how else would you explain the universe sticking us together.

Sent from my iPhone

Sent from: Leahwoods@gmail.com
To: Maudewoodstock@aol.com

I thought time and closeness would help, but she hasn't realized it yet. Look at me, why would she? She's so beautiful, and bright. Everyone loves her. *I* love her. I just want them to look at me the way they all look at her.

Sent from my iPhone

Sent from: Leahwoods@gmail.com
To: Maudewoodstock@aol.com

Wasn't it the hair that made her more lovable? Or the way she dressed? Then, why isn't it working for me? Can't she see we are the same? Can't they? Why am I not enough and she is?

Sent from my iPhone

Sent from: Leahwoods@gmail.com
To: Maudewoodstock@aol.com

She thinks she's so fucking special. Like she has a monopoly on being perfect. Does she even hear the way she sounds when she talks? It's like the whole world just bends to her will, while I have to try twice as hard.

Sent from my iPhone

Sent from: Leahwoods@gmail.com
To: Maudewoodstock@aol.com

Living with me isn't good enough? Fine. We'll see just how much better she is.

Sent from my iPhone

Sent from: Leahwoods@gmail.com
To: Maudewoodstock@aol.com

You know, it can actually be quite fun to play with a Doll. Just look at her move around, never knowing how many times I dictate what happens to her.

Sent from my iPhone

Sent from: Leahwoods@gmail.com
To: Maudewoodstock@aol.com

To family. Did you see that? I fucking knew it.

Sent from my iPhone

* * *

<u>Acknowledgments</u>

First, I want to thank my Puddin', for always supporting me in whatever new adventure I want to try and for being my muse. Thanks for letting me type away next to your sleeping head, and keep the lamp on into the wee hours. I love you most.

To Fart Head, thank you for being the one person who heard most of the details of the book as I rattled off ideas, and still reading it even though you knew the ending. I wouldn't have been able to make it through writing without someone to spill my secrets to. Buckle up for book two.

To Holla Back Gurl, thank you for waiting the whole year to read it without any spoilers, and for naming Leah. Remember ladies and gents… this is all fictional, but never piss off a writer or her friends.

Another special thanks to everyone who beta-read and helped me with edits. As a new author, I couldn't be more thankful for such a supportive community of book lovers!

Last, but definitely not least, thank you to Gramma for being who I want to be when I grow up. Thank you for showing me how to grow through the cracks, and love unconditionally.

Thank you for supporting me as an author! For news on Mel's book in the Glenbrook series, stay up to date with me online! You can find my social media accounts and more information on my website: CassandraRoland.com

9 798992 338508